Blackout

Sam Mills was born in 1975 and studied English Language and Literature at Oxford University. Sam worked as a journalist and publicist before giving it all up to write full time.

Sam is the author of two previous young adult novels, *A Nicer Way to Die* and *The Boys Who Saved the World*, which is currently being made into a film. Please visit www.tbwstw.com for more details.

Praise for *A Nicer Way to Die*:

'I burnt a lot of midnight oil and even more adrenaline reading *A Nicer Way to Die* . . . Mills never lets the tension drop, skilfully weaving into the claustrophobic atmosphere flashbacks which build up a picture of a deeply disturbed boy.' *Sunday Telegraph*

'This is a marvellous, gripping, appalling book – which my own teenage son is begging to read as soon as I have finished it and stopped shuddering.' *Telegraph*

Praise for *The Boys Who Saved the World*:

'A book that is timely and sensitive in its exploration of the forces that make adolescent boys cut off their empathy for others and choose violence and submission to charismatic leaders as a means of channelling their isolation and frustration.' *Telegraph*

Also by Sam Mills:

A Nicer Way to Die
The Boys Who Saved the World

faber and faber

First published in 2010
by Faber and Faber Limited
Bloomsbury House, 74–77 Great Russell Street,
London, WC1B 3DA

Printed in England by CPI Bookmarque, Croydon

A CIP record for this book
is available from the British Library

ISBN 978–0–571–23941–2

2 4 6 8 10 9 7 5 3

For L. K., with love

'Sticks and stones may break my bones
But words will never hurt me.'

Prologue

I am a murderer.

I'm standing in a bookshop, a gun hot in my palm. The bullet that sat in my barrel thirty seconds ago has pierced flesh, blown into brain tissue, metal now fighting consciousness.

The woman slumps onto the floor. Blood begins to trickle from her head. It drips onto a pile of signed copies stacked on the floor.

Time pauses. The bookshop feels underwater, silent, still. Everyone stops staring at the stage. Their heads spin towards me. A sixteen-year-old. Dressed in an anorak and jeans. Standing at the front of Waterstone's. I looked just an ordinary boy when I came in. Now my face is pale with shock. (*The Catcher in the Rye.*) The gun dangles from my hand.

Then panic splits open the silence and screams pour out.

I stare down at the gun. I don't understand. (*The Catcher in the Rye.*) I don't understand.

A man tries to grab me in a headlock but I wriggle away, gasping. I turn to Omar; I seize his wrist desperately. But he shakes me away.

'*RUN!*' he yells.

As I head for the door, a woman blocks my way, scream-ing. I point my gun at her. She throws up her hands, handbag banging her wrist. I shove past her and run down the street.

My heart pumps disbelief round my body. *I've shot someone. A famous writer. Me, Stefan, boring son of a boring bookseller. A murderer.* The streets are swirling with shoppers: mums, kids, pushchairs, grannies, fathers, all battling it out over the pavement. (*The Catcher in the Rye.*) Why did I do, it, why? Sirens steal the air. Don't look back, don't look back, just keep going. I swing into a shop-ping centre, chest heaving. But the eyes of the State are everywhere, CCTV recording my every breath. I pull my hood up over my face and walk steadily, trying to blend into the crowds. In the shopfronts, plastic models stare at me with hollow, accusing eyes. I risk a look back. Where are the police? Are they waiting for me at the other exit? (*The Catcher in the Rye.*) My hand pulled the gun out of my pocket as though I was a puppet and some God above had decided to turn me into a killer. I don't understand. I don't understand.

When I get to the exit, I push my hand into my pocket, feeling the gun again. I edge towards the revolving doors slowly, slowly. I exit through them as a businessmen enters, caught in a spin of circling glass. Outside, the streets are full of shoppers; no police. I run across the road, ignoring a screeching horn, and run towards the docks and down towards the dirty, deserted shanty-town. Here are huts, made from driftwood and debris, where the refugees who lost their houses to the sea used to camp, until the sea began to creep into these too.

Shallow water laps beneath my trainers, erasing the blood. The sea shushes with an angry wind. The gun bangs against my thigh. I keep looking back, but all I see are gulls fighting for sky space, and a woman with a pushchair. I sneak between the huts, claw the doors, splintering my palms. They've been nailed shut with bits of wood but I yank one hard; encrusted whelks split away with a brown crunch. I climb inside, find a wooden board that was once a bed and lie down, the cold seeping into my hot pumping body.

The dark ceiling grimaces over me. Over and over again I see the woman fall; I see myself shoot her a thousand times. Why didn't the police catch me? I almost wish they had. I yearn to be back in the Institution, to feel the spotlight shining onto my face, piercing my irises, forcing my brain to find an explanation, to remember, to rationalise. (*The Catcher in the* —) Stop, stop, why do those words keep coming? I look down and realise I'm clutching the gun to my chest. The barrel is staring up at me. I think of my father and how I may never reach him now. My face will be on most-wanted lists everywhere. I think of my victim, of her dying thoughts, of the people who love her. My fingers curl round the trigger and I'm close, so close . . .

I toss it to one side with a clatter and curl up into a ball. My heart is still now, cold and still with the shock of this new me, this new future chained around my neck. I feel tired. I want to shut the world out, to forget. I close my eyes, vaguely aware of my body shuddering, aching for sleep to wash relief through my mind. But the words keep echoing. (*The Catcher in the Rye.*) They're so familiar; I know they mean something; if I can just remember what, I'll find the key to unlock this mess . . .

Part One

One

How did I become a murderer, aged sixteen? If I look back, I could blame it on Omar, or the Words, or the men who forced me to take the gun. But the seed was planted long before then. It really began with a copy of *1984*.

Up until the age of sixteen, I lived with my dad in a bookshop in Primrose Hill. Our lives were fairly quiet. I went to school; my father bought and sold books. I was only eight years old when the terrorist attacks hit London. At first I didn't really understand why they happened, or why I started to get bullied in the playground for having a dad who was a bookseller. For it was all because of a book that the Houses of Parliament got blown up. A book called *The Exploded*.

The Exploded was a pacy thriller about a group of terrorists who blew up all the main buildings in London. It included details of how they made the bombs, got past the police and set them off. The leader of the terrorist cell read it and admitted later in court that the book had given him the inspiration. I saw the trial on TV and I remember the judge saying before he banged his gavel, *Does art mirror life or does life mirror art?* I didn't really understand what he meant, but it sounded cool.

The leader had used the book as a weapon to recruit half

a dozen teenagers to carry out the bombing. In their good-bye videos, they had stared into the videocams, their eyes flashing anger and fear and sadness, holding up copies of the novel as though it was a religious text. The group was called ArkQ. Dad said they had 'originated from a band of religious nuts' but had expanded to include protestors upset by climate change, as well as all the angry refugees. Dad explained to me that a refugee is someone who has lost their home because our rising seas had gobbled them up – and that the government had refused to help them.

The teenagers all died. The gang leader survived but he got sentenced to death by hanging. It was the first public hanging that happened in our country in over a hundred years. Some people got upset about it but most agreed that it was proper justice: 15,000 people had died in the attacks. I wanted to go and watch the hanging in Trafalgar Square, but Dad said I was much too young. As more terrorists were sentenced, the hangings became popular and one Saturday, when Dad was out, I got to watch one on TV. I felt my heart banging but I couldn't take my eyes off the screen. I didn't really understand how a hanging worked and I kept thinking the rope would slice through his head and his body would hit the ground, leaving his head-stump swinging in the noose. But he just jerked about for a few minutes and then went slack.

As for *The Exploded* – it was banned. It became the first book in the country which carried a fine or even a jail sentence if you were found with it in your possession.

People began to rebuild Parliament and the shrouds of flowers on the streets shrivelled to pink ashes. But life was different. Dad had always been a content man, happy to spend hours muddling about amongst his books. Now he always seemed nervous, upset. Letters came through the post that he cursed over and tore up. Whenever I asked him what the matter was he would snarl, 'The Censorship,' then change the subject. I didn't understand what the word meant, so I assigned my own monstrous meaning to it.

♛

I remember the day I began to understand more fully why my dad was so upset.

It was a cold day in April and I was sitting on the floor, knocking marbles about. I was struck by the way that the sun, passing through the musty windows of our bookshop, hit the marbles and sprayed patterns of spooling light on the walls. They looked like the symbols I'd seen in books about Egypt. I'd just rolled my favourite marble – the one that looked like a pearl – when Mr Jones came running into the bookshop.

Mr Jones was our best customer. He bought at least six books a week. He looked a little like Father Christmas, with little round glasses perched on his permanently red nose. He waved his arms, crying, 'They're coming. *They're coming!* I've seen them – they're going through Waterstone's – Samson's been arrested – I told you they were serious – I told you this would happen – burn the Orwell. Burn it!'

'I can hide it,' my father said, 'we'll put it in the back—'

'Are you insane? They'll find it! They'll be searching – BURN IT!'

'I can't – it's the only copy . . . there are only twenty copies left in the country now . . . I can't burn it . . .'

I wasn't sure what *the Orwell* meant. I watched my father pick up a book. It was orange with *1984* stencilled in black on the front. My father looked as though he felt the same way about it as I did about my white marble.

9

Then he tore the first page out, ripped it into three and put it in his mouth.

'Are you crazy?' Mr Jones shouted.

'It's the only way –' my dad tore out more pages and stuffed them into his mouth, his voice thick with words, '– to preserve it – there are only fifty left in the country –' He kept on eating and tearing, eating and tearing, swallowing down great lumps of papier mâché. 'It might just work – I can't think of what else —' Swallow.

Mr Jones threw up his hands and ran to the front of the shop. I followed him. In the distance we could see them. I realised then that they must be the Censorship. I'd always assumed it must have three arms and sharp teeth. I was surprised, then, to see that the Censorship was an ordinary man with a sidekick. They looked a bit like police, only their uniforms were navy, not black, and their caps had little silver arrows at the front.

We turned back to see my father gagging on the middle of the book.

'Oh for God's sake!' Mr Jones ran to him and grabbed the remaining pages, hurrying out through the back door. 'I'll burn the rest!'

My father looked after him desperately, ready to chase – but then the shop door tinkled.

I can't remember the looks on the men's faces as they came in, but I remember the feeling they emanated. They had the smell of fear about them; they filled my stomach with black smoke. I quickly gathered up my marbles into a little nest in the corner.

They greeted my father with brisk handshakes and curt hellos. They told him they were from the Department of Public Protection and had come to check his stock. They hoped he had complied with the government regulations that had been sent to all bookshops six months back.

'I may have,' my father said. 'Though I can't say I agreed with all the suggestions. I really cannot see how *The Catcher in the Rye* would ever do any harm–'

'Well, that is not for you to decide,' the Censorship said, and proceeded to attack a case of books. He ran a forefinger along a shelf length. Every so often, he picked one out and threw it on the floor, breaking its back.

'Hang on,' my father protested with a nervous laugh, 'this is ridiculous. I mean, for God's sake, we all know there's a War on Terror – but – and this wasn't on the list – this one wasn't!'

'Then clearly you have not read the list.'

'But . . . but . . .' the tips of my father's ears had gone bright pink; he struggled against his temper and put on a polite voice, 'this bookshop was owned by my father and before him, his father. For God's sake, this is England, not Iran! We've never had this sort of mad censorship before, people won't put up with it, you know; people want to read what they want.'

'We may not have had this sort of censorship before,' the Censorship echoed him. 'We've never had this sort of terrorism before, either.' His tone softened. 'New measures are required. The laws have been passed. We are grateful for your help.'

'I don't agree with them. You can take what you like but I'll reorder. I'll print my own copies!'

The Censorship walked up to my father until their mouths were just inches apart.

'Whose side are you on?'

'I . . .' My father's shoulders collapsed. 'I'm just a bookseller,' he said weakly.

This went on for a good hour. I crouched in the corner,

watching. Soon there was a small pyramid of books in the centre of the shop, looking as though they were ready for the bonfire. My father kept on protesting and arguing and the Censorship kept on snapping back, his voice rising each time. Then, just as he had completed his task, he spotted me.

'He's my son Stefan,' my father said quickly. 'He's only nine, he's just playing . . .'

The Censorship leaned down. He had a pudgy, friendly face but there was venom in his eyes.

'Do you like to read, Stefan?' he asked.

'Yes.'

'Well, I hope your father gives you the right thing to read. What's this?' The Censorship bent down and picked up my precious white marble.

'It's mine!' I cried. I tried to grab it back, but he kept opening his palm, then snatching it away at the last minute, the way the bullies taunted me in the school playground.

Bored with our game, he stood up and slipped my marble into his pocket. I listened in clenched silence as the two men said goodbye to my father and warned him that they would be back soon. Did he realise what I'd had to do to get that marble? I had swapped it for ten others. I had saved for weeks.

As he strolled towards the door, I leapt up with a roar and threw myself at his thigh, curling my arms around it and yelling, 'GIVE IT BACK! GIVE ME BACK MY MARBLE!'

The Censorship yelped in surprise. He tried to shake me off, but I only clung on tighter.

Then I felt something cool pressing into my temple and I realised he was holding a gun to my head. My arms fell slack. I wasn't really scared by the gun, for at the age of eight they still seemed like toys to me. I'd seen them fire bullets in cartoons but the little technicolour victims always bounced cheerily back up. It was the sound of my father's whimpering that terrified me; the cruel twist of the Censorship's mouth, as though he might hate himself for pulling the trigger, but that wouldn't be enough to stop him. Yet, still the whisper came from my lips: 'I want my marble back.'

The Censorship's eyes widened. Then, with a funny little laugh, he drew out the marble and passed it back to me, ruffling my head. The bell tinkled merrily as they left the shop.

My father scooped me up in his arms, crying prayers out loud. Then he fled to the bathroom and stuck his fingers down his throat. I watched him with moon eyes. His sick spurted onto the floor, flecked with the chicken and carrots we'd eaten for lunch. He combed his fingers through it, sobbing and muttering. In the swirl of colour, I could see the words of the book crawling about like ants. My father kept trying to fish them out but they would disintegrate in his fingers into paper mulch and the ants died. He rolled up his fist and struck the floor.

Then he caught sight of me watching. He came up and gave me a hug so tight it nearly knocked me over. I wanted to pull back but he clung on. On his lapel there was a little piece of sicked-up paper that said, *–'re a traitor!' yelled the boy. 'You're a thought–*

'Things are going to change, Stefan,' my father said, 'things are going to change.'

Two

Things did change. Just as Dad predicted. A week later, there was another major attack. The HMV on Oxford Street was on every TV screen: a pile of rubble spewing smoke, charred bodies being carried to ambulances. Ninety-five people died. The suicide bomber was only twelve years old. In his bedroom, they found an ArkQ manual and a pile of violent videogames.

Half of the press and State blamed ArkQ. The other half blamed the videogames. Knife crime might be rare these days, they said, but because kids knew they couldn't get away with carrying a blade any more, their aggression was being channelled into terrorism.

A few days later, on my tenth birthday, I received my first Game Boy. I was dying to play *Grand Theft Auto*. It was meant to be for over-eighteens but I knew some boys at school who had illegal copies. The game was based on a guy who rises through the ranks of the criminal under-world through assassinations, pimping, street-car racing and that kind of thing.

I never got to play it. That very day, the police came into every classroom and inspected our bags and desks. Loads of our games and books got confiscated, as well as our iPods. When one of the boys threw a tantrum, the police took him with them and he only came back to school weeks later.

The teacher eventually gave us our iPods back, but most of the music had been scrubbed. I remember sitting and trying to remember the beat and lyrics of a gangsta rap song I loved, but every day it grew fainter and fainter until I could no longer remember how a rap sounded. That upset me at first. But as I grew older, I began to see that Dad was wrong; things changed for the better, not worse. The terrorists were trying to pollute our minds through music and books and newspapers. That was why the government took control of the papers, so that we could be told the truth, rather than disturbing, distorted whispers the terrorists wanted to put about to cause unease and dissent. A lot of bookshops in London closed down, too. The Waterstone's on Piccadilly that was so big Dad once called it 'a cathedral worshipping books'; Foyles, Borders and The Pageturner, the little bookshop down the road who used to cheat us by buying our stock cheap and then selling it at a profit. Dad always used to moan about the competition. Now he moaned about them closing down. In truth, I secretly didn't mind if we did close. Then he could get a proper job.

I didn't much like having to work in the bookshop after school, either. It's hardly the sort of thing you want to do when you're fifteen.

It seemed to me that there was a dark river between being a boy and being a man and I wasn't sure how to jump across it. I'd heard stories about what Dad had done when he was in his teens, how he'd smoked cigarettes and drunk beer and driven a motorcycle through the streets of London. I sometimes wondered if he was just making up how wild and free those days had been. I'd only ever once seen someone smoking and I remember the shocked thrill. We were in Leicester Square, watching a street performer freeze into various uncomfortable shapes, when I saw a man wearing a cap put a cigarette into his mouth and hold a lighter to it. I thought it would burst into flames but the tip simply glowed orange. It looked beautiful, like a firefly. Within minutes, however, the crowd were moaning at him and coughing, and a policeman had tapped him on the shoulder and made him pay a fine on the spot.

From time to time I was gripped by vague, dark impulses.

I wanted to break the curfew and be out in the streets after twilight.

I wanted to roam free.

I wanted to see if beer really would poison me.

I wanted to do something with a girl, something hot and beautiful and swelling, though I wasn't quite sure what.

The blurriness of my desires frustrated me until I sometimes punched my pillow to feathers; I felt that if I could just work out how to relieve my feelings, then I might feel all right again. At school I sat in class and wondered if I was the only one how felt this way; if I was mad or screwed-up. I guess I should've reported my unrest to Mrs Kay, who would have referred me to the school psychologist. But half our class was in therapy and I had no wish to join the queue.

And so I learnt to live with my strange desires, and remained stuck in a shop full of paper that was slowly turning yellow.

♔

Sometimes I had arguments with Dad. Our fights would always go the same way. I'd say I wanted to go out. He'd say I was under age. I'd say I was *nearly sixteen*. He'd say come on, you know the rules, since the attacks no child under sixteen is advised to go out without a parent. Not when the ArkQ were issuing new threats of their next attack and we were on red alert. Everyone else in your class has to stay in too. I'd say Chris doesn't. Nor does Mike. Nor does Henry. And he'd say, 'That's because their parents don't love them.'

It seemed to me that love was a noose that was slowly being tightened round my neck, squeezing all the life out of me.

Feeling mad, I shut myself in my room, reading my spy book. I wanted to be like the heroes – spying on terrorists and winning medals for reporting them to the State.

After a while, I got bored of sulking and went downstairs. Halfway, I stopped.

I gazed out at the silhouette of my father at the cash desk. His shoulders were hunched, his hands trembling as he held the book, and I noticed the bald spot at the back of his head was getting bigger. Suddenly he no longer looked like my father but an old man, a stranger. I felt almost sorry for him and the feeling frightened me. I went over to him and muttered an apology.

Dad didn't apologise back. He never did. He rarely used words to say how he felt; he tended to make up for his spurts of temper by being kind, offering me a treat. Later that evening, when we sat having dinner together, our forks clanging against our plates of baked beans on toast, he asked me if I wanted to go on a special outing for my sixteenth birthday. I told him I'd like to see a terrorist being publicly killed. Though he could not conceal a grimace of distaste, to my surprise, he agreed.

Three

Normally there was a public hanging once a month in Trafalgar Square.

Dad said that if they couldn't hang someone who was guilty, they'd just hang someone who was innocent. He said that the hangings weren't about the criminal, but the public; it gave them a channel to vent their grief and anger and hatred over the loved ones they'd lost in the bombings.

The man who had been sentenced to death was splashed over the newspapers every day. His name was Omar Shakir and his picture was always the same: a drooping black moustache that hung over terse lips, his eyes glinting with evil. He hadn't set off a bomb. He was being hanged because he was an Islamic writer who had written a novel about characters *planning* a bomb; luckily the police had stopped him in time before it was published.

His arrest had upset a lot of people. Especially the Muslims. They felt they were all being victimised and said Shakir had only confessed to the crime because the police had tortured him. They said he was only being hanged for show, to make the public feel safe. They wrote letters and articles and made a big fuss. And in the end the government agreed that, as a Muslim, Shakir could be brought to justice in a Shariah court. Then everyone got even more upset; some said it was crazy; others said it was the best and most fair way.

'What's a Shariah court?' I asked my father. It was the day before my birthday and we were on the train on our way to my 16+ check-up.

'It's part of Islam,' my father explained. 'There's a sura – a section of the Qur'an – that says God has sent to each people a *shari'a* and an open path. So *shari'a* means path to life and the divinely revealed laws that define that path. And the court is a way of enforcing their laws.'

'So they did say he was innocent?' I asked, worried his execution might be put off.

'No, they still found him guilty, but they ordered that instead of being hanged, he should suffer a punishment they have decreed, which means he'll be stoned to death.'

A woman who was listening to our conversation muttered, 'That's barbaric.'

I didn't think it was barbaric; I couldn't help feeling a secret thrill at the thought of seeing him die. Stoning was even better than hanging. I could hardly wait for tomorrow.

♔

'You're supposed to register children for 16+ at least four weeks before they turn sixteen. His birthday's tomorrow – you're late!' the woman behind the desk snapped, angrily twisting her mouse and glowering at the computer screen. 'You know there's a five-thousand-euro fine for late registration?'

My dad kept muttering sulky apologies. People started looking our way. I felt embarrassed. I'd told him we should have come earlier. At moments like this, it felt as though my father's books were sons he took more care of than me.

19

Finally, the woman gave us a pink raffle ticket and told us to wait until our number was called. The hall was full of metal chairs and carpeted in stripy lino. It was just like being at the doctor's, only the room was filled with teenagers and parents. I saw Brian from my class, as he was turning sixteen next month. There was a poster on the wall that said *NOTHING TO HIDE, NOTHING TO FEAR* and he kept peeling the edge off the wall and playing with the Blu-Tack until the woman shouted and told him off. His mum grabbed him, hissing, 'D'you *want* to end up in the Institution?' He quickly sat down, looking sheepish.

Then my dad had to fill in loads of forms while I had a fingerprint check. Next I had to stare into a lens and they took a photo of my iris. It seemed strange to me; I'd always thought eyes were just eyes and that all blue eyes were the same as all other blue eyes. But the woman explained:

'Every single person has a unique eye that is entirely their own. Now, we'll just take your DNA swab and you can go.'

I felt scared. I hated having injections at school. But the nurse showed me a picture on her computer of what DNA looked like: a string of amber and turquoise and purple beads all wound together in a chain.

'Your dad's DNA will have shaped your own, so there's a little bit of him in everything you say and do – isn't that nice?' She stuck a little plaster thing into the inside of my cheek, then put it in a dish. 'That's it. Don't look so surprised! I told you it wouldn't hurt. You can go now.'

As we left, I turned round and looked at the big red community building and felt strange.

Strange to think that my fingers and eyes and saliva and DNA twists were all being stored in a huge machine with thousands of other fingers and eyes and saliva and DNA. If I ever committed a crime, they would find me at once. But then I didn't need to worry. I had nothing to hide, so there was nothing to fear.

♛

The next morning, I turned sixteen.

My dad hadn't bought me the new football I'd asked for. I knew that the moment I saw the shapes of the presents. As I unwrapped them, I hid my disappointment. Books, books, and more books.

I was half-dreading Dad would back out of taking me to the stoning. We had a lunch – baked beans on toast again, with chocolate cake as a special treat – and I could barely eat it for butterflies. The moment we had finished I ran up to the door and hung up the CLOSED sign, crying, 'Come on, Dad!' It was a cold day and we put on coats and gloves and wrapped up in thick scarves.

We took the tube to Leicester Square. It was packed and we had to stand up. Up above, technoposters alternated between advertising hand cream and red letters screaming *BE AWARE AT ALL TIMES*. The security man had a sullen face; he held onto his rifle and scanned the crowds with piggy eyes. He caught me looking at him and I quickly looked away.

When we got off the tube, the platform was suffocating with crowds. It took us fifteen minutes to get to the escalators and push our tickets through the machines and beep our ID cards over the laser sensors. A Security for London Underground team were conducting random searches by the exit. One man with a dark beard had turned out his pockets and was crying, 'I haven't done anything wrong, what have I done wrong!' and the SLUG was waving a copy of the Qur'an and yelling back, 'Well, I don't see your registration number for this!' My dad looked fraught and

21

quickly hurried me out of the station; he seemed relieved to breathe in the fresh air.

Outside, the streets were churning.

We didn't so much walk as let the crowds carry us. A harsh wind was blowing across the city, trying to fight the flow of people. I heard shouting in the distance. As we swept across Charing Cross Road, I saw where the noise was coming from. A road had been blocked off. A crowd was being held back by policemen. The police were perched like kings on top of horses, who hissed steam through their nostrils, their flanks dark and shiny with nervous sweat. Another row of officers held up a row of plastic placards, making threats with stun-guns and truncheons. Behind them, the tide of the crowd pushed and pulled. They waved placards and screamed slogans: *Let Omar Live!* and *This is Murder!* and *This is not the British way!* My dad grabbed my arm and led me on. We stopped at the traffic lights and a black girl with dreads thrust a leaflet into my hand. It was red with white lettering:

BRING BACK PROTEST MARCHES
WE HAVE A
RIGHT
TO PROTEST

I rolled it up and put it in my pocket and the crowd surged on.

Then, finally, we were there.

Trafalgar Square.

My heart pumped with excitement.

Through the crowds, through the chaos of arms and elbows and bumping shoulders, I could see a huge fountain with a statue gushing torrents of water.

In front of the fountain, an area had been cordoned off with tape and boards. Police patrolled, guns thwacking against their hips. Behind the tape was a concrete stage where the terrorist would be brought out for the stoning. There was a large metal pole in the middle and large white bags which seemed pretty mysterious.

We had to queue for over an hour in order to be allowed to enter the Viewing Area. Policemen lasered our ID cards and felt us for weapons. Some men seemed to be refused entry for no reason, and if they argued or hung around the police chased them away.

The stoning wasn't for another hour, so I got my dad to buy me a Sprite from the food stand. There was smoke in the air and I was amazed to see a bonfire burning brightly in one corner by the stage. People were throwing things onto it. Officers were strolling round it but they weren't stopping anyone.

'How come the police let them do that?' I shouted up at my dad over the noise of the crowds.

'They're burning Shakir's *books*,' my dad shouted back. 'It's barbaric.'

I watched a book fly into the pyre and become a red bird, spitting fire. I watched the pages being killed by the flames, shrunken by heat, eaten and spewed back into ashes. And I thought that somehow the whole thing was really pretty beautiful.

A little while later, the police came by and put the fire out and ordered the book burners to clear the way, for the stoning was about to begin.

We were near to the front of the crowd, though I had to stand on tiptoe to see. The terrorist Omar Shakir was brought onto the stage. He was dressed from head to foot in billowing white. He looked strangely ephemeral compared

23

to the bulky band of policemen that surrounded him.

The air filled with shouts and spits and howls of rage.

They cuffed Shakir to the pole. Then several men split open the white bags and started shovelling out sand. I watched, transfixed, as they buried his feet, then his knees, then his thighs. Finally, they stopped at his waist and put their shovels down. I looked at Shakir's face. His eyes were tender with sorrow; a few tears were trickling down his cheeks.

A group of men wearing black filed onto stage and each picked up a stone.

The silence grew louder, until it was painful. I found myself staring hard at one of the stones the men were wielding. I couldn't believe that in a minute's time it would be hitting Shakir's rib; or cracking against his arm; or thwacking his head and bursting it like a rotten fruit into red pulp. I couldn't believe that the men holding the stones would actually be able to hold back the disgust in their stomachs and lift their arms and throw them. I couldn't believe that very shortly Shakir would be a carcass and blood would flow across the stage to the tips of our very shoes. It all seemed unreal, like a nightmare I would suddenly wake up from.

When the men raised their stones, I thought my heart might burst with sick excitement. I found myself reaching for my dad's hand. One half of me wanted to squeeze my eyes shut and clamp my hands over my ears; the other wanted to watch without a single blink and drink in every howl of pain.

When I heard the cracking noise, my fear won out. My eyes flew shut. I forced them open quickly, telling myself not to be such a girl.

Then I saw the fountain of blood in the air. The crowd

filled the square with screams of panic. There was another cracking noise. I realised it was gunfire. *One of the men who was supposed to be throwing stones had a gun.* He was shooting the other men; he was shooting the police; shooting into the crowd. The girl with black dreads who I'd seen earlier ran onto the stage and began to dig Shakir out; the police shot her. Shakir pulled himself free of the sand and began to run. A group of men in black jackets surrounded him, firing bullets. My dad bellowed and crouched down, pulling me with him.

The crowd became a mighty rag doll, pushed and pulled by two forces; some people pushed towards the stage to stop Shakir, others ran away from the bullets. I could hardly stand upright; nails clawed me, bodies shoved me; someone clambered over my back and knocked my temple hard against Dad's elbow. I yelled out and Dad held me close up to him. I tried to pull away, to pull him homewards, but there was another burst of gunfire. I actually saw the bullet split air over the sky above me. Then a big weight slammed down on top of me and I drowned in blackness.

'Dad!' I screamed, 'Dad!' The weight on top of me was human; it spurted warm wet blood across me; it groaned. 'Dad, oh Dad, please don't die. I love you Dad, please, oh God . . .'

I was screaming . . .

. . . and then I heard Dad's voice in my ear crying, 'It's all right, Stefan, it's all right,' and I saw his face brush close to mine, his stubble on my cheek, 'It's all right, we'll get him off you.' Above him, a chaos of faces and mouths contorted into Os and eyes blind with panic and hair wet with blood. 'There's a man on top of you; you're okay, you're okay, aren't you Stefan, aren't you? Have you been hurt did you get hit did you?' I let my body go slack, and

I felt no pain, just the heavy weight of the man crushing me onto the cold cobbles and cried, 'I'm okay, Dad, I'm okay I'm okay.'

Then the winds of panic changed direction and blew Dad backwards onto the ground. Someone stamped across him and I yelled, 'No, Dad, no!' He staggered up and I saw him being sucked into the quicksand of bodies. 'Dad, Dad!' The dead man's weight was so heavy I could hardly breathe; my ribs felt as though they were about to crack open. I clenched my fists and drew up my arms and push push pushed against it. He was shifting, slowly shifting, when suddenly I heard weeping and the man was moving and the cool air spilled over me. I lay there, heaving breaths, my body bruised and battered. A woman with golden hair was clutching the corpse, weeping, her eyes pink blotches, '*Someone help me, someone help me, someone.*' I stood on tiptoe and yelled, '*Dad!*' Someone nearly sent me flying again. I crouched down low and found I could move this way. This was another world, of legs and feet propelled by panic, but easier to negotiate than the one above.

I pushed a path through the forest of people, finger-thorns catching in my hair and scratching my face. A ribbon of red tape glimmered; I fought for it. My hands clawed a board. I realised I had found the stage.

The board was weak and I pushed it down flat. There were pools of sand everywhere. The black girl lay writhing on the floor, her dreads matted with blood; a policeman ran across the concrete, stamping on them. The pole which had once held the terrorist hung at a sad angle, swinging gently in the wind.

I ran up onto the pile of stones. The wind blew sand in my eyes and tears bittered my cheeks. The crowds were still scrambling. They looked like the ants in our kitchen who'd panicked when Dad poured hot water over them last week; all unity gone, each individual obsessed with saving his own heartbeat. Watching them, I had never felt so big and yet so small. I opened my mouth and yelled at the top of my voice, '*DADDDD! DADDDD!*'

Once I started yelling, I couldn't stop; the panic took full possession of my voice.

'PUT YOUR HANDS UP!'

My screams broke off jaggedly. Two police, a man and a woman, were pointing guns at me.

'I'm just looking for my dad – I just want my dad,' I whimpered. 'Please.'

I tried to raise my hands but only my left would lift. There was something wrong with the right and I screamed with pain.

'BOTH HANDS!'

'I can't – I can't – it hurts . . .' I looked down and saw that my sleeve was soaked in blood. 'I just want my dad . . .'

'Come down,' the woman beckoned. 'Slowly.'

I clambered down the stones, stumbling and falling at her feet. Pain smashed through my arm again.

'GET UP!' the policeman yelled.

'He's just a kid,' the policewoman said, stopping him. She helped me to my feet. 'Now – have you got an ID card?'

'In my pocket.' I was close to sobbing.

She reached into my pocket and gently pulled it out, scanning it on the sensor on her belt. 'He's just a kid,' she said. 'I'll deal with him.'

The policewoman guided me away from the stage. A line of men were lying on the ground with their hands over their heads, police pointing guns at them and yelling. We hurried down a side street. She kept her gun pointed, looking left right left right. My head was swirling with black; I didn't think I could manage many more steps. A gang of police came sprinting round the corner; they shouted at her and she shouted back. We reached a police car and the policewoman flung open the door. I sank onto the seat. She told me the ambulances were all full, there were none left, too many people were hurt. She'd drive me to the hospital herself.

Her car smelt of oil and some sort of sickly lavender air freshener. I slumped back, conscious that my blood was seeping all over the leather. She switched on the radio and the report crackled out: '. . . *today the public stoning of the terrorist Omar Shakir was prevented by an attack from a group of armed men . . .*' the words sounded so formal; they were all wrong; they couldn't convey the fear, what it had really felt like '. . . *it is thought that the attack was planned by the Words, a radical terrorist organisation linked with ArkQ who are using violent methods to preserve freedom of speech . . .*'

'Did the terrorist get away?' I asked.

'We'll get him,' she said. 'They're chasing after him. He won't get away.'

'I need to call my dad,' I said, reaching into my pocket. Nothing. I tried all my other pockets. 'Oh God. I've lost my mobile phone, I've lost it!'

She took one hand off the steering wheel and passed over her phone. I couldn't grip it properly with my right hand; I had to let it balance on my knee and punch in his mobile number with my left forefinger.

'Dad?' I cried. 'Dad?' I heard him crying with relief and my head swam. 'Dad, I'm okay, I'm okay.'

Four

We were kept waiting for hours in the hospital. The waiting room was crazy with running doctors and flickering fluorescence and crying people and blood splashing onto the floor and a receptionist who couldn't cope. When I finally saw the doctor, he told me I'd sprained my right arm and suffered a severe cut to the shoulder. I had to have a tetanus injection and wear a sling. I wanted to go back to school but Dad insisted that I stay home. He kept making me cups of tea and fussing round me.

The next few days were very strange. I became obsessed with wanting to put the news on and see the story over and over again. But Dad couldn't bear to hear another word about it. In the end, I had to make do with reading the newspapers. But they didn't satisfy me. They made the day sound matter-of-fact, as though it had been nothing out of the ordinary. They didn't describe the blood and the sweat and the raw agony. I'd never considered before that newspapers might not tell events exactly as they were. Suddenly, I became conscious that there could be a gap between the truth and words. I felt confused, because we'd always been taught at school that newspapers were protected by the government and were never wrong. Maybe, I told myself, everyone experienced that day differently, took away a pain as unique as their own iris. Maybe all the newspapers can do is summarise, and so their words have to sound cold and dry and lame.

At night I revisited Trafalgar Square in my dreams. Back at school, I found I could hardly concentrate. We stood up in assembly for the National Pledge and when everyone raised their hand, it reminded me of submitting to the police. I couldn't raise my right because of my sling so I hastily put my left up. *We pledge to honour and obey our government and celebrate the glory of Great Britain* . . . My mouth was too dry for words; I let the rest of the school recite for me. *It is our duty to serve the State, to always speak the truth and protect others from harm* . . . I suddenly saw the Head looking at my left hand and shaking his head sharply; I quickly lowered it. *We are all different, but we are One.* Would the Head be capable of throwing a stone?

Everyone in my class was jealous that I'd been at the Square; none of their parents had let them go. Some of the girls signed my sling, scrawling out hearts in black markers with giggles, and Sally Harper even offered to carry my bag for me. Sally had yellow hair and green eyes with little flecks of grey and blue.

Out in the playground, I saw Jasper Williams filming me on his mobile. Jasper was one of the boys I hated most in class. He had a habit of just walking round the playground and filming anyone in a random situation, whether they were playing footie or skipping. Immediately, their football would dribble to a halt or the skipping rope would go slack. We were all told to film suspicious behaviour and show it to our teacher, so you never could tell how Jasper was going to slant or edit it. I glared at him and he stared back coldly, holding up his mobile like a gun. Then we heard the noise of a plane overhead. Immediately the playground fell silent. Everyone froze, even Jasper. Some of the girls ran for cover under the trees.

The plane passed over. There was a collective sigh of relief. Planes freaked us out. We'd been warned that the ArkQ could hijack one any day and bomb us. We all knew what to do in the event of such an attack; we'd practised the drills in our National Security lessons. We had to run through the emergency exits to the bunker built under the school – if we were still lucky enough to be alive.

After break, our first lesson was English Literature, and that was when something horrible happened.

English Literature was taught by Mrs Kay. She was tall, with dark, wavy hair and a sexy voice. English was now the least popular subject at school for GCSE. Often it was picked by troublemakers or those who didn't do well at the proper subjects like science and history. I only did it because my father told me to.

We'd all recently been issued with brand new e-copies of 1984, where we could scroll from page to page with a flip of a stylus. I thought of the white marble, now yellowy and dusty, sitting in the pot by my bed at home.

'So,' Mrs Kay asked, with a desperate, beaming smile. 'What do you think of the ending of 1984?'

There was a long silence. Whenever Mrs Kay asked us questions about books, none of us really knew what to say.

'Stefan.' She smiled cajolingly, put her head to her side. 'What did you think?'

'Er, I liked it,' I said. There were titters and I shrugged. I stared back into her eyes and repeated, 'I liked it, Mrs Kay.'

Behind me, Jasper whispered, 'Bookshop boy,' under his breath.

'Go on, Stefan.' She lowered her voice and in the spotlight of her gaze it felt as though there was nobody else in the classroom. 'Why did you like it?'

'Well – it's a happy book with a nice ending. I mean, Winston starts off being a bit of a rebel but in the end he learns the government is right and then he marries and they have kids, so everyone lives happily ever after.' I realised I was rambling and I tried to think of something smart to say. 'So I guess it's about the individual – the individual – learning to live in harmony with society and respect their government.'

'You could say that Big Brother is a symbol of a divine force running through society that wishes to bring peace to all.'

'Er, yeah, that's exactly what I was thinking,' I said, and everyone laughed. Mrs Kay's lips curled up in amusement and I mirrored her smile.

Mrs Kay went back to the book and started asking another question about the Two Minutes National Pledge that Winston joins in at the start of the book. I felt a yearning to pull the spotlight of her attention back onto me. Without thinking, I put up my hand.

'Yes, Stefan?' Mrs Kay asked.

I suddenly felt uncertain, but her smile was encouraging, so I blurted out: 'Why was the old version of 1984 so bad that it needed to be Rewritten by the government people?'

Mrs Kay's smile vanished. My words seemed to spread and hover in the room like a stink bomb. Everyone shifted, looking at me, and I wished I could blow the stench away.

'We don't need to discuss this,' Mrs Kay said sharply. 'This is the version that is on the National Syllabus and that you will be graded on in your final exam.'

'Oh – but what was in it?' Jasper asked, intrigued. I

realised then that he didn't even know there was an earlier version. Nor, judging from their confused expressions, did many of the class.

'Put your hand up before you ask a question,' Mrs Kay snapped.

Jasper put his hand up. Mrs Kay ignored him.

'That's enough.'

I lowered my head. The numbers *1984* all swam together, forming one deformed digit. Oh God, why had I said that? Maybe I ought to go up and say sorry at the end. Maybe I should tell her I wanted to be a Rewriter when I left school.

It was then that I noticed the men through the warped circle of glass in the classroom door: two officers, their chins sliced by the upturned collars of their black uniforms.

They're here for me, I realised. *They must be.*

My heart started to jabber. It must be because of what I'd said about *1984*.

But how did they *know*?

Unless Mrs Kay had some special button or monitor under her desk. Unless there was CCTV in the classroom – they'd sent home letters to our parents last week warning it would soon be in place.

'And do you think Winston is a likeable character?' Mrs Kay carried on, acting as though she hadn't noticed their presence.

You can just explain to them that your dad's a bookshop owner, so you're bound to know these things, a voice of reason assured me. But my stomach was churning nervous vomit. I thought about stories I'd heard in the playground about how they tortured terrorists. Left them with burns and no hair and pulled out their teeth and took away their sleep and broke their minds into kaleidoscope pieces.

What if I ended up in Trafalgar Square in front of a jeering crowd?

The men banged on the door and walked straight in. The plastic cover of my e-book was now slippery with sweat.

'We apologise for the interruption.'

The officer flashed an ID card at Mrs Kay. The other officer scanned the class. Everyone shrunk, their copies of 1984 forming a shield of anonymity. As though smelling my fear, he pinned his eyes on me.

Oh God, they've come for me, they really have come for me.

'We're here to see Sally Harper.'

All eyes turned to Sally, who dropped her e-book in shock.

'Well, can't it wait until the end of my class?' Mrs Kay asked. Her voice was fierce, but her fingers nervously twisted her wedding ring.

'I'm afraid it can't. We've spoken to her parents and to your Headmistress and we have permission to remove her from this lesson.'

'May I ask what exactly this is about?'

The man ignored her, beckoning Sally. She hurriedly shoved her computer into her bag. I tried to give her a comforting look, but she rushed past with her head lowered, tears wobbling in her eyes.

Mrs Kay tried to continue the lesson as though nothing had happened. But everyone was too busy watching the figures through the warped glass; too busy listening to the sound of their footsteps slowly dying away. Then silence filled the classroom and stayed there like a fog. No matter how desperately Mrs Kay asked her questions, nobody gave any answers. Finally, Mrs Kay gave up talking about 1984 and said: 'Today's lesson was a useful example of how we should all be on the lookout for any dangerous behaviour.'

The restlessness in the class calmed. But I thought I saw something flash in Mrs Kay's eyes and it disturbed me, for I couldn't understand what it meant.

The bell shrilled for break and there was still no Sally.

The story rushed through the school in a tidal wave of shock. The gossip was that she'd been arrested over her MySpace page. I came back into the classroom to find Jasper sitting in front of the class computer and everyone crowded round him. Standing on tiptoe, I saw Sally's homepage. It had a pretty photo of her smiling and looking cute. It also had a cartoon picture of our Prime Minister being hanged in Trafalgar Square, the rope squeezing his scrawny neck and twisting his face into a grotesque bulge. The caption underneath read, *It'll be you one day!*

'See, she was planning murder!' Jasper cried. 'That's why they came for her!'

'For God's sake, it was only a joke,' Ava, Sally's best friend retorted. 'She didn't mean it.'

'You can't joke about murder or the government,' Jasper said solemnly and we all fell quiet.

After school I hurried home, feeling jittery about the men. What if Mrs Kay mentioned my slip in class to them too?

I wished I hadn't lost my mobile – now I couldn't text Sally to see if she was all right. Then again, all texts were read by the Censorship. I ran upstairs to my room, keen to lose myself in my spy book.

Something was wrong with my bedroom. It took me a while to realise that someone had been moving my things about. I'd left my notebook lying face up. Now it was face down. My wardrobe doors were open and my clothes looked ruffled. The Censorship weren't due here until next week, so it couldn't have been one of them. It could only be the police. Mrs Kay must have spoken to them.

Trembling, I sat down on the bed.

Thank God I didn't keep a diary, even though I wanted to. Sometimes when I lay awake at night I felt there was so much going on in my mind it was like a paintbox being shaken about, all the colours melding with each other in a manic rainbow, and if I could just write them down they would smooth into one beautiful shade that made sense. But I knew I must always keep my thoughts locked in my head; if I put them down on the page I might inadvertently find my words became trip-wires.

Then another thought scared me. I quickly lifted up my mattress. The drawings were still there. They didn't look as though they'd been touched.

The drawings were a risk. I pulled them out, tracing their curves with my fingertip. They were all pictures of the same woman, naked.

Last year, when we'd had a Sex Ed class at school, I'd thought I'd get to see a picture of a woman's body. But the class had mostly involved putting us off ever having sex after we were told about all the diseases we could catch. At school I found myself watching the way girls' curves swung under their uniform, but a female body was still a mystery to me. A red shame gripped me as I wondered if the pictures meant I was a sick perv. If I was the only boy in my class who wondered about this sort of thing.

Still, I couldn't bear to tear them up, so I pushed them back under the mattress.

I ran downstairs and asked my father who had been looking in my room.

'Nobody,' he said. 'Nobody. I've been in the shop all day

and there hasn't been a soul. And before you accuse me, young man, I haven't touched anything either. You're just being silly. Now help me log these books, we're a day behind.'

The bond that had united us since Trafalgar Square snapped. I punched ISBNs into the computer, stomped across the floor, slammed books onto shelves. It was all my dad's fault for ruining my lesson. Now Mrs Kay hated me and it was all his fault. If I didn't have such a weirdo father I would have been just as ignorant as everyone else . . .

After dinner, I surfed the net. When I looked up Sally's MySpace and Facebook pages, they had completely vanished. A chill went through me and I quickly checked my own Facebook page. Empty, but – thank God – still there. It kept shutting down every few days while the Censorship checked all the messages and suspicious comments that they wanted to investigate. Then it would come back up with all our 'Wall' and 'Info' pages wiped clean. Sally had been crazy to take such a risk, even if she'd been joking.

Once again I typed in my name, uploaded a photo. I thought about putting 'Stefan Burns, super spy' into the summary box for a joke, but figured it was too risky.

That was the night before the phone call came. Then, everything changed, and I came to know what it felt like to be the wrong sort of spy.

Five

The phone call came on a Tuesday afternoon after school. The shop was very quiet. Dad kept on making strong teas and reading the paper. I was sitting on the chair by the radiator, reading and feeling hot pipes blast my back. Next to me was the bookcase for W–Z; the rows of books were iced with dust. At the back of the shop, behind my father's chair, was a large black safe peppered with locks. Even I wasn't allowed to know the combination, for this was where all the Banned Books were kept, awaiting collection by the Censorship. My father said it was better that I didn't suffer the temptation. Every so often, though, I found my eyes flicking to the safe. It was developing an increasingly ominous air, as though the books inside were deadly animals that would hiss and spit and bite if it was opened. I kept wondering what was in those books. I wondered if they had been banned because they had sex in them. I wondered about sex.

The bell tinkled. A large, middle-aged woman came bustling in. She was carrying a big plastic blue bag with pink cows and flowers decorated on the side, and it was filled to the brim with books.

'Hello!' she said cheerfully. 'I've got these books – there are some I'd like to sell, and some I'd like to donate.'

'Donate' translated as 'I'm worried these books are on the banned list, so I'm dumping them on you before I can get into any trouble.'

'That's fine, you're very welcome,' my father said, smiling. 'Stefan!'

'Uh huh.' I put my spy book down wearily.

I pulled out a form from the drawer in the shop and got the woman to write down her name and address. As she pulled out fistfuls of books, I scrawled:

Of Mice and Men by John Steinbeck

Stormbreaker by Anthony Horowitz

Harry Potter and the Philosopher's Stone by J. K. Rowling

'This one!' my father tapped the cover. 'Banned.'

Terror sprinted across her face. Then she quickly composed it into a look of blank innocence, like a label on a bottle.

'You say banned? Why's that?'

'Because the government says so,' I said helpfully. 'The government encourages us to read books that promote the positive development of our minds and the safety of our nation.'

'Well, I really didn't know about it, I mean, I've hardly even read it . . .' the woman blustered.

I looked at her with narrowed eyes. She didn't look like a terrorist. Not like the ones I'd read about in books or saw on the news. But still, you never knew. *Be aware at all times.*

'You can be fined five hundred euros and sent to jail,' I said, giving the woman a very direct stare. Sweat dribbled on her cheeks. I couldn't help feeling a thrill, knowing that even though she was three times my age, she was scared of me.

'Stefan!' My dad reprimanded me. He turned back to the woman. 'I'm sorry. It's fine. You weren't to know Harry

Potter is banned, it only turned up on the list this morning. It was felt that any book with magic in might encourage children to dabble themselves. We just got the text warning through.' He reached out and patted her arm. 'It's not your fault.'

'Well – quite. *Quite*. That's exactly why I brought it in today.'

She gave me a stout, defensive look and I shrugged, feeling a little sheepish. I sat back down with my spy novel.

I was vaguely aware of their conversation in the background. Dad said he was happy to give her twenty euros for the Steinbeck and the Alex Rider novel. Then he wrapped up the blacklisted book and put it in the safe.

'Now, I was also hoping that you might be able to suggest a book for my son's birthday?' said the woman. 'Something which isn't on the list, obviously,' she added with a hearty laugh. 'I don't want him to have an e-book like all the other kids, I'd like him to have the same type of book I did when I was a child!'

'Quite right!' my father agreed. 'That's why I only stock *proper* books. I can't stand all those mini computer things. Modern claptrap! I might be old-fashioned but I say a book should have a cover and paper and a nice font!'

It was then that the telephone rang.

'You get it, Stefan,' my father asked.

I put my book down with a sigh and picked up the phone.

'Good afternoon.' It was a man's voice. 'Is this Burns' Bookshop?'

'Yeah,' I said. 'I mean, yes. How can I help you?'

'I was wondering if you had a copy of *Paradise Lost*.'

'Would you like to speak to my dad?' I asked.

There was a funny sort of pause. I was about to open my

mouth and beckon my father over, when the stranger said in an excited voice, 'Are you his son?'

'Yes,' I said, suddenly feeling uneasy. 'You can—'

'No, this is even better. I'm delighted to talk to you . . . ?'

'Stefan,' I said.

'Stefan,' he savoured my name as though we were the best of friends. 'Now, could you go to the *M* section of your shop and look something up for me. I'd be grateful if you could do it quickly, I'm in rather a rush.'

'M . . .' I wove through the labyrinth of bookcases. Reaching *M*, I found myself completely shielded from my father and the woman.

'Are you there?' his voice was very low now, nearly a whisper.

'Yes.' I found myself mirroring his conspiratorial tone.

'That's it. That's good. Now. *Paradise Lost*.'

'Where . . . where do I look?'

'What do they teach you at school? Or has it become a banned book? Dear God.'

I smarted, then caught sight of it on the shelves.

'Milton, John,' I said hotly. 'We have three copies.'

'Three? Can you describe them to me?'

'Well . . .' I was beginning to feel uneasy but the man had me on a hook and, though I was wriggling, I couldn't quite untangle myself. 'There's two brand-new copies, fifteen euros each, and one very old one, it's tatty, and there's a stain on it, so I don't think you'd want that one—'

'I'll judge that for myself. Open it up. Open the first page. Does it have *W* written in pencil on the top, on the front page?'

I pulled it out, balancing it on my knee and flipping it open with one hand.

'Yes—'

At that moment my father appeared and, startled, my knee jerked. The book fell and a few pages unsnaggled from their weak binding, attempting to fly free until the cover slammed down on them.

'Who's on the phone?' My father demanded crossly.

'It's just a man who wants a copy of *Paradise Lost* —' I stopped. The caller's insidious breathing had been replaced by the dial tone. 'I think I lost him, sorry.'

'Who was he, did he give a name?'

'No, he —'

'This book is not for sale, all right? If anyone tries to buy it, it is not for sale.'

'Okay, okay.'

My father knelt down and picked the book up tenderly, as though it was a wounded creature. He seemed very agitated about the pages and gave me a lecture on being more careful. Taking the book to the front, he ordered me to run up to the stockroom and get some binding tape.

The stockroom was a kooky little hidden room that existed behind my bedroom. My dad called it 'The Narnia Room' because we accessed it from the back of my wardrobe. I slid the panel back, scanning the piles of damaged books and cellophane jackets and pots of glue, and grabbed the tape, then hurtled back down again.

Later, as I filed some books into the *M* section, my fingers brushed the newly bound *Paradise Lost*. There was definitely something strange about that book. It felt to me as though its words were fuses, the book a bomb waiting to ignite.

Six

A hand was gripping my shoulder; my eyes fluttered open. It was dark. I could smell my father's breath on my face.

'What is it, Dad?' I asked blearily.

He flicked on the light and we blinked at the fluorescent sting. I sat up. My clock said 3.34 a.m. Dad's face looked gaunt with worry, the night crawling into its wrinkles and creases.

'Stefan, get out of bed and get dressed.'

'What!'

My father yanked back the covers and I got up. He turned away and I took off my pyjamas. 'Hurry up,' he hissed, and I hastily pulled on the school clothes that were hanging over the back of my chair, staring at his hunched back.

'Dad, what's —'

'We're going to have a visitor tonight.'

My father's Adam's apple was bobbing as though it might burst out of his throat. I hadn't seen him look this frightened since the Censorship first invaded. But now I was too old to be fooled by any act. I could sense the emotions he was struggling to conceal, and they terrified me.

'What visitor?' My voice shook. 'Is it the police?'

'No – not the police. The police mustn't know about

this. Nobody must know – okay? Nobody at school – d'you hear?' his voice was edged with anger.

'You have to tell me what's going on!' I cried. 'Who's coming?'

'I'm sorry.' My father touched my shoulder. 'It's some- one who needs our help.'

'But . . . I've got to go to school tomorrow, I've got to do my homework.' I think it was the first time I'd ever defended it.

'Look. We're all ready for the visitor, I have everything prepared.' He ducked his head and went into the wardrobe, sliding back the panel.

What was he doing in the stockroom?

Then he switched on the light and I saw everything. Over the past few days, while I'd been at school, my father had been busy. Gone were the paperclips and cellophane and jackets; in their place was a small camp bed, the old one we'd had stuffed up against the fridge for years. The lamp that usually belonged in the kitchen was by the bed, cord snaking across the floor. A flannel was folded neatly on the pillow, with a toothbrush in plastic on the top.

'Our visitor will stay here. They won't disturb you, and you won't need to disturb them.'

'Are they – are they going to help us with the book- shop?'

'No. No. They'll just be here, in this room, and they'll keep themselves to themselves. We'll be here, but we'll pretend they're not here.'

'But if they're here, they're here; how can we pretend!'

'Stefan –' my father shoved his thumb under his watch- strap, spinning the face round, '– we'll talk more later. I have to go now. Wait for me here.'

'I can't – where are you going –'

'Stefan, I promise I'll be back within the next hour. Just wait for me, okay? Make yourself some hot milk if you're hungry.'

I sat down on the camp bed numbly. My father attempted to ruffle my hair but in his nerves, his nails nicked my ear. I winced and shied away. I listened to the thump of his footsteps as he hurried down the stairs, the tinkle of his keys, the slam of the door.

I ran to the window, watching him jog down the street, his head spinning to the left, to the right. Then I sat back down on the bed. I picked a nail, kicked the metal leg of the bed.

I couldn't sit here. I couldn't do it. We'd been here before, my father and I.

That terrible night, ten years ago. We'd been woken by the phone ringing. Dad had been fretting for hours because Mum was due home from her shift at the hospital. 'She works too hard, they work her too hard,' he kept muttering, accidentally smashing a plate as he did the washing-up. I was only six and I'd missed my bedtime story; *Treasure Island* remained on pause. Then, in the dead of darkness, *bring-brings* cut the air. I remember waking up and getting up. *Treasure Island* banged to the floor. In the hallway, I looked at up my father's face. I was horrified, struck dumb by the expression. As though all the summer had left it, all the shine and hope and beauty, and an eternal winter had blown in with the harshest and most desolate of winds.

He'd told me that Mummy had had an accident. He'd told me I had to sit and wait.

He should have taken me with him. I should have had the chance to say goodbye like he did, as her heartbeats slowly faded into silence. But he wanted to protect me, and so he left me behind in a dark room for the longest three hours of my life.

I wasn't going to let history repeat itself. Now I jumped up and pulled on my shoes. I tumbled down the stairs – stopped – where were my keys? I'd left them back upstairs – *forget them, forget them*. I pulled on my coat and rushed out of the house. The door nearly slammed behind me; I caught it just in time, pulling it shut with the softest of clicks.

Outside, it was pitch black. The houses watched me with dead eyes. It was the first time in my life I had ever been out in London at night. Every night, the booming of the curfew siren would wake me briefly at ten or tangle with my dreams, giving a screaming voice to monsters. Some people did try to challenge the curfew. Every so often you might see a man walking his dog, or a couple of drunks wandering by; then the police would turn up, zap their ID cards and pack them off into a van.

I crouched down, hurrying along the street, each car an island I paused behind. The cool, pale night mist floated about me like spirits, coating my body in goosebumps.

I came near to the end of the street. Where was he, where was he?

I saw them both at the same time. A car coming slowly down the street, my father's face flashing in the back window. And two policemen, walking their night beat, walking round the curve that led into our road.

I was about to jump up and yell *DAD!* but my voice froze in the air. I saw the car pull up by our house. My father was helping someone else get out. In the dark, it looked as though his arm was curled around a strange, floating dark ghost. Then I realised it was a woman, wearing a burka, which meant she must be a Muslim. She was

46

drenched from head to foot in black cloth; the only thing you could see was the dark blink of her eyes.

The car pulled away and my father helped the woman towards the house. She was hobbling and seemed to be very weak. My father's eyes flitted about nervously, but I could see that he was too engrossed in helping her to spot the police.

They were coming down my side of the road. They hadn't spotted my father yet, but within a few seconds they'd be close enough to. Oh God. I had to create a diversion . . . but how?

My spy novels. I thought about the heroes who were so quick-thinking. They created distractions or diversions. They regaled bad guys with clever speeches about how good terrorism was, tricking them into confessions. But I could hardly do that now. No . . . but I had to do something.

Anything.

The policemen were getting closer. My father was still in no man's land; he'd helped the woman as far as the gate.

Think, think, think . . .

I jumped up from my hiding place. The policemen spotted me at once.

'YOU – FREEZE!' One of them yelled.

My legs became jelly. I turned and looked helplessly at my father. He'd reached the front door and was bundling the burka woman inside. He turned and caught sight of me, his face taut with shock. I waited for him to shout out, 'STOP! HE'S MY SON!' But he disappeared quickly into the hallway, kicking the door shut.

'Name,' one of the policeman snapped. 'ID card. What the hell are you doing out here after curfew?'

I handed on my ID card, numb with shock. Betrayal

raged inside me. Where was my father? He was supposed to be protecting me. I'd saved him and he'd repaid me by deserting me!

'He's only sixteen,' the other policeman said. 'You live in this road, I see. What are you doing out beyond the curfew?'

'I . . .' I gasped, trying desperately to think up an excuse.

'I said, what are you doing out past the curfew?'

'I was just . . . just walking – I was ill and I really needed some air, I thought I'd just . . . I just . . .'

The policemen exchanged glances.

'I think he's one for the Institution, what do you think?'

'I don't know – it seems a bit harsh,' the other said in a low voice. 'He's just a kid—'

'D'you want to get yourself fired?' the other hissed. 'This is our job. You know the guidelines – we find a kid out after curfew, we take him in.'

They both turned to look at me and I saw the last traces of compassion in their faces vanish. One of them reached out and grabbed my arm roughly.

'No – no. NO!' I yelled in panic.

And then I heard footsteps hammering up the road.

'Stop!'

My father. He came pounding up and I felt my insides curl with dread. I knew what would happen now; he would splutter and stammer the way he did when the Censorship came. Now we would both end up locked up.

'Stefan . . . have you been sleepwalking again? For God's sake!'

The policemen were jolted. Then they exchanged dubious glances. As though they didn't believe a word of it.

'It's a condition he has,' my father went on, 'a terrible case of noctambulism. I have a doctor's number for him –

you can call him if you need to. I'm so sorry – it won't happen again, I promise.'

I saw the policemen's expressions change. Now they thought he might be telling the truth, even if it was a strange one. Hope flashed in my heart. I looked up at my father and felt a deep admiration in my gut. It was something I'd never felt for him before.

'Make sure it doesn't,' they said.

In the distance, a dog began to howl. Distracted, the policemen hurried off. I turned to my father and he grabbed my arm and pulled me into the house.

The moment we were inside, he started shouting at me.

At first I couldn't take it in. I was still in shock, still gasping breath. Then I burst out: 'I saved you! I saved you and now you're yelling at me!'

I turned and tumbled up the stairs in a rage. My father tore up after me. I thought he was going to apologise. Instead, he pulled me back and went into my bedroom first. He opened the wardrobe doors. The panel which led to the secret bedroom had been slid shut. My father knocked against it gently. There was no reply. My father muttered something that sounded like a blessing, then turned to me and put a finger to his lips.

'Go to bed now,' he whispered. 'It's been a long night.'

Seven

I woke up a few hours later.

I got up, tiptoed into the wardrobe and put my ear to the panel. I could hear faint noises.

I gently tapped my knuckles against it. No reply.

I stepped back, aware that Dad would be angry with me. Then indignation overcame my guilt. Dad hadn't given me any warning last night. And now I had a stranger in my room and I still had no idea who the hell she was. I rapped sharply and yanked back the panel.

The stranger lowered the mirror *he* was holding. I stared at the scissors in his other hand, the fuzz-scraps of beard that lay scattered in his covers. The burka from last night lay in a ghostly heap on a chair. So that had been a disguise.

He smiled and nodded. I muttered 'Bye' and stumbled out.

Downstairs my father said, 'Okay, Stefan? We'll talk about it all tonight.'

'Okay,' I muttered. I thought – the first crack of the chasm was opening up between us – if he's going to lie to me, I'm going to lie to him.

In the car, the silence was broken intermittently by the windscreen wipers gently smearing away flecks of rain.

'Please do remember,' my father said as we pulled up

outside the gates, 'we must keep this quiet. Okay, Stefan? . . . *Stefan?*'

I nodded and ran out, slamming the door. I arrowed through the kids milling about in the playground, swinging lunchboxes and skipping and playing footie, and dived into the school hall.

My shoes clicked on the polished parquet as I hurried to the Truth Box. It was a large wooden thing, a bit like a phone box. I slipped inside and shut the door. A little bulb came on, bathing me in fluorescent light. I sat down on the metal chair for a while, feeling hot and strange. Then I realised why the man had looked so familiar.

He was Omar Shakir.

The terrorist writer who had escaped the stones in Trafalgar Square.

My dad was hiding a terrorist in the bedroom next to mine.

Before me was a small desk with a sheet of paper and a pen on a chain. And a box with a dark slit, a mouth hungry to feed on secrets. Above them was a plaque, a reminder to all:

THE TRUTH IS THE GREATEST WEAPON
AGAINST DARKNESS
THE TRUTH WILL SET YOU FREE

I looked up at the heights of the booth. A moth was bashing against the light. It suddenly felt as though all the suspicions ever penned in here – a suspicious package, a look, a stray phrase a parent might have said – were crawling up the walls like invisible insects, whispering in corners. My eyes fell to the desk. Students only picked up the pen with care. Once or twice in the past, a few had written false or silly stories. Their punishments had been so severe that the Truth Box was now regarded with awe. Even the wildest of school rebels, the expert graffiti artists, wouldn't touch it.

I wanted to pick up the pen and write:

I don't know what to do. I thought I knew my dad. I thought he was a good man who liked books a bit too much, but a good man. He's always been so afraid of doing anything wrong. He pays his taxes on time. He moans about the inspectors, but in the end he always plays by their rules. Now he seems like a stranger to me.

I sat there for some time, then slipped out of the booth, the words still heavy inside me.

As I closed the door behind me, Mrs Kay caught me. I flushed, guilt painting red all over my face.

'Everything all right, Stefan?'

'Fine – it's all fine,' I said quickly.

All through assembly, lessons, break, lessons, lunch, lessons, I churned and churned with confusion and anger. The moment the school bell shrilled, I ran out of school, ignoring the taunts at my back (*'Go Stefan, go Stefan!'*), footsteps thwacking on the pavement. Halfway home, I stopped, panting, spotting a stone by the side of the road. I picked it up, caressing its jagged edge, then put it into my pocket and kept on running.

♔

'Hello, Stefan,' my father said in a bright, nervy voice as I came in.

I ignored him and pounded up the stairs went to my bed-room. I invaded the wardrobe and slid back the panel. The terrorist was in bed asleep, nightmares frowning across his face. By his bed lay a copy of the Qur'an. I took a step forward; then fear halted me. I remembered how it felt the night my mum died, as though her end had slashed open my heart and left it to bleed grief for the rest of my life. I thought about all those people who had lost their mums in terrorist attacks, or fathers, or sisters, or brothers or uncles or friends or teachers. This man was responsible for wave upon wave of pain and misery. I took the stone out of my pocket and whammed it at him.

He woke up with a bellow. The stone bounced off his shoulder and hit the floor.

'Hey!' he cried, clutching his shoulder, his eye whites wild with fear.

'You should be dead, you deserve to be dead,' I cried. I heard footsteps on the stairs. 'Get out! You shouldn't be here!'

'What the— What are you doing, you stupid kid!'

'Stefan!' my father came up behind me. 'Stefan!'

I whirled round to face him.

'You're hiding a terrorist! A *terrorist*, Dad! If the police find out, they'll hang us!'

'He's —'

'*I am not a terrorist!*' the terrorist cried, sitting up. His shirt spilled open, revealing a criss-cross of wounded skin. There was a flower of blood forming where my stone had hit him. I felt ill; I hadn't meant to harm him; and then I hated him even more, for making me stoop to his level.

'You —'

'I'm not a terrorist! You told me I'd be safe here!' he appealed to my father. 'I'm not safe with him here – not if he starts to talk.'

'He won't talk!' my father protested. 'It's just that I haven't prepared him properly yet. Just let me take him down and explain everything to him – and then he'll be fine.'

'He had better not talk!'

I felt fury roaring up inside me. This was *my* home; he was in *my* room. Only fear of what he might do to me kept the angry words shoved to the back of my throat, but once we were downstairs, they erupted out of my mouth.

'DAD, WHAT ARE YOU DOING —'

'Ssh! SSH!' He made me sit down in the kitchen. 'Have some hot milk.'

Hot milk. His answer to everything. I took an angry sip and burnt my tongue. I felt like smashing the mug to the floor.

My father sat down opposite me, sipping his milk. It left beads over his beard and he wiped them away with the back of his trembling hand.

'I'm sorry – I know what you must be thinking,' my father explained. 'The Words were originally going to take him, you see. But then the assigned hideout went under surveillance. And then Sasha Brooks couldn't take the risk. My bookshop was their last choice, Stefan. It was just a reserve location, and I really wasn't expecting them to call on me.'

'Who are the Words?' I tugged at my memory. 'I've heard of them! They were on the news – they're terrorists! They're part of ArkQ'

'Not at all! The Words are not part of ArkQ – not that ArkQ are as dangerous as the government would have us believe, anyhow. They make out we've never suffered such a threat from any group before, that they made al-Qaeda and the IRA look like angels in comparison – it's all completely overblown and over-hyped so that they can use our fear to control us and make new laws. As for the Words – they're a group who were set up by Kaiser West to help protect writers and bloggers who are being persecuted by the government. Omar Shakir is a very talented writer, Stefan. They're trying to help him.'

'He's not a writer, he's a terrorist!' I objected.

My father got up and went to the safe which held the Banned Books. He twisted the locks quickly – I saw that the combination began with 9, though his body shielded the rest of the code. He drew out a book, kicked the safe shut and placed it down before me. The cover was a grainy black and white picture of London streets, with a silhouette, painted blood red, running through them. At the bottom, in bold black letters, was the title: *The Fall* by OMAR SHAKIR.

I shook my head, unable to find the words to match my outrage. My father believed that those who played with words for a living were gods who could do no wrong. I felt as though I was the adult and he the naïve kid I was trying to educate.

'Listen – all Omar Shakir did was to write about characters – *fictional* characters – who were planning a terrorist attack. The next thing that happens is that he's arrested and nearly stoned to death. Should Shakespeare have been hanged for creating Macbeth, the serial murderer? Should J. K. Rowling be put on trial for encouraging children to indulge in magic? A story is a story. Shakir's strength as a writer was seen as a threat by the government, because he writes with great subtlety and, more importantly, ambiguity. He created terrorist characters who were misguided but sympathetic – i.e. human beings. He wrote something that they could have interpreted as for or against the State. Before this book was even published, Shakir was arrested and the book banned. But the Words set Shakir free – and they set his words free as well. The Words decided to secretly print copies of the book themselves. And, you know, ever since they started selling this underground, the orders have gone through the roof. *Everyone* wants to read this book. And you know why? Because it's fresh. It's *real*. It hasn't been tampered with by some Rewriter who's hollowed out its flesh and guts.'

My father held the book up as though it were a sacred text.

'You know, Stefan, if you were to just read this book, you'd see what a *good* man Omar is. This book – it's so moving, it's so humane – a man who has written a book like this could *never* be a terrorist.'

I stared at my father in disbelief.

'How stupid are you, Dad? Books *are* lies. Stories *are* lies. A terrorist can write anything down. It doesn't mean he's good.'

My father stared at me with disappointed eyes.

'That's where you're wrong, Stefan. There's a part of a book that never lies. A writer puts his soul into a book. Every word is like two sides of a coin – one side is the lie, the story, and the other is the truth, the insight. You can judge someone by the stories they tell.'

He tried to push the book in my direction. I quickly pushed it back. There was no way I was going to read it and let its ideas taint me. What would Mrs Kay say if she thought I was reading a book that hadn't been Rewritten by the government? She'd go mental.

'Stefan, you have to believe that Omar is a good man. All he has done is write books and they've tried to kill him.'

'Look, Dad – the London attacks were *inspired* by a novel. Someone could easily read this book and get ideas in their head about committing another attack. It's *evil*.'

'No, Stefan, no. An author can't be responsible for his readers. People take from books what they want. You know, Stefan, the man who killed John Lennon – he was obsessed with *The Catcher in the Rye*.'

'*The Catcher in the Rye*!' I cried. 'Well, that's top of our list of Banned Books. It's a murder manual, isn't it? It's pure evil, so —'

'It's a perfectly innocent book about a young boy who is struggling with American society in the 1950s.'

'Does it have murder in?'

'No.'

'Guns?'

'No.'

'Well . . .' I was completely confused.

'So you see,' Dad said triumphantly, 'you can't blame Omar or Salinger for what their books have created. We have a duty to do good and help Omar.'

I stared down at the table. I felt my father's eyes on me, bullying me to agree. Finally, I looked up at him sullenly. And then I saw the despair on his face.

'I can't stop you telling anyone,' he said helplessly. 'There's nothing I can do if you do. But you'll end up in the Institution. You know that.'

'Well, what would you care if they took me?'

Dad looked stunned. Then he reached out and grabbed my arm.

'I'd never forgive myself. Your mother would never forgive me.'

'Okay,' I said. 'I promise. I promise.'

I went up to my room to do my homework. But I couldn't concentrate. I could hear Omar reciting his Islamic prayers, the rhythms of Arabic rolling under the door. My father stayed below, sitting at the table, lost in thought.

When I went to bed, I thought about what would happen if the police found us out and I got sent to the Institution. It might not be so bad. The Institution was set up years ago when England was a very different place. Dad had told me that back then, kids did whatever they liked: they answered back to teachers, or bunked off school, or took drugs, or walked round in gangs terrorising neighbourhoods. He said the papers were full of headlines about teenagers knifing each other. That's when the Institution was invented. It made me feel glad to be alive now and not then. Even though I was scared of the police and teachers, I'd hate to go to school every day fearing I might get knifed.

Even though we didn't have knife crime any more, the Institution still existed. You could be sent there if your parents were accused of terrorism. Or if you were caught fighting; or if you were excluded. I'd even heard of one boy who'd been rude to a teacher being sent there.

I'd heard it wasn't such a bad place. It wasn't like prison where they tortured terrorists. You had to be under eighteen to go to the Institution, so they put you in your own room with a TV and gave you special lessons and counselling. Hell, the way my stupid father was behaving, I might be better off there.

Eight

The following morning, after an hour of soul-searching, I slipped out of the Truth Box. I had come into school an hour early and I'd thought there was nobody about except the odd cleaner sweeping dirty water down the corridors. Outside the box, however, I found Mrs Kay waiting for me again. Eyeing up the crumpled ball in my fist, she stretched out a hand, red talons rippling like a bird eager to dig into prey.

'Would you like to give that to me, Stefan?' she asked lightly.

'It's nothing. I didn't write anything,' I cried, quickly stuffing it into my pocket.

Mrs Kay laced her fingers in front of her, fixing stern eyes on me.

'I'd like to see you in my office after school, Stefan,' she said. 'Come to my room at four p.m., okay?'

I didn't say anything. My heart was thumping hard.

'Don't look so worried,' she added ominously. 'You're not in any trouble.'

♔

Back in the classroom, I sat and waited for register to be taken. Soon all the seats were filled, except for one.

59

The empty orange plastic chair where Sally Harper had used to sit beamed at me like a warning. Ever since she had been arrested over her MySpace page, she hadn't been seen in school. Behind me, I heard Jasper and his friends chatting.

'My dad let me have some wine last night,' one of them said.

His friends – led by Jasper – sneered and jeered in disbelief.

'Oh, sure,' Jasper said. 'He'd really let you drink that poison. We'd be visiting you in hospital now if you'd drunk wine, wouldn't we?'

'I heard that Sally Harper was drinking wine when she did her MySpace page.'

'She's been taken to the Institution,' Jasper said, swinging back in his chair and waving a bag of Minty Mints. 'My dad said.'

Jasper's dad was very powerful. He worked for the government and was one of the men in charge of the Institution.

'What happens in the Institution?' someone asked.

'Well, she is a terrorist,' Jasper said slowly, sucking on his sweet, 'so obviously she'd get maximum terrorist treatment – she'll be locked in a dark room for a week without food and they put rats in there who are starving and they waterboard you and then—'

I thought of Sally's soft face and sweet smile and spun round to Jasper and cried, 'That is all a load of bollocks and you know it! The Institution is there to make bad people good, they don't treat you like that . . .'

Jasper looked stunned for a moment that I'd answered him back. Then he said, 'Oh, are we in love with Sally Harper? You and Sally! You can be terrorists together!'

At which point, Mrs Kay entered the room and we all stood up to greet her.

'Good morning Mrs Kay,' we chorused.

I sat back down in my chair. I could feel sweat oozing down my spine and collecting in the little basin of skin at the bottom. Jasper didn't realise how much his words had stung me. In Geography, when we were supposed to be looking up maps on our e-exercise books, I went to Google and typed in RATS PUNISHMENT. One website told me:

> *The Chinese invented a method of torture where rats can be used to eat humans alive. In medieval times, the Tower of London had a rats' dungeon. As the tide of the River Thames rose, rats would enter the cells and tear flesh from the prisoner's arms and legs.*

I shuddered, then quickly flipped back to a map of America. At the end of every day we had to hand our e-exercise books in so they could check the web pages we surfed. Jasper had once got into trouble for putting CCTV into Google to find out where all the cameras were. But if they asked me, I could just say I was interested in rats for a Biology lesson. Something like that.

I looked up at Mrs Kay's face and she gave me a brief, secret smile, as if to say, *Don't be afraid*. I felt reassured, but only for a few minutes. I felt as though I was standing at a terrible crossroads. If I told Mrs Kay about Omar, I would probably be okay. *The government protects those who tell the truth*, said all the signs. *Come clean about a terrorist and you will be rewarded; but withhold information and you will be seen as an accomplice.* Omar Shakir would be arrested and possibly my father too, but I would definitely not end up in a dark place with rats' teeth gnawing at me. But how could I do that to my father? Yet if I didn't say anything now, and the Censorship found Omar in the secret room, then I would be the son of a terrorist, someone who had colluded against the government.

Suddenly I felt furious with my father. How could he put me in this position? Then I cursed myself for ever going to the Truth Box and attracting suspicion.

All through the day the coin of indecision tossed over and over in my mind: *Tell her, don't tell her; tell her, don't tell her.* And all the while, the hands of the clock ticked round and round like the countdown to an explosion.

♔

There were plenty of reasons to tell. For one thing, I wasn't happy at home any more. I thought of my bedroom. Though it was small, it had always been mine, every corner and cranny, from the little hole in the skirting board where whiskers peeped out, to the dirty walls where I hung my posters to cover the dull stains with colour.

Now my books had been taken from their shelves and piled in a corner. Heaps of old books and covers patch-worked the floor; rolls of Sellotape were stacked like rings in a tree-trunk. Every time I wanted to sit down and read or draw or do my homework, to dip into my own world, there would be footsteps on the stairs and the sound of my father humming. *You don't mind if we just use your room as the stockroom, just for now?* he kept saying, in a tone that suggested that, even if I did mind, it wouldn't make any difference.

Nor was I enjoying the company of Omar.

He wasn't what I'd been expecting. He wasn't like Anne Frank. We had studied her diary in school. Anne Frank was a Jewish girl who had been hidden by a family in a secret room during the Second World War, to save her from the horrors of Nazi concentration camps. The picture of Anne's face on the cover looked gentle and serene. She had been brave and kind and wise about her terrible situation.

Omar, however, was rude and ungrateful. I suppose you could forgive his temper to an extent. He was stuck in a tiny room all day and night; he could only risk slipping out to the toilet for thirty-odd seconds. He complained that his muscles were aching from lack of use and I frequently heard the gentle creak of floorboards as he paced round in a constricted circle. My father, who was endlessly patient with him, tried to console him by saying, 'You might not be able to exercise your body, but you can still exercise your mind. You can have any book in our shop.'

At dinnertimes, my father cooked extra portions of food. He often got me to carry up a plate to Omar. I would knock on the secret door and find Omar slouching on his bed. Sometimes he would pick his nose, careless of my grossed-out face, or start tucking in and burp loudly. He never said thank you. In fact, the other only words he ever reserved for me were sarcastic. Once he asked me what I was reading at school and I said, 'I'm reading *1984* – the new improved version.' He had laughed hysterically until my face burnt a violent red.

Some evenings, my father would send me down into the shop as a lookout, in case the Censorship suddenly stopped by. Then he would hurry upstairs and talk to Omar. I used to creep up the stairs and sit on the landing, trying to listen to their conversation. They spoke in agitated voices and there were certain expressions that kept cropping up again and again. *Grain of sand* was one of them. *Paradise Lost* was another. I heard Omar saying in a very loud voice once, 'Can you really be sure that this is the safest place for it?' and my father replying, 'It's always safer to have something right under their noses than hidden away suspiciously.' I crept back downstairs and flicked all the way through *Paradise Lost*, wondering if someone had scribbled a secret message into a corner. But I couldn't see anything.

Their discussions scared me as much as they intrigued me. I feared that Omar was turning my father into a terrorist too. That they might be planning some sort of terrible attack. Every day that went by, my father seemed more and more of a stranger. He stopped asking me if I'd done my homework. I even had to remind him that I needed a new pair of shoes because he hadn't noticed my old ones were falling apart. His mind seemed to have narrowed to only one focus: Omar, Omar, Omar.

Then, yesterday, Omar had done something that made me hate him. Mr Phillips, who was teaching Physics, let us go home fifteen minutes early for good behaviour. I had raced up the stairs . . . to find Omar in my bedroom.

He had found my drawings. The ones I'd hidden under my mattress. He was trying to put them back but I had caught him.

'I was just – checking for bugs,' he said.

I stared at the pictures, flushed. They were all drawings of one woman. And she was naked in every sketch.

'Well, glad to know you're a typical teenager,' Omar added cheerfully. 'You should read D. H. Lawrence. It might help.'

When I got mad at him, he didn't even apologise. He just crept back into the stockroom and shoved the panel shut. I wanted to tell my father what he'd done, but then I'd have to explain who my pictures were of.

Now that Omar had seen them, they suddenly seemed dirty and gross. I went to tear them up, then stopped myself.

I wasn't going to let him censor me. I could draw whatever I liked. Next time I would just choose a better hiding place.

'When will Omar go?' I had asked Dad last night.

'I can't tell you that,' he said. 'I'm sorry, I know this is hard for us all, but please be patient.'

I had stared at my father's face in alarm. He had always seemed such a dry man to me; I had never seen him look so passionate or excited about anything. I felt afraid for him. What if Omar was just using us? What if Omar was leading us into a trap? That was why I'd gone to the Truth Box again this morning. This time I'd written a few words down, then guiltily screwed up the paper. Then Mrs Kay had caught me. I wondered if there was a camera in the Box, for it had seemed that she'd been waiting for me to come out.

And now I was going to have to decide.

❦

Tell her, don't tell her; tell her, don't tell her.

I was so churned up that I spent the lunch-hour unable to eat anything in my nervous state; I just wandered around the playground in a daze.

When I got back to class and opened my desk, it looked as though someone had messed my things around. For one paranoid, crazy moment I thought Omar might have crept into school and hunted through my stuff. Then I heard Jasper's sing-song voice behind me.

'"Rats punishment" – how interesting! Amazing what you can find on the web these days.'

I spun round furiously. Then I picked up my e-exercise book. Jasper must have seen what I'd been surfing.

'You'll end up with rats eating you soon,' I hissed, instantly regretting my lame comeback. Jasper laughed loudly, and so did half the class.

I soon forgot about Jasper. The clock, which was normally so slow, spun round and round and all too soon the last bell had shrilled. It was time for my interview with Mrs Kay. And I still had no idea what I was going to say to her.

Nine

I stood outside the classroom, watching Mrs Kay through the warped glass. She was sitting at the front of the class, marking e-exercise books, her stylus flipping from page to page, electronic ink spooling red cyber scrawl. When I entered, she looked up and smiled.

'Sit down,' she said. 'I just wanted to have a little chat, Stefan.'

Her tone surprised me. As though the bell for end of classes had kicked away the wall between us.

'So, how are you?'

I was thrown off balance.

'I'm – I'm fine,' I said. A silence. Then a bee buzzing lazily at the window. 'I'm enjoying English. I'd really like to be a Rewriter when I grow up.'

I'd been expecting her to look impressed but she just nodded.

'Did you see *Good Boys* on TV last night?' she asked.

'Uh – we don't have a TV. My dad says it's better for me to read, which is just so boring . . .' I trailed off, confused. This didn't seem to be an interrogation at all.

She carried on chatting to me in such a friendly fashion that I found myself relaxing in relief. I wanted to laugh at myself for wasting a whole day tying myself into knots of worry. It was obvious she had forgotten all about the Truth Box.

As we chatted, I noticed that she had a habit of using her stylus to swing a curl of black hair back over her shoulder. I couldn't hold my gaze steady; it kept on slipping down, down, down over the filmy folds of her blouse to the curving creases of her black skirt. I wondered if the body I'd sketched in the pictures resembled her in reality. My cheeks grew a little warmer. Then all of a sudden I realised she had stopped speaking and I sat up, nervous that she had read my thoughts.

'Stefan, I'd like you to do something for me,' she said.

'Um, sure,' I said hastily.

'I'd like you to recite the National Pledge to me.'

'What? Here? Now?'

'Yes. I just want to be sure you know it.'

Suddenly I felt as though a spotlight had been swivelled onto me.

I coughed a few times and then began.

'We pledge to honour and obey our government and celebrate the glory of Great Britain . . .' I broke off, gulping.

'Why don't you stand up?' she suggested.

'Yeah, sure.' I jumped to my feet and raised my right arm. It felt a bit weird, as though I was being asked to take an exam. I was certain this was being taped. I had a scary vision of a room full of police and officers, listening in on me.

'It is our duty to serve the State . . .' I was desperate to sound confident, for my voice to shine with love for my country, but it emerged in a weak and wobbly trill. 'To always speak the truth and protect others from harm . . .' I stared at Mrs Kay's high heels, aware of her eyes pinned on me. What if, right now, my father had already been arrested? What if they were now assessing me to see whose side I was on? 'We are . . .' I suddenly stopped. My eyes flicked up to Mrs Kay. She leaned forward, frowning.

'Start the line again,' she suggested gently.

'We are all different . . . Sorry . . . I just . . . I've said it so many times, I can't believe I've forgotten it . . . I just . . .' I shook my head. 'I'm really sorry, my mind's just gone really blank.'

My legs felt shaky and I was desperate to sit down, but afraid to do so without her permission.

'We are all different but we are . . .' I tried again, but my words hung in the air like a half-built bridge.

Mrs Kay played with her stylus for a minute. I felt hollow inside, as though I'd failed her.

'Stefan,' she said in a low voice, 'I'd like to take a look at your e-exercise book. Can you get it for me?'

'Sure, sure, of course.' I hurried back over to my desk and got it out. Then I collapsed onto the chair, waiting as she skimmed through my work, my notes, my web history.

'Stefan,' she said, in a tone of voice that made me sit upright with a fresh wave of sweat, 'I'm rather concerned. Can you explain this?'

She held out the e-exercise book. I stared at the log, which detailed all the web pages I'd visited that day. All the words I'd entered into Google search. My mouth literally fell open in shock when I read:

Rats
CCTV
Guns
Knives
The Words

'I didn't do this!' I cried.

Her face hardened. When I had failed the Pledge, I'd felt

that she was still sympathetic towards me. Now her eyes were icy with distrust.

'Well, can you tell me how this came to appear in your book, then?' she asked.

'I didn't – I didn't – someone is setting me up, I swear—' Then I realised. 'Jasper!' I spat out. 'Jasper did this . . . at lunch . . . you can look it up on the CCTV, rewind it, you'll see.'

'There's no CCTV in this room, Stefan,' Mrs Kay said in a cool voice. 'So I'm afraid it would just be your word against his.'

I felt as though my body had turned to liquid. I was too shocked to even speak. This is it, I thought, this is it. I'm going to end up in prison.

'Please,' I whispered, holding my forehead, 'please don't . . . don't send me there . . . at least just let me try again with the Pledge . . . just don't send me there . . .'

'Where?' Mrs Kay suddenly reached across and touched my shoulder. I flinched and then looked up at her, sweat streaming down my face, salty on my lips.

'Stefan, are you scared that I'm going to have you put into prison or the Institution?'

I nodded, savouring the feel of her fingers through my shirt, wanting to move over and cling to her.

'Stefan, when you were in the Truth Box this morning you wrote something down that you didn't submit. If there is anything that you want to tell me, then now is the time to say it. You're in a very dangerous position. You've failed at the key tests set by the government to ascertain your com- mitment to the school and State – you couldn't recite the Pledge and now your e-exercise book is full of suspect sites.'

So it *was* all a test: just as I'd thought. Mrs Kay stood up, looming over me.

'Stefan, if there is anything you're keeping back, you must tell me now.'

I stared down at my hands. *Make something up*, a voice cried wildly, *just make it up*.

'It's just my dad,' I improvised. 'He's been shouting at me a lot . . . it's hard to concentrate on my homework and . . . and . . . Jasper's been giving me a hard time . . .'

'Let's return to the subject of your father,' she said firmly and I flushed, wondering if I was plainly such a terrible liar. 'Why does he shout at you? What's wrong?'

'He's just under pressure – he runs this bookshop and we don't make much money and he doesn't even like e-books so we're out of date and . . . you know . . .' I laughed, shrugging, then swallowed. Her close presence was making me hot; the sickly smell of her perfume floated about, making me feel almost delirious with desire and fear. I felt as though she knew there were unspoken words inside me, teetering on the brink; she was hunting for the right way to coax them out.

'And? What else, Stefan?' she whispered. 'What else?'

'He's . . . there's . . . I . . . I can't tell you,' I burst out, shaking my head. 'I just – you'll tell, you'll tell.'

'Stefan, I won't tell anyone. Not unless I think you're in danger or someone's hurting you. I don't work for the government. Remember that I'm your teacher.'

'But you just said that – you just said you tested me for the government—'

'I had to do the test,' she said gently, 'I'd lose my job if I didn't. The paperwork is there and it has to be filled out. But look,' she whispered, leaning in so close that I could feel her breath against my ear, 'between you and me, I'm going to say you passed the National Pledge and tonight I'll take your e-exercise book home and wipe it clean.' She

71

stood up, glancing behind her back, then turned back to me. 'D'you believe me?'

I looked up at her and nodded. Relief came over me, like a cool breeze on my sweat-soaked skin. I knew then that I could fall; I knew I could fall and she would catch me.

'My dad is hiding a terrorist writer called Omar Shakir in a secret room in our house.' For the first time that day, I spoke clearly and calmly.

There. The words were out. I suddenly felt the way you do when you wake up after recovering from a dose of flu: pleasantly sharp and clean, relieved to be back to your old self again.

Then I looked up and saw Mrs Kay's face. She looked absolutely horrified.

'Right,' she said quickly, 'I'm glad we've sorted that for you. I have some marking – can you help me carry it to my car?'

'But—'

'Quick!' she checked her watch. 'Come on. I have to get home.'

We hurried out to the playground. The expanse of grey between the school and her car seemed like a desert that went on for ever. A wind blew around us; I looked up and saw helpless clouds being tugged all over the sky. As she fumbled with her keys to the car, I saw her hands were shaking violently. Then we were safe in the car and she breathed out hard and said, 'I didn't realise. I thought you were just having a little trouble at home, I thought maybe your father had allowed a Banned Book to slip through the system. I thought, at the worst, you'd read 1984 in the original.' She turned to look at me, her face breaking into a terrible smile. 'And then I was going to tell you off and get the copy back. And we'd advise you to take Behaviour Pills for a month and that would be it.' She bit her lip so hard it turned white. 'You weren't joking or lying back there, were you?'

I shook my head, wide-eyed.

'It'll be on the CCTV,' she said.

'But you said—'

'I wanted you to open up. It's procedure. The instructions advise us to tell you that there's no CCTV. But, believe me, there is.'

In her shocked state, she was clearly spilling things she wasn't meant to say.

'But – what shall I do?' I panicked.

'Stefan, you have to speak to your father. He has to get that writer out of your house tonight. If he doesn't, you will end up being taken away and I won't be able to help you.'

I felt panic scream through me. I had thought that, by telling her, everything would be all right. I could already picture the row ahead. My father would never listen. It was hopeless.

'Can't you go and speak to someone? Can't you tell them Omar has forced us to take him in, that he's threatened us at gunpoint?' I cried wildly. 'I mean – it's kind of true. He's brainwashed my father.'

'You'll end up in the Institution,' she said flatly. 'Why the hell is your father taking such as risk?'

'I don't know, he's just stupid.'

'He loves books,' she said sadly. 'I saw his file.' A pensive silence. Then: 'Stefan – I'm going to do something quite crazy now. Something that you must never tell anyone I did. I'm going to go back and get hold of the CCTV recording. And I'm going to wipe it.'

'Thank you,' I stammered, overwhelmed with gratitude. 'Thank you, thank you.'

'There's no guarantee,' she said. 'I don't know if they make copies; I won't know if someone else has a recording that's being analysed. They don't tell us to keep us on our toes. But I will try, for you. Now go home and speak to your father.'

♛

We are all different, but we are One.

I woke up in the middle of the night, remembering the National Pledge word for word. I wanted to push back the covers and run into school and recite it all perfectly for Mrs Kay.

I couldn't get back to sleep after that. I lay awake as pearly light ebbed into the room and the soft noises of the city became scratchy. I hadn't even been able to have a discussion with my father about the terrorist. When I'd tried, he had said, 'I'm not going through this any more with you, Stefan. Just shut up,' with a roughness that had shocked me. I lay and thought about extremes I might go to. I could go down into the shop and find the heaviest tome and then go into his room while Omar was sleeping and smash it down on his—

Just the thought made me shudder. I wasn't capable of murder, not in a million years.

I skipped breakfast, too ill to eat. At school I sat at my desk and waited for Mrs Kay to come and take the register. She was late. I became convinced that she had been taken away and it was all my fault.

When I heard the click of her footsteps, I felt relief.

I tried to catch her eye as she entered, but she ignored me.

At the end of register, as everyone was streaming out, I went up to her. I noticed she looked pale and tired. She nodded abruptly at me and rummaged in her bag. I opened

74

my mouth and then her look closed it. The fear in her eyes frightened me. I felt the eyes of the camera like a knuckle between my shoulder blades. She passed over my e-exercise book and a silent agreement passed between us.

A few days passed and nothing happened.

A week passed and nothing happened.

I began to stop waking in the night in a sweat. And then my father told me that in a few nights' time, Omar would be moving to a new location; it was too risky for him to stay in our place for too long.

I thought that everything was going to work out. Omar would move on, and we would go back to our ordinary, quiet lives. I would no longer read spy books with a sense of longing; I had tasted danger and in real life it was too bitter. I was happy to become a square, to sit and read, to behave myself, do my homework, be good. Anything to sleep well at night and not walk around like a nervous wreck.

And then the Censorship decided to pay us a visit.

Ten

I wasn't ready for them when they came.

My dad was out buying groceries. Omar and I were arguing – as usual – when I heard the bell to the shop door tinkle and I ignored it. Then I heard a voice call up, 'Hello?'

Omar gestured wildly for me to get rid of them.

I quickly slid the secret door shut and hurried down the stairs. A man with dark eyes looked up at me, his cap forming a V of shadow over his wrinkled face. *The Censorship were here.*

I managed to conceal the jolt to my heart.

'Hello,' I said pleasantly.

There were three of them. Normally only two came. I walked forward and shook their hands. They assessed my age and flashed me patronising smiles.

'My name is Inspector Merrit,' the man with the dark eyes introduced himself.

'We weren't expecting you until next Tuesday.' I went to my father's desk, buying time. Anything to avoid the penetration of his eyes. I flipped through the diary, trying to decipher the smudge of his illegible pencil scrawls. 'Normally you come on the fifth, the fifth of every month.'

Was it my fault? Had my confession to Mrs Kay been a domino that sent a row crashing down, that brought them here? But she'd promised me that she'd protect me.

'It's just a random security check,' Inspector Merrit said casually.

'The thing is,' I said shakily, 'my dad's not in. He'll be back soon. Maybe you should wait . . .'

'I'm afraid we're very busy,' he said pleasantly. 'We have other bookshops to survey. We can't wait.'

And then his smile ignited a memory. *I already knew this man.* Seven years had passed, and his lips had shrivelled and drooped, his hair greyed. But his eyes were the same. This was the very man who had invaded our shop and held a gun to my head.

I watched him pass the lists over to his colleagues. They loaded their minds with forbidden key words and started scanning the shelves, waiting for word ignition.

Merrit stared at me carefully. I held his gaze. I talked my fear away. It was good that the men had come. They were to be trusted, not feared.

'Have you got any copies of *Paradise Lost?*' he asked.

I started. He raised an eyebrow.

'I'd be very glad to show you,' I said. I led him to the M section, pointing.

I noticed that he put on a good act. He pulled out all three copies, pretending to inspect each in turn, before settling on the large, ancient tattered copy. I thought about the man who had phoned up searching for it. How I'd overheard Omar and my father discussing it. I had a feeling that book was nothing but trouble.

Merrit took it and marched up the front desk. I followed him uneasily.

'We'd be happy for you to take it away,' I said helpfully.

'Oh? Why? Is there something in it that you feel should be banned?' he shot at me.

I started again. I wished I could show that I wasn't the enemy, yet he seemed determined to circle my every sentence with defiance.

'I haven't read it,' I said. 'I'm sure you know best what should and shouldn't be banned.'

His lips curled as though I was being sarcastic.

He slammed open the cover and drew out a small tube from his jacket pocket. It contained a pale yellow liquid with a faint froth at the top. When he uncorked it, a bitter smell unfurled. He lifted it above the book.

'Hey—' I began.

The tube stopped in the air, the first drop caught on its rim. I shut up. He poured it over the page. It seeped through the ancient words of angels and demons and Man's first sin.

'What are you doing? That's an old book, it's very rare . . .' Suddenly I felt full of suspicion and fear. Were these men really inspectors? I hadn't seen their IDs. What if Inspector Merrit had left the force and was now some maverick? What if these men were really with the Words? If they had stolen police uniforms and . . .

The other men came up to inspect the page.

'There's no sign of anything,' one remarked. 'But you'd really need to take it away for proper testing. Maybe you just try the classic method – waving your lighter under it and seeing what shows.'

'I suspected it was all silly rumours. I don't think there is anything of interest here,' Inspector Merrit said, shoving the book at me. A ringtone zig-zagged from his coat pocket and he yanked it out. 'Inspector Merrit? Yes, we're just round the corner, we'll do the bookshops on Oxford

Street next. Right. Well. It will have to wait.' He snapped his phone shut.

That had sounded authentic, I thought in relief.

'Right,' Inspector Merrit said briskly. 'One last thing. Where's your stockroom?'

It was a golden opportunity. I could have just led them up the stairs and slid back the panel and let the fireworks explode. But something, some nag in my heart, made me splutter, 'We don't really have one at the moment. Because – well – we're going to turn our kitchen – what I mean is, my bedroom is just a temporary stockroom, so . . . it was in the kitchen, but then we felt our kitchen should just be for eating, so for now it's my bedroom.'

'Show me,' he said.

I climbed the stairs with a beating heart. *It's all right*, I told myself. *If they find him, it's all right.* Imagine: you might be praised for turning in a terrorist. I pictured myself in assembly, climbing the school stage, the Head pinning a medal to my chest while applause burnt in my ears, and my eyes met Mrs Kay's, her face flushed with pride. In my room, he let out a little sneer of a laugh at the chaos. Old books; new books; glue; jackets. I felt Merrit's eyes on me. I tried hard not to look at the wardrobe, but my eyes, magnetised, flicked over. The door was slightly ajar, the dark slit like a snake that might strike any minute.

Inspector Merrit walked over to the wardrobe.

'I've a new spy book,' I heard my voice saying. 'D'you think they'll be banned in the future? I really enjoy them, though I do understand and respect that you might have to stop them.'

The Inspector turned and gave me a faint smile.

'I suspect they won't,' He said. His jacket quivered with the buzz of his mobile again. 'Yes? Very well. I'll be there.'

He looked at me hard, then turned and tramped down the stairs.

Now that my moment was lost, something in me clawed after him. All I needed to say was, *I've heard noises coming from the panel*. Why wouldn't the words come out? What was stopping them? *Am I a traitor?* I thought, my mind sweaty with confusion.

I watched them conferring in the shop and opened my dry lips.

'Inspector Merrit?' he didn't hear me and I said more loudly, 'Inspector Merrit?'

'Yes?'

'I —'

Suddenly the shop bell tinkled.

My father came in, laden with shopping bags. Seeing the inspectors, he let them slump to the floor. A yellow melon rolled out and came to rest in the centre of the room.

'What . . .' Panic sprinted through his eyes.

'It's fine, Dad, they're just doing a random check,' I said quickly.

'All right, Stefan, I'll take it from here,' he said, but his eyes were asking me urgent questions and I gave him a brief look to reassure him: it's okay. I felt relieved then that I hadn't betrayed him. As he bent down to pick up the melon, love trembled through me as I realised how close I had been to losing him.

'We have assessed your shelves and checked the stockroom,' Inspector Merrit said.

'The *new* stockroom —' I quickly interjected.

'Oh good, the old stockroom is —' my father cried at the same time.

Inspector Merrit looked from me to my father, my father to me.

'The old stockroom? The new stockroom?' he asked my father. When I opened my mouth to speak, Merrit raised his black-gloved palm.

'We have a new stockroom, in Stefan's room – it was down here in the shop originally but we're about to repaint,' my father said brightly.

Something flashed in Merrit's eyes. Pleasure, I realised in horror – he's actually glad that he's caught us out.

My father still didn't realise that our stories didn't tally, that we'd been had. Merrit started going back up the stairs again, pretending all was fine. I thought, *If we confess now, we might make it sound better than it is*.

'He's in the wardrobe,' I cried. 'He's nothing to do with us. The Words made us put him there.'

'Shut up!' my father grabbed my shoulders so that I half-tumbled back down the stairs. 'Shut up! You stupid bloody boy!' He backed away from me, recovering himself and quickly laughed harshly. 'He's got his head in the clouds – he makes up stories all the time.'

'They know, Dad,' I told him a shaky voice. 'They already know. I told them the old stockroom was in the kitchen.'

We stood there, my father and I, staring at each other. Listening to their footsteps cross the landing upstairs, the slide of the wardrobe, Omar's cries, the scuffles of arrest, the footsteps coming back down the stairs for us.

I will never forget the look in my father's eyes. The way they bored my betrayal into my soul. The way he said, 'Oh, Stefan.'

'It'll be all right, Dad,' I gabbled quickly. 'It's not our fault, Omar's under arrest, we'll be all right.'

The inspectors were circling us now, patient, knowing we would surrender peacefully. My father suddenly leaned in and whispered, '*Paradise Lost* – if you get out of prison before me – take care of it, it's – just – for me – look after it –'

He broke off as the Inspector placed a hand on his shoulder.

And then he turned away.

And I had a terrible premonition I was never going to see him again. I wanted to run after him and hug him tight and say goodbye properly, but he had already been led away into the police car.

Inspector Merrit laid a hand on my shoulder and said, 'The Institution will take care of you now.'

Eleven

'How long do I have to stay here?'

   'If you tell the truth, it won't be long.'

   'But what about my dad, when will you let him out?'

   '.'

   'Please don't hurt him – this is my fault – I should never have told you, I've let him down, it's my fault, please don't hurt him.'

   'No, Stefan, you were right to tell the truth.'

👑

'Tell me how you feel about your father. Do you see him as being a good man, or a traitor?'

   'I don't know . . . I think he's a good man, he just . . .'

   'I don't want you to tell me what you think I want to hear. Just speak the truth.'

   'I think he got brainwashed by the Words, and the thing is, they *made* us keep Omar in that room, one night I came downstairs and I saw them hold a gun to his head, we didn't want Omar there, they made us.'

   'The truth will set you free, Stefan.'

   'You're hurting me, please stop, that hurts, please stop. I'm only sixteen, you can't torture me, I'm only sixteen, this isn't allowed, this isn't fair, it's breaking the law—'

'This isn't torture. This is an enhanced interrogation technique. You may experience some pain, but it will only be mild.'

♕

'Please don't hurt me again. I won't tell any more lies, I promise, I'll tell you everything.'

'We don't want to hurt you, Stefan, we just want to look after you. Look, we are going to give you a gift to show you that we are on your side. See? Now how do you feel?'

'The light . . . it's hurting my eyes . . . but I mean, it's beautiful, it's beautiful, please don't take it away, please keep the light on.'

♕

'The reason that you're hungry and that you haven't eaten for two days is because of your father. This is his fault, do you see?'

'Just fuck off. I hate you. You're evil, this is meant to be an Institution looking after kids and you're being evil, when I get out of here I'll tell everyone what you did to me.'

'You're currently classified as a terrorist, Stefan. Your punishment befits your behaviour.'

'Oh sod off. I'm not listening to you, I'm not listening to you, tra la la, go away, I don't care if I don't get any food, go away.'

♕

'Please can I have some food? I'm sorry I said those things. I'm just hungry.'

♕

'The reason you went hungry is because of your father. This is his fault, do you see?'

'I hate him, I hate him.'

'Why do you hate him?'

'Because he's a terrorist. He hid a terrorist in his house. He aided and abetted terrorism. He is a danger to society.'

'What do you think is the definition of a terrorist?'

'Someone who . . . who terrorises, who is horrible to the government, who's evil.'

'What else?'

'Someone who plants bombs and has stupid ideas about killing people.'

'You have correctly summed up the acts of terrorism. But what about the mind of a terrorist? How does he think?'

'He has an evil mind. He reads books that are banned, he puts bad ideas into other people's minds.'

'Your father was a bad influence on you: he allowed Banned Books to potentially fall into your hands. Do you understand the dangers of this happening?'

'I think so.'

'What is the difference between a good book and a bad book?'

'A good book makes people feel they should be good people. A bad book puts evil ideas into people's heads. But – but – bad books – you can't always tell if they're bad because they seem ambiguous. My dad said that. But ambiguity is evil because you think you're reading something good but really it's bad.'

'You are beginning to make progress, Stefan.'

♛

'Are you enjoying your new room?'

'I really like it. Thank you for helping me to be good. Thank you.'

'We feel that you deserve to have a good father and a loving family. Would you like that?'

'Not my father – I don't want to see him ever again . . .'

'We understand that, Stefan. We will place you with a family who will help you to be good. It will be a new start for you.'

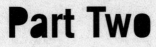

Part Two

Twelve

We were being watched. There was a woman with frizzy brown hair across the street, wearing a bobbly green coat. She wasn't even making a pretence of waiting for someone; she just stood and stared at us. I looked up at Marie, my social worker. She smiled down at me. Marie was very pretty, with short blonde hair and a beaky nose. I think she sensed how nervous I was.

We were in a part of London called Holland Park. It seemed to be rich area. The houses were big and white, like birthday cakes.

Now we were standing at the door of number 32.

Marie rang the bell.

We waited.

The door opened and I stared at my new parents.

'Stefan!'

'How do you do,' I said, shaking Mr Kelp's hand. He was tall and thin, with a fussy grey moustache.

Mrs Kelp was a large woman, with a jolly face and hair like a butterscotch whip. I went to shake her hand but she pulled me into a big hug. I felt really embarrassed, but she was warm and cuddly and I held on tight. Up until now, the only adults who had taken an interest in me had prodded me, measured me, lasered spotlights on me or asked me questions. Even Marie had been a little distant with me; kind, but detached, as though by touching me she might become tainted. But there were no barriers with Mrs Kelp. She was the first adult in a long time to show me real affection.

'There, there, Stefan,' I heard Marie say.

I realised that I needed to let go. But I couldn't help it: I hung on until Mrs Kelp prised my arms away and I felt the cold air coming up between us.

Then she guided me into my new home.

We sat in a big living room. Everything seemed to be covered in either stripes or flowers. A small, fluffy dog came up and snuffled at my feet. Marie had warned me that I might find my new home strange and it would take time to get used to it. But I drank it all in. After the cold cell, this place felt like a palace; I kept smoothing my palm over the arm of the sofa, feeling the expensive cloth and the thick rose brocade. I felt both relieved and panicked: desperate to fit in and be accepted, and nervous that I would mess up and be sent back. The Kelps asked me pleasant questions about how old I was and would I be happy to go back to my old school and what my favourite dinner was. I thought very carefully before I spoke, testing every word in my mind before I allowed it out of my mouth. I said what I thought they wanted to hear.

'It's nice weather out there, isn't it?' Mrs Kelp remarked, nodding at the last of the sun, as though it was every day that she fostered the sons of men who hid terrorists in secret rooms in their bookshops.

Except, Mr and Mrs Kelp *did* do this sort of thing every day. Marie had told me that they worked for the government. They had taken in loads of children over the past ten years. They had a reputation for being kind.

'They'll sort you out,' Marie had said, and she had given me a look, as though expecting me to disagree, but I had nodded obediently.

'I want to be good,' I said.

I meant it.

After Marie had gone – reminding me one last time to be good – Mr and Mrs Kelp gave me a guided tour of the house.

I was really enjoying it, until we came to Mr Kelp's study.

There was a bookcase in the corner. It had a glass case and a lock. Behind the glass were books that I recognised, for I had seen them in the safe in my father's shop. I felt so scared I thought I might be sick. My fingers curled instinctively around the scar on my left arm.

'Why – why have you got those?' I asked in a pale voice.

'Don't look so worried,' Mr Kelp laughed. 'I'm not like—' he broke off, looking awkward. 'I – it is part of our job to advise on which books should be banned. We are the regulators, not the sinners. Look!' He gestured to the certificates on the wall.

I was glad to hear it, and glad to leave the room.

Upstairs, I was shown my new bedroom. Mr Kelp brought up the small bag Marie had packed for me and then left me on my own, 'to settle in'.

My bedroom was plain and simple. On the bed was a small bottle of pink pills. When I held them up to the light, they seemed to writhe like worms. *Good Behaviour Pills*, said the label. The government sent a bottle to each family, so that if their kid started breaking rules they could keep them under control. Whenever my father had received our monthly supply in the post he had sneered at them and chucked them in the bin.

The pills made me feel uneasy. I would have felt happier if the Kelps had just told me to take them. Leaving me the choice made me feel as though I was being put to the test.

I decided to focus on unpacking. I opened the small brown envelope which contained a new ID card for me. Under my photo it listed my date of birth and 'Parental Contact', with the Kelps' details. As though my father had never existed.

Some of the clothes in my bag were mine; some were second-hand ones issued by the Institution. They looked worn and when I sniffed them, beneath the washing-powder smell was a scent of musty loneliness. At the bottom of the bag I discovered something that gave me a shock.

It was a framed photo of my father. It had been taken a few years ago and he was staring away from the camera, into the distance, looking thoughtful.

I couldn't believe Marie had packed it. She had probably thought it had sentimental value. Like I wanted to remember my stupid father.

I recalled the voice in the Institution warning me, *You can cry out all you like but your father isn't here to save you. If he loved you, he would be here.*

I threw the picture onto the floor and kicked it around like a football until the glass cracked into spiders over his face.

'Stefan?' I heard Mr Kelp's voice on the landing.

I was afraid he'd heard the banging. I quickly kicked the picture under my bed and hurried out into the hallway.

'Stefan?'

Mr Kelp had a funny look on his face. I was just opening my mouth to explain when he said, 'Stefan, we'd like to introduce you to your foster sister. One of the reasons Marie felt we'd be the best people to look after you is because a month ago, we took in a girl who goes to the same school as you. I'm sure Marie told you all about her?'

Foster sister? Marie hadn't told me anything. But I smiled quickly and nodded.

'Well,' Mr Kelp said, looking brighter, 'we'd like you to come downstairs and meet her . . .'

I followed Mr Kelp down the stairs and into the hallway.

I saw a girl in a school uniform; saw a turned-up nose with freckles and a flash of blonde hair. Sally Harper.

'Sally!'

'Hey,' she said, grinning. 'It's good to see you.'

The last time I had seen her had been the day she was arrested.

My eyes swept over her. Though she still looked the same, there was something different about her from the girl I'd known back in school. She fiddled with her ear-rings, her collar, her hems. Her fingernails were bitten down to their raw rims. I noticed a scar on her wrist, and I realised where she'd been. We smiled at each other with a sense of affinity, a pain we both recognised – but our smiles were sad and suddenly it seemed as though we were decades older than the Kelps.

We sat down to have dinner together that night. It was probably the best meal I'd ever tasted. After the grey slop of the Institution, it felt as though my mouth was swirling with an incredible rainbow of flavours. But Sally hardly ate anything; she pushed the food nervously round her plate, forcing herself to take an occasional nibble.

'Eat up, dear, it's good for you,' Mrs Kelp said gently.

Sally looked up and forced a quick, apologetic smile. But she still struggled to eat even two mouthfuls.

After dinner there was nothing much to do. The Kelps didn't have a TV set and there were a few e-books with approved Rewritten stamps on them, but I'd become allergic to reading anyhow. As far as I was concerned, I was happy to never touch another book again.

I offered to do all the washing-up for the Kelps. They said how helpful I was, over and over. Once I'd done the washing-up, I did the drying-up. I wiped the tea towel with manic strokes. Every so often my scars would throb and I'd wipe even harder. Then I set about finding the correct places for them in the cupboards. I was just handling a large cream jug when Sally entered. She had a smirk on her face, as though she thought I was sucking up. I was so surprised that I dropped the jug. It shattered into pieces on the floor; the handle came to rest by my feet.

Immediately Sally's eyes widened in horror and I heard the swift patter of her footsteps on the stairs as she fled the kitchen.

I heard heavier footsteps and then Mr Kelp appeared. I tried to make an excuse, but my scars throbbed as though they were burning. I found silent tears running down my face. I tried to brush them off, feeling like a kid. I knew I'd be sent upstairs and told to pack.

When Mr Kelp came forward, I thought he was going to hit me. When he patted me on the shoulder, I jumped in surprise.

'Go to bed – you're tired,' he said, smiling softly.

Upstairs in the bedroom, I wept tears of relief, so glad that Mr Kelp had become my new father.

I grabbed my pyjamas and went to the bathroom. I noticed that the door was slightly ajar. I understood why Sally hadn't locked it; since I'd come out of the Institution, closed doors scared me too.

Then I saw a sliver of her naked body. Water was streaming down over her breasts and the V of dark hair between her legs. She looked so beautiful, but so skinny. Her ribs showed through her skin like a rake and when she turned her back I saw the notches of her spine sticking out like barnacles. Then I saw her standing on the scales with an anxious look on her face. I realised then why Mrs Kelp had been pestering her to eat up. If she weighed too little, the Kelps would be forced to send her back to the Institution. Children were not allowed to be *potentially* anorexic (or obese), as the government ads warned.

Too late, I realised I was breathing hard. She turned and I saw a flash of shocked iris before I hurried back to the bedroom.

I hardly slept that night, scared that the Kelps were about to launch into my bedroom and accuse me of being a perv. In the morning Sally gave me a dirty look but nobody said anything; I felt relief wash over me. I went back up to the bathroom, opened up the scales and adjusted them so that we'd all be three pounds heavier.

Thirteen

I had been back at my old school for three days when I had a shock.

At first I had dreaded going back. Facing Jasper again wasn't easy. On my first day he tripped me up as I was going into multi-faith assembly; on my second he gave me an illicit kick during footie practice. But after my experiences in the Institution, Jasper's bullying seemed trivial. At times I was even able to detach myself and feel completely unmoved by his taunts and his smug face.

I kept my head down. I did my homework. I walked to and from school every day with Sally. I still didn't feel like myself. I still felt more ghost than human, floating through the day on autopilot. But I was surviving.

And then I saw her.

I'd been very disturbed to discover I had a new teacher for English: Mr Wilson. I'd spent hours in the Institution tearing myself apart, knowing that Mrs Kay was also being tortured, questioned, humiliated. All because of the risks she'd taken for me, by hiding that CCTV recording. Yesterday, I had sat in English class and realised, with a terrible chill, that Mrs Kay might never come back. She might spend the rest of her days in jail. And I hated myself so much then that I nearly broke a rule, just to put myself back in the Institution so I might suffer more punishments.

And there she was.

Mrs Kay.

I bumped into her in the corridor. She was clutching a bunch of books to her chest. She looked rosy-cheeked, well fed, carefree.

Her eyes caught mine. She stopped in shock. A book fell to the floor. A boy picked it up and blushingly handed it back to her. She took it and hastily hurried on.

I took me a while to get over the shock and analyse the truth.

Mrs Kay was unscarred. She hadn't destroyed the CCTV recording at all. Maybe she'd intended to, but lost her nerve at the last minute. Realised what was at stake.

She had *given* the recording of me confessing my father was a terrorist to the State. She had got us both locked away.

She had betrayed me.

♔

Where was Sally?

Every day we met at the school gates and walked home together. I liked our routine because we never had to fill the silence with meaningless words. It felt as though we shared the same dream world. Every so often we'd look at each other and grin. Or she'd say something smart.

But today she hadn't turned up. I waited until the playground was deserted and the wind blew through empty sports nets. I hunched my shoulders with my hands in my pockets and started to walk home alone.

I was still feeling bitter about Mrs Kay. I'd stopped fantasising about revenge: setting her up against the government so that she got arrested, giving her a taste of her own medicine. I knew, deep down, that I was to blame for the arrests. But I still felt that I would die hating her.

Maybe my churned-up state was the reason that I took a detour on the way home. I found myself getting onto a bus towards my father's old bookshop.

On the bus I saw a man fiddling about with one of his pockets. He looked suspicious. Automatically, I drew my mobile out to film him. Then I stopped. What if he ended up suffering what I'd suffered? I put my mobile away, then felt guilt flood me as I got off the bus. If an attack did happen, it would be all my fault.

I tried to put him out of my mind, and it was soon easy to forget him when I came to the shop.

I was quite shocked by the state of it. Our shop had always looked cosy from the outside, its golden glow spilling onto the street, with the silhouette of my father pottering about amongst his beloved books. Now it was a cold, derelict wreck. The windows were boarded up and there were notices plastered all over the door. GOVERN-MENT PROPERTY, they said. NO TRESPASSING.

Suddenly feeling self-conscious, I turned my back to the window, checking my watch as though waiting for some-one. I noted a CCTV camera twist its head and linger on me, debating whether or not I was suspicious. I pictured the man at the other end of that CCTV camera, sitting in a room filled with tiers of screens, hundreds of faces and colours and streets, trying to assess that one look or smile or style of walk that signalled a terrorist.

The camera turned away and lingered on a crowd across the street. I broke into a grin. They were the Ecos, as we called them at school. They claimed they had no affiliation with ArkQ because they were peace-loving Christians who cared about the environment. I'd heard that they were allowed to hand out leaflets in the streets because they were now officially classified as a religion, which meant they were 'converting' people rather than protesting. There were about a dozen or so of them, some old, some young, wearing clothes decorated with green and blue tie-dye splashes, waving wacky umbrellas decorated with fishes. One little girl, who was only about eight, had a sign strapped to her chest that warned: IF WE DO NOT STOP SINNING, THE FLOODS WILL KEEP COMING.

While the camera was distracted, I grabbed my chance. I turned my head to one side, my eyeball straining against the periphery of my lid. There was a gap in the boarded window. I could see books splayed on the floor. And then something that made my heart leap. *Paradise Lost*.

My father's words flooded my mind: Paradise Lost – *if you get out of prison before me – take care of it . . .*

I gazed at the camera. It was still perusing the crowds. Before I could lose my nerve I slipped down the alley and round to the back of the house.

The garden was choking with weeds and wild flowers, rustling with new insect invaders. There were more white notices plastered all over the back door and windows. Then I noticed that some of them had jagged edges, as though they had been broken along the doorframe and pressed back into place. I curled my hand around the back door handle and was surprised when it opened.

I stood in the place that had once been our kitchen. Where my father had once lit candles on the oak table and I had eaten baked beans on toast before starting my homework. Now it looked like a squat: electric wires spindling out of the walls, the lino torn and cracked, the shards of a broken bulb lying on the floor. The dank walls still seemed to hold the memory of the horror of our arrest.

I heard the voice of the Institution telling me to leave right away.

It was the first time I'd ever disobeyed that voice. It took tremendous physical will, for my entire body screamed and wept in outrage and I nearly threw up with the fear. But I was overwhelmed with curiosity. And, perhaps, a sense of sadness for the life my father and I had once had. I closed the door behind me and tiptoed into the hallway.

Wallpaper hung from the wall in strips and the carpet had been torn up to reveal bare boards. I went into the main shop. All the bookcases stood empty, with the forlorn air of artefacts in a museum. The remaining books had been flung onto the floor, covers cracked and broken, pushed into a pyramid as though gathered for a book burning.

And there it was. On the edge of the pile. *Paradise Lost*.

I grabbed it and stared at the front page, still wrinkled from the weird test the Censorship had conducted on it. Holding it felt as though I was holding my father's hand. For a moment, before the revulsion came, I felt a flicker of brief affection.

Your father is a terrorist, I reminded myself. *You should take* Paradise Lost *back to the authorities and ask them to assess it for secret plots.*

I held onto the book, telling myself I'd leave in just a minute, just a minute. But first I wanted to see my old bedroom.

There was no carpet on the stairs and the bare treads were studded with nails. Some of the boards had been ripped away, flashing the intestines of the downstairs cupboard.

I reached the landing and went into my old bedroom. Nothing remained except for the bed, covered with a bare mattress, and one of my pictures.

Mrs Kay. Naked. Some joker had taken it and pinned it up on the wall. I pulled it down, ready to tear it into pieces – but when I stared at her face in the sketch, I couldn't quite bring myself to destroy it.

I put the picture aside and sat down on the bed. I felt the ghost of my old self haunt me. A teenager who didn't have nightmares or scarred skin, who had read spy books and idled on his bed feeling bored. I couldn't imagine ever feeling relaxed enough to experience boredom ever again.

I thought then that redemption is a path back from experience to innocence, but I had no idea if I would ever be able to get back to it. Maybe in time, with the love and help of the Kelps, I would get there.

The thought of the Kelps filled me with hope. I didn't need to be here any more. I'd go downstairs, put *Paradise Lost* back on the pile, say goodbye to my old home for ever and get back to my new one. I'd take a shower, start my homework, maybe even cook the Kelps a nice dinner.

I got up to go, then I heard a noise from below. I froze, listening to the creak of footsteps. Sweat began to slime across my forehead. What if the Censorship had come to clean up? Then I heard voices. Two men. One had a deep voice; the other's was high, shrill with nerves.

'I can't see it. I can't see it,' said the one with the high voice.

'*Of course* it's here. Look, just check the bloody pile again. The Censorship said they'd left it behind. You find it, otherwise it really will be *Paradise Lost* for you.'

'Oh, I'm scared. Okay. I'm sorry, I'm sorry, just give me a chance to look, okay?'

I stood very still. I listened to the frantic sound of books thudding to the floor, pages being torn impatiently.

'It's got to be here somewhere . . .'

'Have you tried that bookcase?'

'Yes, I've tried that one!'

A loud groan of frustration.

It's all right, I told myself. *Just wait until they've gone and then creep out. Just wait it out.*

'It's definitely not down here. Let's try upstairs.'

'No,' I whispered. 'Please, no.'

I spun round desperately. Their footsteps began to boom on the stairs. Where to hide, where to hide? I nearly slipped under the bed, but at the last minute I opted for the Narnia wardrobe. I tiptoed over, sliding back the panel, wincing as it squeaked. Here was the secret room where we had once hidden Omar Shakir. It had been stripped so thoroughly that even the wallpaper had been removed. I slid the door back as their footsteps reached the top landing. I wondered if they'd heard the noise. I closed my eyes, praying and pleading for them to just go.

I listened to their footsteps stomping across the landing. Then they separated. One went off into my father's bedroom. Another came into mine.

I stood very, very still. My breath fluttered like a tiny bird in my throat. I looked down and saw my knees were shaking violently.

I listened to the creak of the mattress being lifted up, then the *thwack* as it hit the bed-springs. I heard the sound of Mrs Kay's picture being torn up. They were obviously troublemakers and terrorists.

I heard the man open the doors to the wardrobe. My heart rate trebled. I listened to him smashing the empty coat-hangers with a clatter of frustration.

Then I heard him let out a sudden noise. A small cry of joy.

'Interesting,' I heard him mutter.

My eyes widened. He wasn't going to do it, was he? He wasn't going to slide back the panel? My knees felt so weak I thought I was going to faint.

As I heard the door slide back, I quickly darted over to the side wall, pressing myself against it. I saw a man enter. He was small, with stumpy legs and a thick, hoary beard. I could hardly believe that he was just a foot away from me; that I was staring at the back of his head. For one ridiculous moment I thought he was going to see the room was empty and walk out without noticing me. But, of course, he turned. And saw me.

He cried out in shock. Then his eyes fell to the book I was hugging against my chest.

I tried to run for it. I'd managed to make it back into the wardrobe when I felt a hand gripping hold of my shoulder. His grip was so savage I could feel his nails slicing through my jumper to my skin and my collarbone screaming pain. Then he was in the wardrobe too, our bodies banging against the wooden walls as he tried to wrestle *Paradise Lost* from me. The dark claustrophobia provoked a horrific déjà vu. I was back in the Institution again. Back in that tiny cell where there was only room to sleep and stand. The eyes of the man, glinting in the darkness, became the small camera that watched me, interrogated me, ordered me, taught me. Rage overwhelmed me and I heard myself whimpering. And then my teeth were sinking into flesh, into the salty muscle of a hand, and his hot cry rang out in my ear. I burst out of the wardrobe, howled as my knee hit the bedstead. I heard the other man crying out, 'You okay in there?' I dashed out into the hallway, tumbled down the stairs, falling down at the bottom, picking myself up. '*Get him!*' I heard a voice scream from above and then the man started coming down the stairs after me. I looked at the distance from the hallway to the back door and knew I'd never make it. I turned, saw the pile of books gathered in the centre of the room. I grabbed the biggest one and, with all my might, I chucked *War and Peace* up the stairs. It flew and hit the man in the stomach. Though the blow was mild, his surprise made him lose his balance. He tumbled down the stairs and I ran out with the sound of his head banging against wood in my ears.

I tore out through the back door, through the garden and out onto the high street. I was so disorientated that, when I heard the shouts, I thought that they were aimed at me. I saw a policeman strolling up to me and I shrank before him.

'Stand back,' he said roughly, 'we need to clear the street.'

'I'm sorry, I'm sorry,' I whimpered, holding out *Paradise Lost*, when I realised that he was giving me a bemused, impatient look.

'What's this? You want me to do your homework for you? Now, move on!'

I realised that the commotion on the street had been caused by the Ecos. Either their fervour had got the better of them or they had upset the public with their assertions of gloom and doom and torrential rain; I couldn't tell which, for the crowds were too blurry to see what was happening. There was an upturned umbrella in the middle of the road, sitting in a pool of blood, causing cars to swerve around it.

Then I turned back and froze. The men were coming out of the house. They spotted me and ran in my direction. Immediately, I hugged the book to my chest.

'Look, look,' I cried to the policeman.

'What?' he snapped.

'Those men – look – they're on government property,' I cried. 'They're not meant to be in there!'

The policemen's eyes widened and he nodded abruptly, then approached the men. When they started to shout at him, he lost his temper and called to his colleagues for back-up. I didn't hang around to watch their arrest. Instead, I just ran.

I ran and ran all the way home, the book so heavy I had to swap it from hand to hand so that it banged against alternate thighs.

Back home, I pounded up the stairs to my bedroom. I shoved the book under my bed, then wondered if I ought to burn it. What if those men recognised me? What if they knew who I was and came back to find me? But they had been arrested, I reassured myself. Justice had been done. The men most probably had been terrorists from the Words and now the State would take care of them. I was innocent; I would be all right.

Then I turned back to the bed, and saw it. Spread out on my duvet.

'*What the hell!*'

Fourteen

Lying on the bed was a chain of Scrabble pieces:

V₄ O₁ Y₄ E₁ U₁ R₁

Immediately, I ran to the window. I threw back the net curtain, looking for the woman who'd been watching the house a few weeks back when I'd first arrived.

The street was empty.

I turned back to the letters.

The Words.

It had to be them. Maybe they had seen me run away from the bookshop with *Paradise Lost*. Maybe they wanted it back. Maybe they had broken into the house and left this stupid message as a warning.

Then, suddenly, I heard laughter. I froze. There was someone in the hallway. Footsteps creaked closer.

'Hello.'

Sally.

She was standing in her school uniform, holding a big bottle of Coca-Cola in her hand. I quickly jiggled the Scrabble letters into nonsense.

'I —' I swallowed. 'I just came up and found – these letters on my bed. Someone left me a message.'

'Really?' She cocked an eyebrow. 'Weird.' Then she took a swig of Coke and giggled.

'I'd better go and call Mr Kelp—'

'Why?! It's just a Scrabble word. Have some Coke.'

I stared at Sally. There seemed to be something slightly strange about her.

Her face had a faint sneer on it. I grabbed the Coke from her. I was about to taste it, when the curious smell lingering around the neck of the bottle stopped me. I sniffed, and sniffed again. It smelt strange: of sour apples and acid autumn. My lips curled back in disgust and I passed it back to her.

'I think it's gone off,' I said.

Sally giggled again.

'Uh uh. I found some vodka in Mr Kelp's study,' she whispered. 'In a drawer. I thought it might make my Coke taste better.'

I stared at her in horror. Then I pushed past her into the hallway and hurried down the stairs. She caught up with me in Mr Kelp's study. Just as I was picking up the phone, she said, 'If you ring him, I'll tell him you spy on me when I'm naked in the bathroom.'

'*What!*'

'I saw you, watching me like a *perv*.'

'Uh – *you* put those letters there!'

'I might have done.'

'It's not true, it was just a mistake, I wanted to use the bathroom—'

'Oh yeah? Why did you do it three nights in a row, then?'

She cocked her head to one side. I was lost for words. I imagined Mr Kelp's face if she told him; I'd blush so violently he'd never believe my protests. My eyes dropped to the bottle of cola she was carrying. What if he smelt the vodka on her breath when he came back? What if he found out I knew that she'd taken it? I thought of that cold white cell and the eyes of the Censorship boring into me and my stomach clenched in terror.

'I can't believe you're doing this,' I yelled. 'Do you *want* to go back to the Institution?'

'It's because of that that I have to drink now and again,' she screamed back, tears suddenly lacerating her voice. 'Otherwise I get nightmares and I start to shake really bad. It calms me down – I'm not like *you*,' she spat out, 'I'm not *cold*, I can't just be all nice and normal.'

'I . . .' I gulped and said quietly, 'I had a bad time there too, you know.'

There was a silence and we both inhaled and exhaled shakily.

'Look,' she said. 'I won't tell if you don't tell . . .'

She looked upset and suddenly I felt sorry for her.

'It's okay,' I said at last. 'But seriously, I've never spied on you.'

We looked at each other and broke into smiles.

'Doesn't . . .' I felt confused and suddenly a little foolish, as though I was a kid asking an adult for advice. 'Doesn't the vodka . . . make you sick?'

'No,' Sally said. 'The first time I took it, I thought I'd puke or end up in hospital, though I didn't care. But I felt fine. I reckon the stuff they tell us in school is just rubbish they feed us, to keep us down.'

I blinked in surprise and then shook my head slightly. There was no way the teachers would lie to us; it was more likely that Mr Kelp's vodka was just very weak.

'You shouldn't drink,' I repeated firmly. 'You should – you should eat properly instead.'

'I feel like I don't deserve to eat,' she said in a small voice. 'I feel as though I ought to punish myself.'

I was shocked and tried to think of the kindest thing to say.

'I think we were both punished in the Institution. We did wrong, but we've paid for it now. They've set us right. And we're here, with the Kelps, which means we must be good people now. So we have to be grateful and be *good*. I think you should just go and pour that drink down the sink and I'll forget it ever happened. I won't tell Mr Kelp, okay?'

'Okay.' Sally nodded and left the room.

Back upstairs, I sat down on my bed, letting out a deep shaky breath. The aftershock of the fight kept hitting me, again and again; the sensation of my teeth sinking into that man's flesh. Although I had assaulted him, somehow it felt as though I was the one who had been violated; there was a terrible taste in my mouth, as though his blood, his essence, was lingering ugly on my tongue. I was still furious with myself for going back to the bookshop. What right did I have to criticise Sally for a drop of alcohol when I'd broken into a forbidden property and stolen a book?

I ought to take *Paradise Lost* out from under my bed and pass it over to Mr Kelp. That had been my plan, after all. But here and now, in reality, the idea seemed unbearable. I had only been in my new home for a few weeks; surely I deserved a little longer than that before I risked ruining everything?

The book would stay under my bed. For now. I'd . . . I'd wait until the time was right, and then show the Kelps.

My eyes fell on the bottle of pink Behaviour Pills on the dresser. Maybe they would help to keep me on the straight and narrow. I quickly grabbed the bottle and took two.

And then I began to feel different.

Fifteen

I woke up.

The birds were singing. I stared at my wallpaper. There were roses on it. It looked nice.

As I got out of bed, I saw a Scrabble piece fall to the floor.

I picked it up. My nice mood trembled. The V seemed to glare up at me, warning me that I'd done something wrong.

I took my pyjamas off. My school uniform looked nice.

I was buttoning up my shirt when I remembered.

Sally.

She had accused me of watching her in the bathroom.

I had denied it.

I had lied.

I had lied to the Kelps and gone back to the bookshop.

I now had a stolen copy of *Paradise Lost* sitting under my bed.

A sense of shame came over me.

When I'd left the Institution, I'd wanted so desperately to become good. To start over. To fit in.

Maybe I was dirty and sick. Maybe there was something fundamentally evil in my soul, some seed that was just waiting to blossom into the same terrorist tendencies as my father had.

I reached for the pills and took another double dose.

And then I started to feel nice again.

Mrs Kelp was in the kitchen, making breakfast.

When I went into the garden, she asked me where I was going.

Then when I came back in and gave her the flowers I'd picked, she looked happy.

'Aren't you a good boy?' said Sally.

'Thanks,' I said.

At school, I felt nice. Not too happy, not too sad.

As though I was filled with a clean, white lightness.

Everything seemed so simple. I wondered why I hadn't liked school before.

Mr Wilson was back. He looked nice too.

He told us to sit down and carry on reading *1984*. But I found it difficult to read. The words seemed to disappear from the page and the page was just whiteness. I liked staring at the whiteness.

'What do you think Orwell felt when he was writing this book?' Mr Wilson asked.

When nobody answered, he picked on me.

'I think he feels happy,' I said.

'Really? What else?'

I didn't know what to say. I wanted to tell Mr Wilson that I didn't see the point of books, but I didn't want to upset him.

I came home.

I did my homework.

I helped Mrs Kelp lay the table.

I took two more pills.

I said hello to Mr Kelp.

We had dinner.

A happy family.

I went to sleep.

I woke up.

I took two pills.

I went to school.

I did not get very good marks for my English essay.

But I still felt nice.

I came home.

I had a nice dinner.

I took two pills.

I went to bed.

I had no dreams.

I went to school.

I took two pills.

I had no dreams.

I woke up.

I woke up. I had no pills left.

I told Mr Kelp that I had no pills left.

He said I could have some more soon.

On the way to school, I felt funny. I saw the leaves twirling from the trees and they looked so sad, torn down by the wind to turn to mulch on the streets. Their sadness drifted inside me. My stomach hurt.

When I got to my English lesson, I realised I was behind with *1984*. I found myself reading fast, drinking in the words.

I went home and sat on my bed, trying to do my homework. But I kept wondering what Sally was doing in her bedroom. I pictured her brushing out her long blonde hair and painting pink gloss onto her lips. I got up and knocked on her door.

She was curled up in bed; I tried not to stare at the pale skin of her arms.

'Have you got any pills? I really, really need some.'

'Sorry,' she said, laughing. 'I flushed mine down the toilet.'

'Why did you do that? You should have kept them!'

'Boy, you look rough,' she laughed.

I left her room quickly.

I did my homework. At dinner, I stared at Mr Kelp and felt a strange wave of dislike for him. When I took the pills, people seemed to float around me, distant; now they seemed close up, full of loud cracks and flaws. I tried to ignore the bad feeling and I asked him once more, in a very polite voice, if he had any pills.

'I forgot to pick them up for you. I'll get some more tomorrow.'

His tone was so cheerful. I felt like sticking my fork into him.

I went to sleep and I started to dream and I woke up in the night clutching my head and I shook it as though all the thoughts might fly out. I lay awake until it was morning and then I got dressed and went to check the medicine cabinet but there were no spare pills, nothing, and I ran out of the house, ignoring Mrs Kelp's cry to ask if I wanted breakfast. I looked at a car and felt I wanted to smash it; I looked at the sky and felt so happy I could cry; at school, I said the National Pledge in a voice soaked in cynicism. I came home from school and searched my bedroom for more pills, just one stray pill that might have fallen from the bottle, but there were none and I wanted to sleep but I was scared of my dreams. And then I was standing by the bathroom door, looking in at Sally and she turned to look at me and cried, '*You're naked!*' her laughter filling my ears and shame burning me until my skin turned purple and flaky and Sally's laughter became a scream. I woke up soaked in sweat in the dead of night and I thought, *I can't stand this any more*, and I got out of bed and crept down the stairs striped with moonlight to Mr Kelp's study. I knocked gently on the door and I could hear my heart hammering in the silence and I went inside, not daring to turn on the light, and waited for my eyes to find their own light in the dark as I searched through his drawers. My fingers had just closed around a bottle when I heard a creak and I froze, praying, but nothing happened and I held the bottle up, praying in relief, nearly crying at how beautiful they looked when . . .

. . . the door opened and light flooded in and there was Mr Kelp, standing in the doorway.

Sixteen

'I see,' Mr Kelp said in a small, strange voice. 'I see.'

'I wasn't . . . I was just looking for some Behaviour Pills,' I explained. I found myself letting out a nervous laugh; unfortunately it sounded guilty. 'You said you were going to get me some and I just thought – I just thought it would be good to take them, Mr Kelp! Just so that I stay good and you're pleased with me.'

I thought that he would understand. But instead he just said, in a terrible tone, 'I'm very disappointed in you, Stefan.'

'I'm sorry, I'm really sorry, I should have waited . . .'

'I think we both know you didn't come here to take Behaviour Pills.'

'What! Of course I did. I—'

'I think you should just sit down and we can discuss this properly.'

I sat down on the chair, unable to believe this was happening. I opened my mouth to defend myself again, but Mr Kelp held up a palm. He silenced me, and let the silence stretch out until it became unbearable.

'Let us be honest,' he said. 'You came into my study for one reason, and we both know what that was . . .'

'I—'

'To break into my bookcase and get your hands on those Banned Books!'

'NO!'

'Your father was a bookseller who sold corrupting material. You have suffered from his influence. You can't help that.'

'No – you've got it so wrong – you don't understand – that's the *last* thing I'd ever want – I *hate* books – I hate them.'

Mr Kelp looked unconvinced. To my bewilderment, he got up and went to his cabinet. He unlocked it and removed one of the Banned Books: a copy of *1984*. And then he laid it out on the table in front of us.

'This is what you wanted to read, isn't it?'

'No,' I said, shaking my head, hardly able to speak. 'No. No, no. *No!*'

Mr Kelp smiled. But it was an odd smile; the smile a snake might make before sinking fangs into its prey.

'There might be a way forward with this situation, Stefan.'

'How? How? – I'll do the washing-up, I'll cook you dinner, just please don't send me back to the Institution.'

'How would you feel,' Mr Kelp said in a conspiratorial whisper, 'if I told you that this book – *this Banned Book* – was *yours*?'

'I don't want to read it,' I said quickly. 'The government version is superior, for it has been Rewritten to nurture and purify our minds. This – this is filth,' I said, feeling genuine disgust for it.

'It *is* filth,' said Mr Kelp, 'of course it is. But let me explain our situation, Stefan. We at the government are in rather a difficult position at this moment in time. Mrs Kelp and I are, as you know, Rewriters; indeed we oversee all the Rewriters who work so hard and dutifully to convert swine into pearls of reading pleasure. But on our committee, there has recently been some . . . uncertainty . . . We laid out from the very beginning a set of clear moral guidelines outlining how a book should be Rewritten. But there are now two growing schools of thought on our committee. There are those who feel that more words should be chopped, that the rules should become more vigorous, that all the Rewritten books should be called in and Rewritten once more.'

I shifted uncomfortably in my seat. Despite myself, I could not stop my father's voice from entering my head. He had always feared Rewrites of Rewrites, saying, 'It will be disastrous. It'll be like making a photocopy of a photo-copy. All the rich colour of their ideas will leach out until we are left with insipid pastel versions.'

But my father was an evil terrorist who knew nothing.

'Then there are those who feel we ought to be more *liberal*,' Mr Kelp continued. 'They feel that our Rewriting measures have gone too far. They feel we have taken too many liberties with books like *1984*. After all, you protect a child, you tell a child there is no evil in the world, you wrap him up in cotton wool – and then what happens?'

I wondered if I was meant to reply to this, but Mr Kelp answered the question for me:

'When he comes face to face with evil, he doesn't know what it is! He doesn't know how to handle it! The liberals in our group feel that we should teach children about sub-versive ideas in order that they may recognise them and reject them. So that they may understand what weakens society.'

'I think they're wrong,' I said.

'I agree with you there, Stefan,' he replied, and I felt relieved that I'd chosen the right answer. 'Because once an idea or an image has been put into your mind, can you ever get it out? The more you try to forget it, the more you remember it. The mind becomes *stained*.' He said the word with empathic relish and then that snakish smile returned to his lips.

'There has been much debate about this in our group. We put forward proposals for research. The idea would be that a group of children from the Institution would be allowed to read various forbidden texts as a test. Unfortunately, it did not receive official vindication, for those tiresome psychiatrists who argue for child safety said that Institution children were already disturbed, and we would hence create a generation of dangerous intellectual psychopaths. Others agreed that, indeed, a *group* of children reading these books and *sharing* these ideas would attain an outsider complex and grow up to band together to form a group of *terrorists*.

'Then we agreed that we could conduct a small study with selected subjects, perhaps those who have been through the Institution but are still mingling with ordinary, well-balanced others. We also felt it would be unfair to *pick* children as guinea pigs. No, we hoped we might find some who would *volunteer* to read these books and then advise us on how they felt. Of course, this would all happen in the strictest confidence. It would be *our* secret.'

A long pause. Mr Kelp stared at me, waiting.

'I . . . I . . .' I thought of the lesson where I had first upset Mrs Kay just by mentioning the alternative version of *1984*. I was trying to start a new life; I was just getting the hang of being *good*. If I read these books, how would I fit in any more? Everyone else would be thinking and dreaming and reading within the same fence but I would be wandering outside that arena, into dark and dangerous woods of ideas and thoughts.

'I think . . . I think . . . I would find it hard . . . It would be difficult . . .'

'But Stefan, I have just come into my study and found you trying to break into my banned bookcase in the middle of the night. I ought to have called the police and sent you straight back to the Institution. Volunteering to be my little literary test case would be a nice way of saying sorry. Don't you agree? It would also give me good reason to allow you to stay here.'

'I . . .' I felt a sense of outrage at his blatant blackmail. Then I stared at the copy of 1984 and thought: I could just pretend to read it. Or I could just skim it. Or I could say it made me feel awful and that I can't bear to read any more.

'Okay,' I said at last.

'There will be three texts for you to read in the first week,' Mr Kelp carried on, looking very pleased with himself. 'I'll just dig them out, as well as a diary for you to keep to monitor your feelings.'

Then an idea tickled my mind. It seemed unwise to voice it, but curiosity overwhelmed me.

'I'll agree to this if I can read *The Catcher in the Rye*.'

Even as I suggested it, I didn't really think Mr Kelp would say yes. *The Catcher in the Rye* was the most banned book in the country. There weren't even any Rewritten versions about, for it had been deemed beyond redemption. And whatever my father said, even I knew it was toxic waste for your brain and, once you read it, you were pretty much guaranteed to become a psycho.

'I can't *possibly* give you that,' Mr Kelp blustered. 'Don't you realise that John Lennon was murdered after an innocent victim read that book and felt compelled to pick up a gun? Another was inspired to kill an American president, Reagan.'

'But I've heard it's really not that bad – it doesn't even have any guns in it . . .' I trailed off, seeing Mr Kelp's face.

He looked a little like a Christian who had been forced to discuss the Devil. There was a loathing in his expression and a fear too, as though just by mentioning the book it might appear in evil spirit.

'Okay,' I said quickly. 'I was only joking. So what else do you want me to read, apart from *1984*?'

'Here,' Mr Kelp said. '*Lord of the Flies*'.

The books were white, with little serial numbers in the corners, as though they belonged in jail.

'We've not read *Lord of the Flies* yet at school – we're going to soon.' Just the title alone was ominous. 'I won't be able to tell the difference between the normal version and the Rewritten one.'

'Let me summarise the Rewritten, official version that's allowed in schools,' Mr Kelp offered. '*Lord of the Flies* is about a class of boys who survive a terrible plane crash and end up on a desert island with no adults.'

I sat up. This sounded good. But Mr Kelp looked uneasy.

'*Lord of the Flies* was Rewritten during a time when the government lacked money. They raised some sponsorship from Sweets R Us. I said at the time it could never be a good idea. The Rewriters were forced to do a new draft of *Lord of the Flies* with lots of sweets in the plot.'

I smiled, realising how naff it would be, and Mr Kelp smiled too in brief affinity.

'So, after the plane crash, the boys end up on an island with no adults. They have no food or drink either. But then they discover a big treasure chest full of sweets. They spend a few weeks eating Minty Mints, Tasty Toffees and Raspberry Rizzles. At one point, a fight nearly breaks out over who will get to enjoy the Liquorice Twirls – but Jack, one of the boys, makes an inspiring speech about the values of learning to share and everyone calms down. They've just eaten their last Liquorice Twirl and are starting to panic when the police helicopter comes down and the boys are rescued.'

'Oh,' I said, thinking that the story sounded as though it was aimed at six-year-olds.

'I think you'll find that the original – apart from the fact it doesn't have a free coupon for a packet Minty Mints in the back – is quite different. More . . . *savage*,' Mr Kelp said with a shudder of almost pleasure on his face. Then he shook himself and looked stern.

'Now. If I am to give you these books, you must adhere to certain rules.

'Rule One: you will only read these books in your bedroom. You will *never* take them out of the house.

'Rule Two: nobody must ever see you reading them. Keep your bedroom door locked at all times.

'Rule Three: you will read this book in the strictest confidence. You will not show it to any of the other children. If you do, we will have to assume that you are seeking to form a group of radical thinkers and you will be sent back to the Institution.

'Rule Four: if someone happens to see one of your books, you will report them immediately.

'Rule Five: all of these books will be returned in one week's time with a full report detailing your experiences.

'Okay?'

'Okay,' I said. And then hesitated. I thought about the pink pills. If I was to take them while reading the book, that lovely blank feeling would come over me, act as a buffer between my mind and the words I read. They might keep me clean.

'I was thinking that I could do with a few Behaviour Pills,' I said casually. 'You said I could get a refill.'

'Oh. I'm afraid I couldn't possibly . . . they would interfere too greatly with the process.'

'I need my pills,' I cried in a ragged voice. How could I explain to him how it felt to be without them? When I took them, the world seemed to narrow; it was like living in a room where everything was clean and white. Without the pills, the room was suddenly full of doors that let shadows fall in and vignettes of noise and cacophony and colour and confusion. 'Please,' I begged him. '*Please!* Could I just have *one* more pill?'

Mr Kelp was about to say an automatic 'no' but then I think he took pity on me. He passed a single pill over and I swallowed it without water.

Upstairs, however, I kept waiting for the blank feeling to come and wipe away my confusion. I was still shocked by this new side of Mr Kelp that I hadn't seen before. I had thought he was an amazing man, a wonderful father, and that in years to come he would still be asking me fondly if I'd done my homework or thank me for doing the washing-up.

How could he really care about me if he wanted to use me as a guinea pig?

Maybe he would go back to being nice again if I behaved. Maybe this was just a test. Maybe, in a way, I was lucky; he thought I was special enough to be trusted with State secrets.

After all, I told myself, *they're only books.*
How much harm can reading a book do?

Seventeen

How can I explain how it felt to read those Banned Books?

There are common stories that we all know, that have been passed down from generation to generation such as *Cinderella* or *Sleeping Beauty*. Everyone knows that a fairy godmother can solve a ballgown difficulty or that a princess lost in sleep for a century will flutter her eyes open when kissed.

If you were to suddenly find out that Cinderella had murdered her Prince Charming or that Sleeping Beauty refused to wake up, then imagine how odd it would feel. You'd probably smile and find it funny . . . but you'd also be disturbed, too. It's a little like when you're a kid and you discover that Father Christmas doesn't exist. Later, it seems ridiculous that you ever believed in him, but at the time you suffer consternation as fiction and fact untangle and find new places in your consciousness.

'Have you ever read *Lady Chatterley's Lover*?' I asked Sally as we walked home from school.

'Uh? Yeah,' she said. Sally wasn't really a big fan of reading. 'I thought it was *so* boring, the way that stupid woman and the gamekeeper just go for walks and pick flowers and stuff. It was like, so what?'

'Yeah,' I said.

Sally turned to look at me and cried, 'What are you smiling at?'

'Nothing,' I said. In the version I'd read, Lady Chatterley and the gamekeeper didn't just go for walks. She had realised that she couldn't find intimacy with her husband who was 'all mind', that she needed to be alive physically.

When I started reading the book, I'd felt heat burn my cheeks and gradually flood through my whole body. I'd read things about the way a woman might enjoy pleasure from her body that I'd never imagined before. I'd been left wondering whether I could take the book as fact or fiction – did D. H. Lawrence really understand women and sex, or had he just written it from his imagination, the way he wished women might be?

Ever since I'd finished the book, I'd suffered red dreams at night and found my sheets damp in the morning. At school, I'd been acutely conscious of girls around me – the fullness of their lips, the swing of their hair, delicious flashes of skin between skirts and socks, sleeves and jumpers. And their scent: I'd felt like a bee with antennae prickling, breathing in the perfume of the soap and hair and essential girliness like pollen. I'd restrained myself from watching Sally in the shower, but when I'd lain in bed, listening to the drum of water from the bathroom, I'd felt myself harden and had to pretend I was sick in order to avoid embarrassing myself at dinner. I felt as though something had opened up inside me, something strange and aching, something hot and hungry, and I had to do something about it or I'd go crazy.

When we got home, we went into the kitchen to make a drink. I watched Sally bend down in front of the fridge and her hair part coyly at the back of her neck, as though revealing a secret.

I crouched down next to her and whispered in her ear, 'Why don't we drink some *Coke*?'

I felt her start in shock. Then she turned to me and smiled.

'Sure,' she said. Her eyes dropped to my lips. I held her gaze until she looked back at me.

Our eyes burnt.

Buzzy with the excitement of rebellion, we invaded Mr Kelp's study. There we discovered his vodka supply and sloshed some into the Coke bottle.

'Hey, why don't we play Scrabble?' Sally said.

I felt a bit disappointed. But then I shrugged and grinned. Scrabble could be fun, if we made it fun.

Upstairs in my bedroom, we sat cross-legged on either side of the board. Sally put all the pieces into the black velvet bag. When I put my hand in, she grabbed it through the bag and wouldn't let go. I laughed and pulled out seven pieces and we started putting words on the board. Then I saw her pick up the Coke bottle again. She took a cautious sip, as if nervous that this was a trap and I was testing her. To reassure her, I grabbed the bottle back. I peered down the neck at the dark liquid glinting inside. I tipped it back and let it slide slowly into my mouth. Then swallowed.

'Ah!' I cried. 'It's – it makes your throat burn! Is it meant to do that?' I flushed as Sally giggled; feeling stupid, I quickly downed nearly half of it to prove I wasn't scared.

Sally clapped her hands over her mouth in mock horror.

'Oh my God, you are going to be *so* drunk.'

I blinked, trying to hide the burn tearing through my stomach and the spin in my head. Then the drink settled in my tummy.

It felt warm. It felt nice.

We carried on playing.

Sally put down L₁ O₁ V₄ E₁

I put down V₄ E₁ G₂

She put down G₂ I₁ V₄ E₁ N₁

I was ten points up.

Suddenly, Sally started giggling.

'What?' I cried. 'What is it?'

She put her hand over her mouth. A clump of blonde hair had fallen messily onto her cheek. It looked out of place, so I tucked it behind her ear. When my fingers touched her cheek, she froze. For one scary moment, I thought she was going to hit me. Then she started laughing again.

'If I put down a bad word, will you tell Mr Kelp?'

'I might do,' I said. 'Go on then, put it down.'

Her fingers shaking slightly, she laid down the letters:

V₄ A₁ G₂ I₁ N₁ A₁

'I think,' I said in a solemn voice, 'I might have to go and tell Mr Kelp.'

Sally's laughter died away. For a moment she looked terrified. Then she saw my face and screamed. She picked up a handful of letters and shoved them down my T-shirt. Letters bumped and rippled down my spine. I cried out and grabbed her shirt and threw some down her front. I heard the rip of a button and realised I'd pulled too hard. I stared at her naked skin, at the creamy hint of her bra. My eyes flitted nervously to the corner of the room and then back at her lips. She leaned in and our noses bumped and our lips touched and we kissed.

We kissed and I heard my breath growing light and I felt embarrassed until hers did the same.

I wanted to touch her but I felt scared she'd slap my

hand away. I'd always thought – from the stories whispered in the playground – that sex was something you had to persuade a girl to give you, like getting pocket money out of an adult. Now I thought of Lady Chatterley, how she had desperately craved the touch of her gamekeeper. I felt Sally's fingers furrow through my hair and grab my neck; I realised she was pulling me in for a deeper kiss; I realised she wanted me too. Happiness fizzed like sherbet in my stomach. My hands trickled down her neck to the bump of her collarbone. At the last minute, I lost my nerve and slipped my hand between her breasts, caressing her rib-cage. Her bones stuck out so badly the skin looked as though it must tear.

'You're so thin,' I murmured. Then I saw the hurt in her eyes and said quickly: 'You're beautiful. You're really beautiful. But you don't deserve to be punished, you should eat.'

Sally managed a smile, but it was a fragile one.

'I'm going to kiss you,' I whispered, 'and when I kiss you, you'll be absolved of all guilt. You'll be wonderful. And then you won't need to punish yourself ever again, and you'll be able to eat.'

Her smile widened into something strong and radiant. Before I could kiss her, her lips were already on mine. She unbuttoned my school shirt and her fingers slid over my chest, pausing on an Institution scar. She leaned down and pressed her lips lightly against it. Then she searched my body for every little scar or bruise she could find and each one she healed with a kiss. She brought her face up to mine and I saw her eyes were shiny with tears.

'Are you okay?' I whispered.

She nodded quickly and whispered, 'I want my first time to be with you. Please can it be with you?'

I felt euphoria and fear flood through me. I wanted to take away her tears, take her away from the boredom of school, from the fear of the Institution. But I was also scared. I'd never touched a girl before. I thought about the gamekeeper, how he'd taken his time with Lady Chatterley. I caressed her thighs, up and down, watching her face intently. I saw stars of pleasure light up her eyes. Her sigh of impatience tickled me. I began to tease her, flirting with the edge of her knickers, until she touched me back and I lost control.

When we heard the first creak on the stairs, we both blinked, but we were too excited to realise that someone was creeping up on us. Our breathing was shallow, our eyes closed; we floated in hot darkness. Then the door blasted open and we fell apart, the cold air coming up between us. Sally let out a small scream. We tried to pull on our clothes, and act as though nothing had happened, but Mr Kelp wasn't fooled.

He asked us, in a cold, stern, voice to come down to his study and speak to him in turn.

I had to go first. Outside in the hallway, Sally gave me a secret kiss and whispered: 'Good luck.'

I sat down on the chair opposite him, bracing myself.

'I see you're enjoying the book,' Mr Kelp said. There was a smile on his face that was somehow smug, as though I'd done just as he'd expected. I suddenly felt stupid, as though I'd fallen into a dirty trap.

'You may go,' Mr Kelp said.

It was strange: I felt disappointed that he didn't tell me off. But, as I went outside, I reassured myself that at least Sally wouldn't get into trouble either.

For the next half hour, I stood in the hallway, listening in furious bewilderment as Mr Kelp ranted and raved at

Sally: *You're only fifteen . . . what do you think you were doing, going into his bedroom . . . do you want to return to the Institution?* I was close to barging in and punching Kelp, except I was afraid it would only cause more trouble for Sally. I leaned against the wall, closing my eyes, trying to get a grip. And then a sweet flashback entered my mind: her dimpled smile, a warm gasp in my ear as I pulled down her knickers. Tomorrow we'd be alone in the house again and Mr Kelp wouldn't be able to stop us. He might think he'd manipulated me, but I hadn't kissed Sally because of a book: all the book had done was liberate what was already inside me. We would make love in pure rebellion.

I thought then that Lady Chatterley might not have loved the gamekeeper if she hadn't had a husband to betray. And I felt confused, wondering why Mr Kelp's anger made me feel so much more excited about sleeping with Sally.

✦

The next day, Sally wouldn't look at me during breakfast. The morning light fell through the window, pale on her hair. I felt hungry to stroke it again. Mr Kelp might have said that we had been wrong, but I couldn't feel guilty. Mr D. H. Lawrence kept whispering to me that what we had done was right. I thought I might try to explain his ideas to Sally on the walk to school. But when I went up to get my rucksack, she left the house without me. I raced after her, crying, 'Hey! Wait for me!'

But she kept on running.

She wouldn't walk with me to school. Or walk home with me. Or even look at me during meals. I once knocked on her door and she warned me she would scream for the Kelps and tell them I was a rapist.

On Sunday morning, Sally suggested we all go to

church. We sang empty hymns and I felt as though all my desire to hug her and hold her had shrivelled and fallen rotting to the bottom of my stomach.

Back home, I took the copy of *Lady Chatterley's Lover* and nearly ripped the cover in half. Only the thought of the Institution stopped me. *I hate you*, I said silently to the book, *I hate you*.

I swore then that I'd never read another book Mr Kelp gave me.

Books were more trouble than I could ever have realised.

Eighteen

A week later, I got into a really bad fight with Jasper.

I hadn't meant to read another one of the Banned Books. I was beginning to feel angry with Mr Kelp and the little game he was playing with me; I figured I'd just pretend to read it, then make up a fake response and hopefully mess up his experiment. And so the original copy of *Lord of the Flies* sat under my bed, untouched.

But when you're feeling lonely, there's no better friend than a book. I no longer walked to and from school with Sally and every time I entered the same room as her, she walked out. I lay on my bed feeling hurt and bitter. And that was when I reached for the novel. I wanted to forget my pain and lose myself in another world.

I started *Lord of the Flies* at 5 p.m. that day and read it into the night; I fell asleep sometime around 4 a.m. with three chapters to go. The next morning I felt too hungry to wait for the ending and I buried it at the bottom of my schoolbag under my books. I figured I could go into the toilets during my break and hide in a cubicle to finish it.

Our first lesson was English and – with terrible timing – we were about to study the Rewritten version of *Lord of the Flies*.

Even before the fight, I became aware that something had changed inside me during the night – it was imperceptible but it was there. I tried to analyse why I felt different and I realised that I wasn't experiencing the anxiety that I usually suffered in lessons. I wasn't worrying about Jasper. I wasn't scared of being asked to read aloud. I had a secret: a copy of the real, uncensored, raw *Lord of the Flies* sitting in my desk like a bomb. I looked at Jasper and thought: *I'm reading things that you will go through your entire life and never, ever know about.*

It made me feel something I hadn't experienced in a long time: fearlessness. Studying a fake book made the lesson seemed like a surreal illusion. As though the desks were made of paper, the computer-board at the front a sheet of black card.

'So, class,' Mr Wilson said. 'What do you think *Lord of the Flies* is about?'

The usual restlessness and blank looks.

I put my hand up. Jasper looked surprised.

'I keep thinking,' I said. 'What if *Lord of the Flies* turned out differently? What if the boys who crashed onto the island ended up turning savage and turning on each other? What if Piggy ended up being killed? Murdered?'

By now, everyone was looking bewildered. Mr Wilson smiled broadly, but doubt clouded his eyes. I sensed he was aware of the original.

'That's a very novel idea, Stefan,' he said quickly. 'But *Lord of the Flies* is a *classic*. I do feel it is a little *presumptuous* of you to feel you could rewrite it, and in such an unpleasant way.'

I looked into his eyes and saw a warning: if I pushed this any further, there would be trouble. I shrugged and nodded. I felt Jasper's gaze on me and I turned to stare at him, challenging him with my eyes. To my surprise, he looked a bit nervous and averted his gaze.

The bell shrilled for lunch. I was about to leave when I suffered a flash of unease – was it safe to leave the book behind in my desk? Mr Kelp had warned me never to let anyone else see it. I quickly shoved it into the inside pocket of my blazer.

In the playground I saw Jasper and his gang heading for the canteen. I followed them at a distance. I felt shaky and strange, as though all the anger I'd stored up during the months of his put-downs was bubbling up inside me.

In the canteen, I saw them lounge at a table by the back. It was their usual place, from which Jasper could lord it over the entire canteen. Next to their table was the Sweets R Us machine. I walked up to it. Everyone turned and gawped at me. I examined the sickly choices, my heart beating – but more with a sense of liberated excitement than fear. There was a notice on the machine that read:

CHILDREN ARE ONLY ALLOWED
ONE PACKET OF SWEETS PER DAY

OBESITY KILLS

I slotted in some coins and out came a bag of Banana Boffins. I leaned casually against the machine, aware of Jasper watching me. My eyes travelled round the canteen. Boys eating, chatting, showing off, looking shy. The air of civilisation seemed fragile, held in place by threatening notices and CCTV cameras poised everywhere like techno teachers. I pictured boys smashing the cameras, turning on each other, the whole place seething with kicks and punches and venom.

'Hey, careful there, you might turn into a fatso,' Jasper called out.

'Sticks and stones may break my bones, but words will never hurt me.'

Jasper's gang howled with laughter. I ignored them and toyed with some more coins in my palm. Then I slotted them into the machine.

I saw Jasper's eyes widen.

'B-but you're only allowed one,' he hissed.

'So?' I said. I grinned and bought three more bags of sweets, tossing them to his gang. 'Fuck the rules. Eat whatever you like.'

They stared at the packets of Minty Mints and Banana Boffins and Raspberry Rizzles in amazement. Jasper looked both mad and confused. Then his gang started laughing. Soon their mouths were crammed with them, flashing pink and fizzy on their tongues.

'We'll get into trouble,' Jasper said, his eyes flicking to the CCTV.

I wasn't scared of the CCTV any more. I had the perfect excuse. If I got into trouble, I could just explain I was volunteering for Mr Kelp's secret experiment. I'd got away with going to bed with Sally, so I was hardly going to get told off for a few sweets.

Which made me feel rather powerful.

'Are you chicken?' I called out to Jasper.

Jasper opened his mouth and then closed it again.

Feeling reckless, I bought another packet of sweets. I felt the forbidden book jabbing against my ribs and I couldn't resist: I pulled it out and started reading it, waiting for Jasper to take the bait.

'What's that you're reading?' he called out.

'*Lord of the Flies* – Golding's original version,' I said. As soon as I said it, I thought to myself, *You shouldn't have done that*. But it was worth it for the look on Jasper's face.

'I don't believe you,' Jasper cried.

I was about to tease him some more when he suddenly leapt up from his chair and grabbed it. At which point I lost my cool very, very quickly.

'Hey!' I yelped in panic. 'Give it back!'

Jasper's eyes lit up. Realising he'd got me rattled, he tossed the book to one of his gang. He tossed it to someone else, who tossed it back to Jasper.

'I'm warning you,' I said in a shaky voice, 'you're going to be in trouble. That book is banned and you're not allowed to touch it. It will be *your* fault if —'

'Well, how come you're reading it, then?' Jasper asked.

He held the book up high, taunting me as I jumped. Anger fired my adrenaline. I jumped with all my might, felt my fingers brush it . . . tasted triumph . . . and then I was falling, smashing to the floor, laughter slapping my face. I lay there, staring at Jasper's expensive shoes, his taunts punching my ears. I thought of the way Jack had dealt with Piggy in *Lord of the Flies*. I pictured Jasper lying on a rock, a smashed rag doll of blood and bones.

I got up.

Jasper was doubled up now, his laughter theatrical. I curled a fist and smashed it into his face.

It was the first time in my life that I'd ever hit anyone.

I was shocked by how it felt. The physical sensation of my knuckle bouncing his skin back against his cheek. The joy of seeing pain on his face. And then a sudden sense of ugly shame, for becoming less than human, animal.

A moment later, he punched me back.

I stumbled backwards, grabbed a chair. Faces whirled; my hand sprang up to my throbbing cheek. Jasper saw his opening and took it. He pushed me. I heard the chair scrape away and then I was on the floor again.

Jasper's weight was heavy on top of me. A group surrounded us, silent in their shock. Rage roared through me. I saw beyond Jasper's face, the O of his mouth, to his little pink protruding ear. I grabbed it and twisted it. He screamed and I kicked up, knocking him off me. I tried to roll over so I was on top of him, but he fought me back and we tussled sideways.

We kicked and grabbed and punched each other. Our blows became more heartless; our bellows more savage. A part of me seemed to be watching myself, appalled by my own behaviour, yet secretly thrilled at the boundaries I was breaking. No more Stefan the good boy, no more Stefan who walked about with his eyes downcast, scared of what the world might throw at him. My anger possessed me so intensely that I forgot I was fighting another human being. He became a dark thing, a punchbag, a force to pummel and claw. Then, suddenly, I felt his fist break something in my mouth. Warm fluid slipped over my tongue and there were broken pieces in my saliva and my gum was soppy as paper. I heard myself cry out. Jasper was apologising, weeping, but I was wild for revenge. I was aware of the distant voice of an adult telling me to stop but I had to do it, had to get one last blow in, make him suffer for knocking out my tooth. I balled up my fist and smashed it into his face-flesh. His yowl of pain made me grin through the blood.

'STEFAN, WILL YOU STOP!'

And then cold reality dawned on me.

The Head was standing above us, his face thunderous.

It was the first time I'd ever been in our Headmaster's study. In fact, I'd hardly ever spoken to him before. He was a very stern man, with the face of a Roman emperor, a jutting chin and a grand walk of sweeping strides. But his eyes were kind. They were patient. They promised fairness.

His study was dark-panelled and on the wall behind him was a large framed copy of the National Pledge. Jasper and I were sitting on two chairs before his desk. I could feel blood trickling warm on my lips again and I went to wipe it off with my hand. The Head passed me a tissue and I said thank you.

Then I realised Jasper was crying.

'I don't want to go to the Institution, this wasn't my fault, he started it.'

'Shut up,' I cried. I was still stoked up from the fight. My anger, which had reduced to simmering point, now boiled to the surface and I bunched up a fist. Unable to control myself, I went to hit him.

'SIT!' the Head burst out.

I quickly sat back down.

'I didn't mean—' I began.

'You will both sit in silence until your parents come,' he said.

I'm doing all the wrong things, I realised. *It looks bad now; it looks as though it's all my fault.*

As I began to calm down, my anger was replaced with anxiety. I was desperate to make excuses, but every time I looked at the Head, he silenced me with a glance. The banned copy of *Lord the Flies* sat on the middle of his desk and every so often he picked it up, pursed his lips, flicked through it and then put it back down again. When the Kelps came, they would explain everything.

I was lucky: they arrived first, before Jasper's parents.

When I saw them, I leapt up, ready to hug them. But, to my shock, their faces were unforgiving.

'I want my mum,' Jasper snivelled.

'It wasn't my fault,' I explained. 'It was the book – I felt all funny – and I didn't show it to Jasper – he grabbed it and stole it off me.'

I turned to the Kelps, waiting for them to explain.

'He's been difficult at home for the last few weeks,' Mrs Kelp said tersely. 'We haven't been able to control him there either—'

'*What!*' I cried. An arrow of pain shot through my mouth. 'That's not true, you're lying!'

'And now this – he picks on some boy in the playground for no reason whatsoever.' She crimped her lips and her chin wobbled as though she might cry.

I felt as though she'd punched me in the stomach. They're afraid of the Institution, I realised. Afraid they might be smeared by my behaviour, blamed for being bad parents. So now they have to disown me.

'Stefan, can you tell me how you came to be in a fight with Jasper?' The Head asked me.

'We were just arguing about . . . homework,' I said, knowing the excuse sounded lame. I began to panic, aware that if I didn't come up with a better explanation, I would soon end up under a spotlight. I racked my exhausted brains . . .

'The truth is . . . we were arguing about that book, *Lord of the Flies*. I know I wasn't meant to show it to anyone and I'm sorry – I was wrong. But it made me feel strange – I'm a guinea pig, you see. Mr and Mrs Kelp – they can explain it all.'

I looked over at the Kelps, who looked back at me. Their expressions were rigid.

'I'm a guinea pig,' I said. I wiped my mouth with the corner of the paper hankie and let out a faint laugh, then broke off as pain throbbed in my tooth. 'It was a little bit crazy of me to volunteer but I thought it would help important government work. I help the Kelps decide which books need to be Rewritten, so they test texts out on me.'

'I'm afraid I have no idea what he's talking about,' Mr Kelp said. 'I can only think that he stole the book from my private study.'

I stared at him in horror, unable to believe what I was hearing.

'Mrs Kelp – he's lying – you have to help me,' I appealed to her.

Mrs Kelp pinched her lips until they nearly disappeared. And then she shrugged helplessly.

Everyone turned to look at me.

A trickle of blood spilled over the corner of my mouth and ran down my neck.

Nineteen

The white room faded away as darkness filled my mind. Time became vague, swirling grey hours. Then I blinked awake. I found myself lying on a black floor. I got to my feet slowly. I realised that I was standing in a boxing ring. It was empty, except for a rifle lying in the middle. The auditorium was full of empty seats, tiers of loneliness that dissolved into darkness.

I felt compelled to pick the rifle up. I gripped it tightly, waiting, sensing something was going to come at me.

And then they sprang up. On the edges of the ring, in the seats. Metal posts with words written on them. Forbidden words. All the things I'd read, all the ideas that had polluted my mind.

'Fire at them,' a deep voice boomed.

I swivelled the gun this way, that way. The bullets hit the metal targets with loud *pings!* But no matter how many times I fired, I couldn't hit them all. They kept flying up, mocking me, and I couldn't kill them all, I couldn't —

'All right now, Stefan.'

Dark and light swam against each other.

Then I came to.

I was awake. Lying in a dentist's chair. The Kelps had dragged me here after the Head's study, my mouth still streaming blood. *I've been excluded*, I remembered, with a heavy thud in my heart. The dentist had clamped a mask over my face and pumped anaesthetic into me. I could feel a horrible throbbing in my gum. I rolled my tongue around and started when I felt a foreign presence.

'I grafted a new tooth onto your gum,' the dentist explained. 'Now just take a mouthful of disinfectant and spit, will you?'

I spat out, then lolled back weakly into the chair. I didn't want to leave the room and go out to face the Kelps. For all I knew, these might be my last moments of freedom before I got sent to the Institution. My body was still throbbing with cuts and bruises from the fight. But worse was the state of my mind.

I had been wrong to think that the Banned Books had liberated me. They had corrupted me. In a few weeks' time my eye would heal and my throbbing jaw would quieten. But I would never be able to undo the damage those books had done to me. I might avoid the Institution, I might end up at a new school – but what might happen tomorrow, or the next week, or the next? The more books I read, the more I questioned the reality around me, the more I risked saying something dangerous in class or starting a fight. I was destined for the Institution sooner or later.

I realised, with a sense of horror, that for the first time I understood why my father had become a terrorist. He *had* once been a good man; it was his profession that had destroyed him. All those books, those ideas, that had slowly snaked into his mind over the years, making him doubt and question. I had done all I could to be good, but in the end I was becoming more like him than ever. Maybe it was all a matter of DNA; maybe I had been doomed since birth.

I glanced up at the dentist. I wished he could fix my mind as easily as my tooth. Clamp a mask over my face and delve his tweezers into my brain and pull out all the new ideas that I had digested over the last few weeks. I pictured his tweezers grabbing hold of sentences like long flickering white eels, pulling them out and throwing them into a dish and striking them dead. Then I'd wake up with a clean, clear mind; then I would be the old Stefan again.

'I think we're done,' the dentist repeated, looking awkward.

I got up off the chair very slowly.

The Kelps drove me home in silence. I couldn't stop rolling my tongue against my new tooth. My old one was now wrapped in a tissue in my pocket: a white pearl with roots like little red fangs.

Back home, the Kelps took me to their study. They sat behind the desk, looking so smug and calm. They didn't care for a minute that I'd been excluded, that they were ruining my life. I felt as though I wanted to punch them too but I had to control my rage. I kept reminding myself to be polite, so that they'd let me stay. Even if it made me feel sick to be nice to them.

'You betrayed me,' I said in a shaking voice.

'Look, Stefan,' Mr Kelp reasoned, 'we had to deny the experiment to the Headmaster. This was classified government work. You shouldn't have mentioned it to him at all.'

'But you – you and Mrs Kelp – you were slagging me off, telling him I was difficult . . .' I was close to shouting again.

'We had to. Nobody could know that your behaviour was a result of the books. We simply couldn't disclose this level of information to him.'

'You know what,' I hissed, 'I'm wondering if this experiment even is official. I'm wondering if this is something you and Mrs Kelp have cooked up for your own novelty.' I was certain I saw something flit across his face, but it passed too quickly to know if I had hit on the truth.

'Anyway, I'm definitely not reading any more books.'

'But Stefan, you're coming on so well,' he cajoled me. 'Today's fight really proved that Mrs Kelp and I were right to keep these books off the shelves. You are really doing something very valuable – you're helping the children of the future to be protected from these terrible books—'

'Don't try to manipulate me. I'm not reading any more and that's it.'

'Calm down, go to bed early, and we'll see how we all feel in the morning,' Mrs Kelp suggested.

'But I can't! I can't read any more books.'

'We said,' Mr Kelp repeated in more vicious tone, 'calm down and go to bed early.'

'Please,' I said desperately, 'instead of me just reading these books, maybe I could help to Rewrite them. I want to stop good people like my father turning into terrorists.'

'I'm afraid you can't become a Rewriter until you've left school,' Mr Kelp said in a patronising tone. 'But you can help us now. Our books are here for you to read anytime.'

I could see the delight sparkling in his eyes as he glanced over at his wife. I was proving to be a very exciting guinea pig for them. There was no way they were going to stop now. To think I'd been stupid enough to think they cared about me as though I was their own son. They would continue this experiment until the bitter end, until I was taken away and the next victim was brought to their house.

I lay in bed. Awake for hours. I could hear the loud snores of Mr Kelp rumbling through the wall. It made me feel even more furious that he was sleeping soundly while I was lying awake in turmoil.

It was then that I heard the knock on the window. I sat up in bed. The knock came again, a little louder. I drew back the curtain and jumped.

A face was staring in at me. A man wearing a black baseball cap. He was crouched uncomfortably on the garage roof. He looked familiar. He gestured at me to open up. Then I realised who he was.

He looked different now: he had a beard and his face was gaunt. There was a scar on his cheek that was still so raw it shone with little droplets of blood.

Omar Shakir.

I stared at him in astonishment. In my nightmares, I had seen my father's and Omar's faces floating in darkness, bruised and bloodied by prison guards, whimpering and begging for their interrogation to stop. My heart leapt as I realised: *If Omar's alive, then maybe my father is too.*

I was about to open the window when fear froze my hand. Why hadn't Omar escaped jail with my father? What if he knew I had been the one to betray them and now he was coming back for revenge? My eyes flitted to the shattered face of the CCTV camera above my window. If I let him in and Mr Kelp found him, no amount of Banned Books would be able to excuse me. I would be back in the Institution tomorrow.

'Open up,' Omar mouthed. He banged gently on the window and nearly lost his balance on the roof. I went to close the curtains, but his expression stopped me. His eyes were as wounded and vulnerable as a little kid's. I found myself reaching out and undoing the latch.

'Let me come in,' he said, trying to push his way into the room.

'I – I don't know . . .' Suddenly this was all happening so fast.

Before I could stop him, Omar was squeezing through the window. He tripped on the ledge and stumbled onto the floor. The bang reverberated through the floorboards. I froze, waiting for footsteps and Mr Kelp's shouts.

Silence. The central heating gurgled. Through the wall came the rumble of Mr Kelp's snore.

I let out a shaky breath of relief.

'Come on, we have to go,' Omar whispered. He pulled out a plastic oblong from his pocket and unfurled a carrier bag. Turning to the wardrobe, he started tearing my clothes from their hangers. Aware of me watching him, he turned and gave me an impatient smile, then carried on stuffing them into the bag.

Omar didn't know I had betrayed him and my father. Otherwise, I would have been on the floor with his fingers around my throat by now. I felt relieved and then scared, for he would find out sooner or later. I wanted to ask him if my father was alive, but the thought of a negative reply overwhelmed me. 'Is he okay?' I whispered, but too quietly for Omar to hear; he carried on folding and packing articles of clothing. My heart trembled and I cleared my throat and asked again: 'Is Dad okay? Is he below?'

'He's in a prison ship off the coast of Liverpool,' Omar whispered. 'The Words will arrange his release.'

'How come they got you out of jail and not him? What makes you better?'

Omar put his hand on my arm, accidentally squeezing a bruise I had suffered in the fight. I flinched.

'You'll see your dad soon, I promise you that.'

I stared down at his arm, my chest burning with pain.

'I hope my dad is dead,' I whispered savagely.

Omar's expression twisted into one of such deep disgust that my cheeks grew warm with shame. 'What the hell have they done to you?'

'It's not them,' I hissed, 'it's *me*. My dad was stupid enough to hide you and get himself put into jail and get me into the Institution and he chose to do it. He chose to. He was always ranting on about the nanny state and how everyone is telling us what to do. But we do have choices and he chose to become a terrorist—' I broke off as Omar gestured for me to quieten my tone.

'I don't have time for this,' he whispered. 'I told your father I'd bring you back and that's what I'm going to do. Now, have you got *Paradise Lost*? He said he told you to go back and get it – did you?'

I didn't reply. I stared at the carrier bag, and then down at my bed, at the warm impression my body had left in the mattress.

'I'm not coming with you,' I whispered. 'You're a terrorist. Go away or I'm going to call the police.'

'Look,' Omar hiss-whispered at me. 'You've been brainwashed. I don't have time to deal with brainwashing. I've risked coming out of hiding just to track you down, because it's what your dad would have wanted me to do. D'you think I'm glad to be coming out here on a cold night and climbing onto a bloody garage roof to save a teenage brat? No. So just get a move on.'

I shook my head slowly.

'You can go,' I whispered quickly. 'I won't tell them you were here. I promise. Nobody will know and you won't get into trouble.'

This way, I wouldn't get into trouble either.

Omar paused, undecided.

'Okay. Okay. I'll tell your father you wanted him dead and you didn't want to come,' he said sourly. 'Just give me the copy of *Paradise Lost* and I'll be on my way. You've got it, haven't you?'

I reached under the bed for *Paradise Lost*. When I felt my fingers close around it, I still pretended to carry on looking, buying myself time.

As though sensing my doubts, Omar whispered, 'If you stay here, you won't last much longer. The Kelps will put you back in the Institution sooner rather than later.'

'How do you know about the Kelps?' I hissed.

Omar didn't reply. He just stared at me, his expression faintly pitying. I remained crouched by the bed, my fingers taut around the book. My mind became a mouse, scurrying through a maze, hitting dead-ends. Omar was right: I was on borrowed time with the Kelps. I could go to school, tell the Head about the Kelps and their guinea-pig game . . . but he wouldn't believe me. Nor would any of the other teachers. I thought of Mrs Kay with a fleeting hope, then told myself angrily that she would only betray me, and probably enjoy it too. Omar was right. No matter which way I looked, all my paths of destiny led back to the same centre: the Institution.

The very memory made my scars throb, as if they might burst open and pour out blood with the sickness of remembering. I couldn't go back there. Ever.

Running away with Omar was crazy, but it was the only option. I'd play along, pretend that I liked him, until I figured out what to do. I put on my tracksuit and zipped *Paradise Lost* inside it.

'Okay,' I whispered. 'I'll come.'

Omar didn't blink.

We crept out into the hallway and down the stairs. As we passed by Sally's door, I had an urge to say goodbye, but Omar pushed me on.

The car waiting for us outside had white stripes. A police car.

'Is this a trap —' I began, but Omar shoved me in roughly.

It is a trap, I panicked. *They're in cahoots with the Kelps, they're taking me to the Institution*. Then the woman sitting in the driving seat turned and gave me a reassuring smile. Marie. My social worker. I saw she wasn't wearing a uniform and there was no police radio.

The car pulled away and Omar hissed at me to get down behind the seat and keep my head down. I squeezed down on the dirty floor, breathing in a dank, leathery smell. I was still in shock from discovering Marie was in the Words; she had always seemed so dedicated and sincere. I saw that she kept smiling flirtatiously at Omar and broke off from driving to pat his arm. Women seemed to find him handsome, though I didn't get it – I thought he was just an annoying jerk.

I listened to them talking in low voices. I heard the words 'safe house' and I figured the Words had found us somewhere to stay. I pictured some grimy squat in a basement in Camden, where we'd have to stay in sleeping-bags while rats scuttled about. Then I saw a sign flash above us:

BETHNAL GREEN:
LONDON'S FIRST ECO ROAD

We drove through a ghost road of empty houses. In a week's time, Omar explained, a load of immigrants would move in, the first guinea pigs for the Eco project. The car pulled to a halt and Marie passed Omar a key, then gave him a kiss goodbye on the lips.

Inside the house, everything looked as though it was made of Lego. The furniture was either yellow, blue or red. We squeaked from room to room like mice, for everything, from carpets to beds, was covered with plastic. The house was supposed to have solar panels and collect and purify rainwater and save gas and do everything a house could do to save the environment. And in every room, in every corner, there was a CCTV camera, installed to make sure the new family didn't waste energy or throw away unnecessary food or consume too much. Next week, they'd be switched on.

Before we went to sleep, Omar said to me, 'Look, I want you to know that your father did what he did because he believed in a cause.'

I fell silent as Omar carried on trying to persuade me. His words only made me feel more angry. So my father loved a cause. Did a cause live or breathe? Did it have bones or a beating heart? Did it have feeling? The cause was like some twin brother who had stolen all the love I should have had.

My father and Mr Kelp, I realised, were two of a kind. I didn't mean anything to either of them: they were willing to sacrifice my happiness for their own ends. Suddenly I felt weak with despair: who could I trust or count on any more?

'I need to sleep,' I interrupted Omar.

He broke off, then shrugged curtly and showed me where I would stay.

I lay in a red room on a blue bed of plastic. There was a yucky taste in my mouth from not having cleaned my teeth and I kept prodding my new tooth with my tongue. I craved sleep but I felt too jittery, wondering how long this would go on for. I pulled my ID card out of my pocket, staring at my photo, the darkness smudging my face into shadows. Would I have to spend the rest of my life on the run? I tossed and turned in frustration. I didn't want to rebel against the government, run undercover, spend my nights in unknown houses. I wanted a simple life, a warm bed, my school books, my spy novels. I wanted to know that CCTV was a friend protecting me, not an enemy looking for me. Several times I was on the verge of sneaking out of the house and finding the nearest police station, telling them Omar had kidnapped me. I just wasn't sure they would believe me. What scared me as much as anything was spending too much time in the company of a terrorist. Listening to his warped ideas. *If there's one thing I have left*, I thought, *it's my belief in the government and my hatred of terrorism*. I wouldn't let Omar corrupt me the way the Banned Books had. If he started pushing his ideas onto me, I would shut my ears and chant the National Pledge.

For now I needed Omar. I needed him to feed me, shelter me, protect me. But one day, one day, I'd get away from him. I'd find someone who would believe me, someone who would help me. I'd be put into a new home with new parents; I pictured them now, warm, kind people, like the Kelps, but without an agenda. The thought relaxed me; sleep began to spread its tentacles through my mind. Yes, they would be good people. And I would have a room with nice wallpaper, and a comfy bed, and it would be a house with no books in it . . .

Twenty

'Give me the book,' Omar instructed me. 'Give me *Paradise Lost*.'

'No,' I said, 'it's mine. My dad gave it to *me* to look after. I'm keeping hold of it.'

'But I thought you didn't give a toss about your dad. That's what you said last night.'

I ignored him, feeling the comforting chunkiness of the book against my chest, under the zip of my tracksuit top. I knew that *Paradise Lost* was very important for some reason and hanging onto it gave me a sense of security.

This morning, before we'd left the Ecohouse, Omar had revealed something fascinating: an alternative map of London, drawn up by the Words. There were areas shaded in pink. Omar explained that these illustrated where the Words had control of the CCTV network.

'That's what control means in this country now – those who monitor the CCTV, who can watch through the eyes of the country,' Omar said. 'These pink areas mean that we've either tampered with the cameras, or we've got people working in security there who can blank the tapes if necessary.'

The thought of this secret rebellion thrilled me; I quickly reminded myself that the State had introduced CCTV to protect us all.

Now it was early morning and London was washed in the grey pearl of dawn. Omar pulled a cap down over his head.

'We're going to be passing through some safe areas today,' he said, 'and some dangerous ones – that's unavoidable if we're going all the way up to Liverpool. But we've got to watch out.'

Omar told me to pull my trackie hood up to cover my face.

'Whatever you do, don't stare into a CCTV camera. They've developed a recognition program.'

'What?'

'You remember when you went to have your DNA test and they photographed your iris? Well, if you look similar to a photo on their suspect list, the CCTV will freeze your image. Then it'll analyse your iris pattern and compare it to the files in the database. So keep your head down, okay?'

It was horrifying to think my face now belonged on a 'Wanted' list. I had only ever wanted to serve the State and now I was officially a terrorist. I wondered if it would ever be taken off; if I would spend my whole life from now on unable to look up at the sky and stars.

We got onto the tube at Bethnal Green. It was busy with commuters carrying briefcases, jostling their way to work. We ended up sitting a few feet away from a guard. Omar seemed relaxed but I felt as though every muscle in my body was pulled taut. I kept expecting someone to look at our faces and cry, 'IT'S THEM!' I wondered if we had been reported in the news yet. I pictured the looks on the Kelps' faces when they saw my bed was empty. They'd probably be glad that I'd gone and, despite my loathing for them, a little part of me withered inside. I pictured Sally's face when she found out. I thought she might be upset and that made me feel a little better. Then I felt bad that I'd left her on her own with them. I'd probably never see her again.

At Euston, we didn't need to buy tickets – the Words had already supplied Omar with prepaid ones to Liverpool Lime Street. We sat in silence in the waiting room. As I watched the crowds, I no longer felt scared, just sad. Maybe it was just the tiredness getting to me, but I felt conscious of how easy their lives were. They obeyed the State and everything worked like clockwork for them. Their minds were full of an innocent, white emptiness. At least Omar was in the Words and he could enjoy being an outsider. I didn't belong to the crowd and I didn't belong to the Words, either: I was on my own.

Our train departed from platform seven. We were just getting on board when we saw the police coming down the platform.

'We'll get the next train,' Omar said quietly, and we slipped off and wandered over to platform six, pretending to check train times.

We had to wait another hour for the next train and I grew anxious. I asked Omar if the police had been looking for us or conducting a random security check. He didn't reply.

The next train pulled in and we got on. This time, there were no police. I slept for most of the journey and then Omar woke me up for some food from the buffet. Normally I hated egg sandwiches but I was so hungry, I wolfed them down. I could feel the carrier bag with my clothes in brushing my leg; I found its presence comforting.

Finally, the train began to pull into Liverpool Lime Street Station. I rose, grateful that the journey was over. But then Omar suddenly yanked me back down.

'Hey, we're not getting off 'til the next stop,' he said, his eyes flashing.

I sat back down, glanced out of the window and saw what he meant.

'I'm thirsty – be a good boy and get me a coffee from the buffet car, won't you?' Omar suggested, passing me some euros.

I paused, my heart racing, wondering if Omar was trying to lose me. Then I looked out of the window again.

The station was swarming with police.

There was no doubt in my mind that they were waiting for us.

The coins felt hot in my hand. Temptation whispered that I could cry out to them, have us both pulled in. But if Omar was right, if my face was now on a wanted list, what hope did I have of them believing me? Now that I had been labelled a terrorist, how could I ever clear my name? The more I tried to deny it and assert my innocence, the more they would think I had something to hide. That was a cruel lesson I had learnt from the Institution; my scars throbbed once more with the pain of memory.

Under the table, Omar suddenly gave me a sharp kick. My cry of 'Ouch!' prompted a confused glance from the old lady sitting across from me. I quickly stood up and hurried down the coach towards the buffet car. I realised that the police had probably been told to look for a man with a teenage boy, so separating was a smart plan. But what if the police got onto the train? I paid for the coffee, hardly daring to look the assistant in the eye, and gulped some back without thinking. I burnt my tongue and the raw area on my gum flared up in such agony that I spat some back out, staining my top. The assistant made a sympathetic noise and handed me a napkin. I smeared my top, which only made things worse, and started hurrying back to my seat.

I reached the front of our carriage. I could see policemen walking down the aisle with their backs to me. I stood on tiptoe, looking for Omar in alarm.

His seat was empty.

He'd gone. The bastard had deserted me and left me to handle the police. I saw the toilet was empty and I pressed the red OPEN button, diving inside. I put the coffee down next to the dirty sink, checking my watch frantically. The next station was Liverpool Central . . . it probably wasn't far from Liverpool Lime Street. Liverpool was a big city; it no doubt had a number of stops dotted around, just a few miles from each other. I could just hide in here until the next stop . . .

And then what?

I had no money. No way of getting back to London. Nothing.

The train suddenly swayed and the coffee cup twirled on its side, then turned over, pouring its entire contents all over the tiny floor of the cubicle.

'Oh hell!'

My trainers were getting soaked with hot liquid but I didn't dare open the door. I felt angry with Omar but, for some reason, even more angry with my father. I should have been in school right now, scribbling in my e-exercise book, drifting out into the playground sunshine. None of this would be happening if it wasn't for my dad.

'The train is now approaching Liverpool Central Station . . .'

I waited until the train had pulled into the station before I slammed the red button. As the door swivelled open, I saw there were quite a few people waiting. They looked bemused as I hurried past them, my footprints sopping coffee stains. I dived off the train just as the doors were beeping.

Crowds were pouring out of the station. I shoved my hands in my pockets and figured the best plan was to go with their flow.

We spilled out of the station and into the city. There were bus stops and a taxi rank and cars picking people up; everyone was moving with such energy and pace and direction. I drifted uncertainly, wondering whether I should head into the city centre, when I heard a voice behind me.

'There you are.'

Omar.

I was so relieved and yet so angry, I wanted to hug him and punch him all at once.

'Where were you – you left me!' I burst out.

'Keep your voice down,' Omar hissed. 'Just follow me. I have a friend who lives near here who should be able to put us up.'

'A member of the Words?' I asked.

'Why don't you just get a megaphone and shout that into the nearest CCTV?' Omar said, quickening his pace.

'Sorry . . . You could at least apologise for deserting me,' I cried. 'I was freaked out.'

Omar ignored me and carried on walking.

I got the feeling Omar was the sort of man who never apologised for anything.

I also got the feeling that I was starting to hate him.

❦

'You still got that book safe?' Omar asked.

'Yeah.'

We had walked for about twenty minutes now, away from the city and into the suburbs. At first the houses looked posh, with fancy blinds in the windows revealing vignettes of middle-class life; then, gradually, they became smaller and hunched up, as though ashamed at how scruffy they looked.

All the way there, Omar had been on the alert, constantly looking up, down, around, behind, for fear of being followed. Every so often he looked at me and frowned. I noticed that the scar on his cheek had started seeping blood again; I saw him rummage in his pockets for a tissue, then give up and dab the wound with his fingertips. I tried to convince myself that he had got the injury from climbing onto the garage roof, but I knew it was more likely he'd suffered it in jail. *If he knew I'd been the one to betray him, would I be dead by now?* I wondered. The thought made my stomach churn and I pushed it away quickly. Even if I hadn't told Mrs Kay, the authorities would have found out sooner or later.

Finally, he stopped outside a small, detached house with a messy garden. He lifted the gate to one side, for it had been torn from its hinges and was balanced against two posts, and rang the bell. There was no answer. Omar peered through the window.

'He's away – he said he might be,' he muttered, and then headed for the back gate.

It was locked, so Omar leapt up and climbed over it, telling me to wait.

I hung around nervously. There were slits in the wooden gate and I peered through them. I saw Omar pick up a stone and smash the kitchen window, then slip his hand through the gashed glass to open the door. And this was meant to be the home of his *friend*?

I went round to the front of the house. A few minutes later, he opened up the door and let me in.

The house had a musty smell and it seemed messy but homely; there was a thirsty-looking ivy plant on top of a table and books scattered everywhere.

It felt a relief to be inside, somewhere warm and safe. In the kitchen, I stood still in exhausted paralysis, torn between all the things I was desperate to do: drink, eat, sleep, wash. My trainers were still also damp from the coffee I'd spilled. To my surprise, Omar took a glass from the cupboard, filled it with water and passed it to me, giving me a gentle pat on the back.

'Thanks,' I said and he grinned at me.

I was just musing that maybe I didn't hate Omar quite so much after all when his smile became a frown.

'This isn't right,' he said.

'What?'

'It can't be a coincidence,' he cried. 'They *knew* we were planning to be on that first train and they were waiting for us at the station.'

'I'm on your side,' I said quickly. 'You know I am —'

'You might well be,' Omar said, shaking my shoulders, 'but the Kelps might have bugged you with a listening device. Take off your clothes.'

'Wait!'

'Bloody take them off! We need to search every pocket, every stitch, every hem. Go upstairs and borrow something from the wardrobe up there, but bring these down right away. We *have* to check them.'

'What about my other clothes?' I suddenly remembered. 'The bag with my clothes in!'

'I – we must have left it behind on the train,' Omar said, looking a little sheepish.

'But they were *my* clothes.' It wasn't really the clothes I cared about, but the fact I had lost my last reminder of home.

'Stop whingeing and get upstairs – we don't have time to argue.'

I ran upstairs and into a bedroom. I flung open the wardrobe, but all I could see were clothes like the type Islamic men wore – flowing white tops and baggy trousers.

'HURRY UP!' Omar shouted from below. 'If we don't get rid of the bug soon they'll be turning up and knocking on this door!'

I unzipped my tracksuit top and placed the copy of *Paradise Lost* on the bed. I pulled off my jumper, undid my trousers, kicked off my boxers. Shivering, I pulled some trousers off the hanger. They were far too big and immediately slid to my hips. Then I took a flowing top and pulled it on; it ghosted down over my wrists. I yanked my ID card out of my old trousers and shoved it into my new ones. Bundling up my clothes, I carried them down to Omar.

He took one look at my outfit and laughed. I flushed angrily – what else was I supposed to put on? *He* was the one who had lost my clothes. I watched as Omar took each item of clothing and turned them inside out.

'Nothing.' Omar sat back on his heels, shaking his head. He looked me up and down, scowling. 'Your trainers!' he cried, pointing at them. 'Take them off!'

They were still damp with coffee stains. I pulled them off, then winced as he took out a penknife and tore them to shreds.

'Hey – they're the only pair I've got!'

Omar ignored me, sifting through the butchered neon plastic. In his frustration he took one of the laces and started hacking it into frayed pieces.

'Great – now I'll have to borrow a pair of the guy's stupid sandals.'

Omar turned to me, narrowing his eyes.

'You're sure nothing fell out when you got changed up there?'

'I don't think so.'

Omar sighed. I sat down on the sofa. In my nerves, I started to roll my tongue against my new tooth. It was getting to become a habit.

'Why do you keep doing that?' Omar asked.

'What?'

'That thing with your mouth.'

'I've got a new tooth – I was in a fight and they put this one in.'

'*When?*' Omar asked urgently. 'When did this happen?'

'Urm, yesterday – the afternoon before you came to get me.'

'Oh God!' Omar rubbed his face with his hands. Then he let out a strange laugh. 'Clever.' He looked at me. 'That's where it is. In your new tooth. That's where they've put the bug, the listening device – or whatever it is they're using.'

'What! But that doesn't make any sense, that was before we even went on the run,' I objected, already feeling horrified at the thought of what was going to happen next.

Omar looked confused.

'Did they give you a false tooth? Can you just take it out?'

'No – they grafted it onto my gum.'

'Well that only confirms it,' Omar cried. 'You know how much money it costs for them to graft a tooth on? Thousands. It's not NHS treatment, certainly not for some kid who's being looked after by the State. You're bugged. They obviously thought you might try to escape. Go upstairs to the bathroom.'

'Oh God,' I groaned.

Upstairs in the bathroom, there was a thin layer of dust

on the blue sink. A moth was fluttering at the window, trying to get out. Omar had found a toolbox in the cupboard under the stairs and now he threw the contents into the bath with a heavy crash. From this shiny metal mess he pulled out a pair of pliers.

I tried to play it cool but I could already feel the backs of my knees trembling. As he tested the pliers, I cried, 'You have to sterilise them!'

'Good point,' Omar reflected. He ran downstairs and came back up with a cup of hot water and a salt-shaker, half of which he emptied into the cup. He waggled the pliers about in the mixture. I tried desperately to think up more reasons for delaying.

'Okay.' Omar's tone suddenly became gentle. 'I know this isn't easy. Let's face it, this is going to hurt like hell. Just grab me if it gets too much, okay?'

I nodded weakly, trying to put on a brave face and not seem like a wimp.

'It might help if you recite something to distract you,' Omar said, swallowing.

'How the hell am I going to recite something when I've got a pair of pliers shoved into my mouth?'

'I meant in your head, moron!' Omar cried.

I could tell he was nervous, and that made me even more nervous. But there was nothing else for it: it had to be done. I leaned back on the sink and felt the warm pliers enter my mouth. Recite something, recite something, I thought – but what, what? I felt the pliers grip the tooth and the first arrow of pain shot through my gums. *We pledge to honour and obey our government* . . . I found the National Pledge leaping into my mind and I clung to it . . . *and celebrate the glory of Great Britain* . . . He began to pull and I couldn't scream through my mouth so my heart screamed instead. *It is our duty to serve the State, to always speak the truth* – I tried to make him stop but he forced my mouth open with one hand, the other still yanking, ripping the tooth out of the gum. 'NEARLY THERE!' he bellowed. The pledge danced through my head faster and faster. The pain was so bad that I thought I might faint; I gripped his arm so tightly I heard him howl; and faces flashed before me – Mrs Kay's and my father's and Jasper's – and then it was over and I collapsed onto the floor.

'There!' he held up the tooth, triumphant. 'See?'

Wound around the tooth were two wires, thin as cotton.

Omar went to the bath, jostled amongst the tools and pulled out a hammer. He put the bug on the floor and proceeded to pound it. I felt every bang shudder through me, echoing in my raging gum.

Grabbing hold of the sink, I pulled myself up. I spat out and blood splattered across the sink. I opened my mouth and saw the gaping hole. I saw that tears had streamed down over my cheeks, though I had been in such pain at the time that I hadn't even been aware that I was crying.

Twenty-one

Omar and I were standing by the New Liverpool docks. Seagulls cawed above us and the air was sharp with salt. A week had passed since we had broken into the house and this was the first time we'd risked going outside. Omar had warned me that we needed to keep our trip brief. We had followed his map, found a route free from CCTV, protected by the Words – but he was still uneasy about being recognised by the general public. Apparently our faces were plastered across the news and the net. As he passed me the binoculars he made a loud comment about the joys of birdspotting. Every so often he turned and looked at the crowds with a nervous look in his eyes.

There were signs by the docks that cried SEE THE APOCALYPSE – JUST TEN EUROS. The boatmen weren't here to fish; they were here to ferry people across the waves so they could get a kick out of the destruction. Tourists and families were queuing up, snapping pics on cameras and mobiles. Dad had never been keen on summer holidays, so this was the first time I'd seen a ruined shore. Yes, I'd seen pictures of the famous floods on TV a few years back. I'd been transfixed by the pictures, the lines of houses underwater, as though they were floating. They had seemed ethereal and beautiful, like something out of a dream. But here, in real life, they just looked surreal and shocking. Some of the buildings were half-submerged; some just peeked out of the waves. Some were ancient-looking; there was one building of white stone, with a large clock-tower and a domed roof. Some were red-bricked and modern, looked as though they'd once been blocks of flats.

I swept the binoculars across them. I could see a bedroom window, frilled by waves. Through the window I caught sight of a poster on the wall that I recognised, for everyone at school had been given one. A silhouette of a man creeping up towards a station and a figure in white watching him with the logo: BE VIGILANT AND SAVE LIVES.

Omar nudged me and I swung the binoculars back to the sea. Then I saw it. My heart leapt.

A black dot on the horizon. The prison ship where my father was being held.

When I imagined meeting him, I didn't picture the sentimental reunion I knew Omar was hoping for. I saw him trying to hug me, but my arms remaining limp by my sides. Or I saw my fists on his face, breaking it into pieces.

'See it?' Omar whispered.

I nodded and he yanked the binoculars back. I noticed one of the boatmen eyeing us up and I felt uneasy. Omar, however, was a good actor. He smiled cheerfully.

'We've just seen some cormorants,' he remarked and the boatman grinned back, visibly softening.

'I don't suppose you can tell us where the World History Museum is? We were hoping to drop by there tomorrow.'

'You need to go into the city centre, down the high street – you'll see the signposts.'

I'd thought the museum was just a random cover story, but I noticed that Omar listened attentively. We hung around a little longer. Then the last boat pulled up at the shore and customers spilled out of it, looking frightened and excited. Omar checked his watch and started. Curfew was hanging over us like a black curtain about to fall. We had to hurry back to the house; by the time we slipped in through the back door, we were both panting.

♛

Something felt wrong. I couldn't quite put my finger on it, I just had an intuition that Omar was planning something he didn't want me to know about. I asked Omar about his friend, but all he would tell me was that his name was Raf. We'd only stayed in Raf's house for one week so far, but it was already becoming claustrophobic. Omar prayed five times a day and alternated between talking a lot or ignoring me altogether. He seemed obsessed with *Paradise Lost* and often stayed up into the early hours of the morning, reading and analysing the book by the flame of his lighter, terrified of putting on the lights and risking too much attention.

I was sleeping in the bedroom that belonged to Raf's teenage son. I'd been grateful to borrow a pair of jeans, a T-shirt and a tracksuit top. It felt odd, though, wearing someone else's clothes; they smelt different and carried an unfamiliar vibe. I couldn't go out, or surf the net; I was able to play chess on Raf's computer but I got bored after losing ten games. I kept thinking, *This will all be over soon. In a week's time, you'll be back at school, in class. Somehow, this will sort itself out.* I realised that, in my helplessness, I was waiting for some higher force to take over and make everything good. I wasn't sure if I had faith in God, but there was something I *did* have faith in: the State. They punished terrorism and rewarded honesty. Sooner or later, things would work out.

After our trip to the docks, I went down to the kitchen. Omar passed me some paracetamol; my gum was still flaring pain. After extracting my new tooth he had also made me gargle with some warm salty water so that it wouldn't get infected. I'd found a bottle of Good Behaviour Pills and thought they might help too, but Omar had gone crazy, throwing the bottle on the floor and crying, 'Do you *want* to be brainwashed and walk about like a zombie? Don't you realise what these pills do to you? They repress the ability to *think*.' I had flushed and muttered that paracetamols were fine.

Now I watched Omar cook a simple meal, opening up a can of mushroom soup.

'Does Raf mind us stealing his food?' I asked.

'Oh, he won't kick up any fuss at all,' said Omar, though there was something strange, almost sing-song in his tone.

'What does Raf do? Is he in the Words?'

'He's a writer and he's accepted by some factions of the Words, yes,' Omar said, after a moment's reflection.

Like my father, Omar clearly thought that all writers were beacons of moral light.

'Raf may be returning tonight,' Omar remarked. 'It might actually be a good idea if you stay out of the way when he comes.'

'Why?' I asked, tensing up. 'I thought the Words told you to come and get me.'

'They did,' Omar said quickly. 'But Raf doesn't like children.'

'But Raf has a son. Anyway, I'm not a child – I'm sixteen.'

'You're a child.'

I rolled my eyes.

After dinner, Omar told me that he needed to pray. He passed me the copy of *Paradise Lost*.

'Make yourself useful and start looking through this. Take a pen and paper – that pad lying by the phone will do – and note anything odd, any strange words that might suggest a hidden code.'

'So that's why everyone's making so much fuss about this stupid book,' I said.

When I picked the book up, I felt a shudder of revulsion tingling up my arm. The book would always carry dark memories for me: my father's face as the Censorship came, being shoved into the back of the police car, that last look at my home as they drove me away.

'So what kind of code is it?' I asked. When Omar didn't reply, I persisted: 'I don't believe there's a code in this book. If someone had a secret message, they'd just use email or whatever.'

My tactic worked. Omar looked annoyed and blurted out, 'Because every bloody email that is ever sent is analysed by the State. So is every phone call. So the Words have ended up resorting to old-fashioned spying tactics—' he broke off, clearly conscious that he was revealing more than he'd intended.

'But if the Words have put a message in here, how come they don't just tell you?' I went on. Winding him up seemed to be working, so I needled him some more: 'Have they thrown you out or something?'

'No!' Omar cried. 'I'll get the list of traitors soon enough, but— You don't need to know any more.'

'A list of traitors?' I asked, confused.

'The Words have enemies. We will deal with them effectively. I would appreciate your help,' Omar said stiffly. 'Now sit down and read. And by the way,' he added, as though reading my mind, 'if you find a code and don't tell me about it, thinking you can save it for the police, then think twice. I'll make you very sorry indeed.'

'Then why should I bother looking for the stupid code? If you don't trust me, then don't give me the book.'

'Because you're a smart kid and you might just crack it. So get on with it.'

He left, slamming the door behind him, making it clear that there would be no further questions.

I sat down and forced myself to make a start, but it was written in some kind of ancient English that was hard to understand. The first page was still crinkled and a little yellowy from the test the Censorship had run on it. If they hadn't been able to find the code, how the hell was I going to? I tried a few more pages, but I was too tired and I started to lose track of what I was supposed to be looking for.

Then, suddenly, I heard a key turn in the lock. I jumped to my feet, clutching *Paradise Lost* tightly, ready to use it as a weapon if necessary.

A man came into the living room. When he saw me, he started. He was Asian, in his fifties, with a balding head, greying hair, a round face, and eyes as soft and dark as olives. He was wearing a dull suit and a brightly coloured tie: blue, with clouds patterned over it.

Omar came up behind him. I was surprised by the expression on his face; it was almost close to loathing. Then, when the man turned to greet him, Omar quickly smiled and clapped him on the back.

'Raf – this is Jon's son, Stefan.'

I was afraid that Raf would recognise his son's clothes on me and tell me off. But his eyes were warm with admiration and he shook my hand as though I was important.

For the first time in a long time, I felt proud to be my father's son.

'Your father is a very great man,' Raf said, his palms still clasped around mine.

'He's a terrorist,' I blurted out.

Raf blinked and Omar laughed.

'I'm afraid Stefan is your typical indoctrinated teenager,' Omar said.

'Your father is a great man,' Raf repeated firmly, looking straight into my eyes. Perhaps it was my guilt rattling me, but I suddenly felt terrified that Raf could sense I was the one who had put my father in jail. I quickly yanked my hand away and stuffed it into my pocket, then stared at my feet.

A few minutes later Raf had settled in with a cup of tea and we were all seated in the cosy living room. Omar made a few apologies for having broken into his house but Raf didn't seem that bothered; he remarked with a wink that he'd send Omar the bill for the broken glass in the back door.

I listened to them chatting for a while, aware that anything I picked up would be useful ammunition to pass on to the police if I was arrested. It might just save me from being put back into the Institution. But they just chatted amicably, mentioning various names that meant nothing to me. And then, once again, there was that expression. Omar said it casually, but it tugged at my memory; I'd heard him say to my father several times when he'd been in hiding:

The whole world is contained in a grain of sand.

Before I had time to puzzle over it, Raf went to the stereo and clicked on a CD. I felt my heartbeat begin to quicken in rhythm and a new, unexpected energy rocked my body.

'I play this to my son,' he said, chuckling and shaking his head. He smiled at me. 'He's about your age. I sometimes risk letting him listen. And then I always have to threaten him not to tell his friends. We can never enjoy it absolutely. It's called 'Bitter Sweet Symphony', by a band called The Verve. They were around some time ago.'

I could feel Omar watching me. He seemed amused by my response to the music. I was so used to hearing the classical tunes played in train stations and sometimes at school in break-times – music that had been scientifically proven to calm the population down. Beige music with tinkly pianos and pretty violins. The type that makes you feel that you're somewhere between waking and sleeping.

This music cut through me. It made me feel raw and utterly alive. It stirred a distant memory; I'd heard it once before, maybe when I was around nine years old and I'd had an iPod. It suddenly filled me with yearning for Sally, to dance with her and hold her and feel the music reverberating on our lips as we kissed.

'I suppose this is a shock to you,' Omar mocked me. 'Your generation – you've not heard The Verve or Jimi Hendrix or Eminem, you've not read *The Catcher in the Rye*, you've not seen a classic film like *Terminator* or *Blade Runner*. All you've done is read dross, listen to crap and watched Disney movies with happy endings. And what kind of generation have we produced? A slow, simple, dull one who never questions anything. A stunted generation. It's devolution because in order for society to progress, you need to be able to debate ideas, to question, to see the dark and the light in things.' He broke off, scowling at me as though I was something he'd scraped off his shoe.

'I've read Banned Books,' I laughed, suddenly feeling triumphant. 'I've read *Lord of the Flies*, actually. The real version where they all attack each other.'

'Rubbish,' Omar said. 'I don't believe you.'

'I have. The Kelps were Rewriters and they used me as a guinea pig; they got me to read the originals, that's why I was in a fight at school on the day you got me.'

Omar was silent for a moment and then he suddenly burst into laughter.

'That's one of the funniest things I've ever heard – *you* – a guinea pig! Well, now. How did the books make you feel?'

'They . . . they kind of messed me up.'

'You're very different from your father,' Omar said, in a tone of disappointment.

'Well, I think you're stupid,' I burst out. 'If you think that reading Banned Books frees you, then you're wrong. In the end, they only made me feel the government is right. Anyone who reads *Lord of the Flies* can see that if it wasn't for laws and rules and the State keeping everything under control, there'd be chaos everywhere. We'd be fighting and murdering and stealing and it would all be so ugly—' I broke off, afraid he was going to laugh at me. But Omar sat up, his eyes shining, relishing a potential argument.

'That,' he said, 'is an interesting question and one that the Words have debated many a time. But personally I feel that we must have freedom at any price, even if it results in anarchy. The State is not here to act as God and take away our free will. We left Eden so that we might make our own choices.'

'The question is,' Raf asked me, 'in a country that makes a lot of laws – and every day, a new law is introduced into our society, whether we're being fined a thousand euros for failing to recycle or failing an ID check every month – does that society become weaker or stronger as a result?'

Omar shook his head, muttering, as though the answer was obvious.

'I think we need some laws,' I said, feeling a little excited. I had expected Omar and Raf to be black and white about their terrorist manifesto, so I was pleased that they seemed genuinely interested in my response. It made me feel more like a man; perhaps I could even educate them. 'I mean – *some* laws – just not too many.'

'I agree with you,' Raf said, to my surprise. 'The trouble is, the pendulum always swings too far one way. Back before the Great Wars life was very strict – although it seems free compared to the life we're living now. Then in the 1960s, the years of rebellion soared with pop music and free love. Our pursuit of freedom went further and further until it had to stop. I remember once coming home from work – I was only nineteen at the time. There was a pack of boys surrounding my car. I told them to go home, but they started slashing my tyres and kicking the windows in. When I yelled at them, they laughed at me, called me names. One of them even brandished a knife at me. I was so furious that I balled up my fist, like this –' he demonstrated, '– and punched the boy nearest to me. I was so angry I wasn't even afraid of the repercussions. Though they carried on calling me names, they ran off. And the next day the police came to arrest me. They said I had assaulted the boy and I was put in prison for two months.'

'But that's crazy!' I said, wondering if Raf was making the whole thing up.

'No,' said Raf, 'it's just the way things used to be. I, for one, was glad when the government hired a team of psychologists to censor books and films. I thought to myself at the time – even though I wasn't yet a father – there's no way I'd want my son watching violent movies aged ten and turning into an animal. At first it *was* a good thing. Knife and gun crime went down. But then, with the panic of the terrorist attacks, it all went too far. Much too far. Terrorism is being used as an excuse to create any law the government likes. And when we protest, they tell us it's for our own protection. Here,' he broke off, picking up a bottle and pouring out three glasses. 'Have some wine.'

I hesitated. I was starting to like these men and I was scared that the drink would only help them brainwash me. Then I remembered the vodka Coke I had drunk with Sally, how it had tasted hot and sweet. Wine was something I'd never tried before.

I tipped the glass back, saw the liquid swirl towards my lips like blood. I closed my eyes and let it fill my mouth, then swallowed. I put the glass down quickly, my palm flying to my throat. A few minutes passed, and the burning sensation faded.

'You may find,' Raf said kindly, over the top of Omar's laughter, 'that you grow to like it.'

'Why . . . why did my dad join the Words?' I blurted out.

Omar and Raf looked at each other, as though debating who should tell the story.

'I want the truth!' I cried.

'Your father joined the Words,' Omar said, 'for the same reason we all join. You see, Stefan, we're all living fantasy lives. We love lying to ourselves. We construct our lives as stories with ourselves at the centre. We tell ourselves everything will turn out well for us – after all, we all love happy endings, don't we? The woman who ignores her husband's affairs and reassures herself that he loves her really. The man who keeps drinking but assures himself that he's not an alcoholic because alcoholism is something that happens to other people. The kid who thinks the State will protect him when the State feels nothing for him – he's just another statistic. Life is harsh, Stefan, and sooner or later reality always bursts our bubble – and reminds us that our stories are just stories. Those moments – when our fantasies rub up against reality – create a friction. People often fall apart when it happens, because there is nothing more terrifying than facing the truth. But they are also the moments when we can open our eyes and see. That's when people join the Words.'

'But that still doesn't explain anything! Other than that you pick on people when they're feeling weak! Is that what you did with my dad?'

'Stefan,' Raf said gently, 'it was your mother's death that prompted your father to join the Words. You won't remember much about it – you were very young at the time.'

'What happened to her?' I had a sensation of a dark unease gathering in the room; now the rhythm of the rock music in the background took on a threatening vibe. I had the urge to get up and run out before Raf could reply.

'She was arrested by the State for a terrorist crime. Unfortunately, it was a mistake – the DNA found at the crime scene was matched to her by mistake – an erroneous record.'

'But – but – my mum wasn't arrested,' I cried. 'She was killed in a car accident – she was a nurse and she was on her way home from hospital and they'd made her work for days, so she was so tired she fell asleep at the wheel . . .'

'That's what your father told you, to protect you. He

didn't want to tell you the truth about your mother's death,' said Raf, looking uncomfortable.

'What?' my voice seemed to be shrinking. 'How did she die?'

'Oh, I'll tell the kid, then,' Omar snapped as Raf hesitated. 'After your mother was arrested, she was brutally tortured for a few days. They went too far, and she went into hospital and died that night. Your father joined the Words as a result.'

'You're lying!' I cried. 'If that had happened, my dad would have told me.'

'Actually, he was ordered by the police not to tell you,' Raf said. 'It was part of protecting the young, shielding you from such horror—'

'Part of protecting the State, more like,' Omar snorted.

Omar checked his watch and gave Raf an urgent glance.

'Perhaps you should go to bed now – it's nearly curfew,' said Raf. 'We'll talk more in the morning.'

'Raf and I need to speak alone,' Omar cut in as I tried to protest. 'You have to go.'

I got up, dazed, and left the room. As I climbed the stairs slowly, I heard Raf say to Omar, 'D'you think we should have told him that? D'you think he'll be okay?'

'The truth will set him free.'

I lay in bed. I could hear the curfew siren ringing through the streets. Usually I found the sound comforting, knowing that everyone would soon be tucked up safe in bed. Now the siren sounded like a ranting screech and I clamped my hands over my ears. I squeezed my eyes shut, whispering to myself, *They're lying, they're lying, they're lying* . . .

There was a bottle of Good Behaviour Pills by my bed. I grabbed them, pouring a handful into my palm, stuffing them into my mouth one by one. I stopped at six, scared they might knock me out for good. Immediately, a soothing, abstract whiteness seeped into my mind. I fell into a deep, dishonest sleep . . .

Twenty-two

The next day, there was a strange atmosphere in the house.

Omar and Raf seemed to have had some sort of row in the night; they barely said more than two words to each other, except to bicker. The only time they found peace together was when they knelt down to chant their Islamic prayers, when they seemed to declare a silent truce and offer up a unified devotion.

Omar also warned me that I would have to go to bed very early that evening because they would be holding a meeting in the living room.

'A meeting of the Words?' I asked.

'Why?' Omar asked, narrowing his eyes. 'Now that you know the truth about your father, would you like to join?' His smile seemed mocking, but there was a serious intensity flashing in his eyes.

'I – no,' I said. My voice sounded pale and I struggled to inject energy into it. During the night I had tried to persuade myself that the State was not to blame; now I needed to voice my arguments out loud. 'I think – I think that what they did was wrong. But I guess the police and the government made a mistake. It happens now and again, and they were only doing their best to protect the country from terrorism. I mean, my mum sacrificed her life

177

for an ultimate good, didn't she . . . it was unfair . . . but I'm sure now we have a DNA database, it won't happen again. I mean, I understand why my dad joined the Words now – I think he was a good man who meant well – he just got led astray.'

Omar's disgust was palpable. I shrugged miserably and stared down at the table. Raf carried on preparing lunch in the background. I watched him and I felt a terrible, burning pain in my chest. When my mum had been alive, she had always cooked me my evening meals. After she had died, every time I came home from school, my father would say brightly, 'I'll cook us spaghetti tonight – we'll have it with a real tomato sauce!' or 'How about some sardines on toast, won't that be a feast!' Then he'd serve up a pile of orange mush on soggy brown which turned out to be baked beans on toast. Or black shards which had once been pasta in a pan, a sauce bleeding all over them. I remember that he always looked at me with a desperate face, pleading for me to like it. I remember feeling angry that she had died and that I hadn't got to say goodbye to her. I pushed away every meal and told him that it was disgusting. Until one day I came home from school and stopped hearing her voice in the house, looking at her old clothes in the wardrobe. He served me burnt chicken and I forced myself to eat it and told him that it was delicious.

Raf put down a plate of vegetables and rice for me. I could barely eat more than three mouthfuls.

♔

We had discussed torture in National Security lessons at school. I could still hear Mrs Kay's soft voice explaining: 'There's a thought experiment that proves that torture is justified and it's called the "ticking bomb". What do you do if you kidnap a terrorist and he knows the location of a bomb, but refuses to tell you? Torture may be the only answer. One terrorist is hurt – but you save the lives of thousands of people who would have died from the bomb. It is the lesser of two evils.' I had always believed that torture was a simple necessity, that without it explosions would flare across cities on a daily basis.

I sat in the living room of Raf's house, alone, and folded up my sleeves. I had tasted brief flashes of pain in the Institution. My scars were pale and minor. But they were enough. They made it all too easy to multiply my experience and imagine what they might have done to my mother. I saw her face screwed up in agony. I saw the blood on her body. Her exhaustion, her head flopping against her chest, as she begged for mercy. I saw my father driving like crazy to the hospital. Dashing down the corridor to find her ward. I felt his rage when he saw the cuts and bruises on her face. I saw her find one last brave smile for him, I heard her whisper to him, *Say goodbye to Stefan for me —*

They're lying, they're lying —

I put my head into my hands, trying to push the images away. I turned to Raf's bookcase, desperate to fill my head with words. I wanted someone to tell me what to think, how to make sense of this turmoil.

There were two copies of *1984* on the shelf. I pulled one out, then the other. I realised there were different versions. One the original, one the Rewritten one. Except – how I could know for sure that the original was the original, the Rewritten the Rewritten one? What if Orwell's version *did* end happily for Winston? What if the Words were lying? What if the story about my mother was all just a lie, concocted to bring me onto their side?

I heard my mother's screams once more. The story made sense, too much sense. It explained why my father had left me behind the night he had gone to the hospital. Because the police would have forbidden him to take me. *They* were the ones who had robbed me of my chance to say goodbye.

No, a voice that sounded like Mrs Kay's argued back. *The police just made a mistake. It's not their fault. They're here to protect us all from terrorism'* —

Oh Dad, I thought. Oh Dad. I had let them persuade me that he was a monster. But he was just a human being. A man who must have burnt for years with a silent rage he couldn't release. He must have taken solace in his books, tried to escape into fantasy worlds at first. And then he found solace in a quiet rebellion; by joining the Words, selling Banned Books on the sly, a way of getting revenge on the people who had murdered my mother—

Not murder, they just made a mistake—

I jumped to my feet, put one of the copies of *1984* back on the shelf and kept one in my hand.

'You okay?' Omar asked, entering. 'D'you want some supper? We're eating early – we need to prepare for the meeting.'

'I'm not hungry,' I replied, storming upstairs to my bed-room.

There, I sat down on the bed, shaking. I couldn't bear to speak to anyone right now; I needed to work this out for myself. The streetlamp outside the window cast amber ripples over my bedspread. I opened up *1984*.

I could hardly believe how different it was from the one we'd read at school. I'd always thought that *propaganda* was a nice word, because it meant that that government published articles to tell us what the terrorists were up to.

But 1984 made me realise it could be a darker word, for Winston has to work for the government and falsify records and newspaper articles in order to put out *propaganda*. It made me wonder if the word 'Orwellian', which Mrs Kay had said was an adjective meaning 'people who are happy obeying the State', had once meant something else entirely. There were times when reading the book seriously disturbed me, so that I felt close to putting it in the bin and just taking a Good Behaviour Pill to blot it all out. It wasn't so much the plot that shocked me, or the characters, it was the way that Orwell used words. For example, there was a government body in the book called The Ministry of Love which was responsible for torturing people. I suddenly realised that words cannot be trusted, that words can be as dangerous as bombs and as confusing as fog. They can be used like coins; flick them one way and they come up with a smile head, flick them another and they have a nasty tail.

When I got to the bit in the book where Winston was tortured, I felt like throwing up. He had to go into a place called Room 101 where prisoners suffered their greatest fears. For Winston, it was rats. I wondered what my mother's greatest fear had been. I made myself read every word though, because to skip over any of it felt wrong, like taking a Good Behaviour Pill. By the end of the book I felt confused and little headachy, but I also felt a relief in my heart, a sense of a new knowledge that might disturb me at first but would console me in time.

I understood then what my father had been trying to teach me all along. Books might be lies, words might be ambiguous, but the greatest fiction could reveal the greatest truths in a way that newspapers never could. When I turned over the last page, I felt strangely close to my father.

I knew it was his favourite novel; by appreciating it, it felt as though a silent understanding had passed between us.

Then a sadness came over me. I had misunderstood him.

And I had betrayed him. I had passed him over to the State. For all I know, they might be doing the very same to him right now: torturing him to the point of death.

I got up and went to the window, tearing back the curtains. I gazed out at a necklace of gold lights that winked from Liverpool city centre. Just beyond them was the sea and the prison ship where my father was being held. *Hang on*, I whispered silently to him. *Please just hang on. We're coming to get you soon.*

The curfew siren faded. One by one, the lights of Liverpool went out. And then the amber of my streetlamp died, plunging my room into darkness. I realised that, reading the book in one gulp, I had lost several hours; I felt tired and very hungry.

It was then I became conscious of the noises below: surreptitious footsteps, whispered voices. I frowned, opened my door ajar. It was the Words, I realised. They were holding a meeting.

Twenty-three

Slipping out of bed, I crept down the stairs, nervous step by nervous step. At the bottom I paused, listening to the mingle of excited voices coming from the living room. They were all male, so the sole female voice sounded like a thread of beautiful music in the baritone babble. I waited there, listening to them discussing *Paradise Lost*, and I wanted to put a face to the voice. I saw that the living-room door was slightly ajar, so I crept up to it, peering through the doorframe.

The woman had auburn hair that flowed over her shoulders like autumn leaves and a smile like an angel. I heard someone call her Sasha, and realised she must be Sasha Brooks – a woman my father had mentioned many times in the past. As well as Sasha and Raf and Omar, there were about eight other men and women of different ages and ethnicities; one of them wore a Jewish skullcap, another a turban, another a sari. They all looked so ordinary in their suits and ties, it was hard to imagine they belonged to a secret terrorist organisation. And yet there was an undeniable energy zinging through the room. It reminded me of the mood that the rock music had evoked yesterday. They were all bound by a fierce belief in an ideal that beat secretly in their hearts, day and night. For the first time, I yearned to be part of them.

The copy of *Paradise Lost* had been laid on the table. I saw Omar opening a page and then holding out his lighter. Was he going to set fire to the book? I tensed up, wondering what my father would think of that.

'I'm not sure we should really be doing this . . .' Raf muttered.

Omar ignored him. Everyone fell so silent I was scared they could hear my breathing. I wanted to cry out as Omar held one of the pages stiff and then shimmered the lighter under it. Then my anger turned into confusion. They all huddled in close, examining it – *for what?* Omar had mentioned a code – was the heat meant to miraculously reveal it somehow? A moment later, however, their faces were shadowed with disappointment.

'Well,' Raf broke the silence finally, 'the texts are always changing. This one may be out of date now anyway.'

'I don't think so,' Omar said. 'I've heard it's a key text for Faction One.'

'Well, perhaps we ought to respect those above us. That's the *point* of the Words – none of us know too much, so that if we're ever caught we can't give too much away.'

'We're supposed to be a democracy,' Omar rounded on him, 'we're supposed to share everything. It doesn't make sense that a select few above us should have access to this information – and we don't.'

'But that way, we're all protected,' Sasha said, putting her hand on Omar's arm and smiling softly at him. 'You know that as well as I. If any of us get caught, we can't give out the names of those above us. We must stick together, Omar. If we don't stick together, we become weak.'

'Well,' Omar said sullenly, shoving *Paradise Lost* to one side. 'It hardly matters. We've found nothing. We *deserve* to know who the traitors are – and we deserve to know now. Why should we wait? I've heard some of them are on the prison ship—'

'This is precisely why they're keeping it from you!' Raf said. 'You're too hot-headed, you'd just go and murder them and—'

'They'd deserve it. If there are traitors in our organisation, we need to hear about it. That's what makes us weak!'

There was a terse silence. Raf's eyes suddenly slid from Omar to the doorway.

'Hey!' he cried. I tried to press myself against the wall but it was too late. They were all staring at me. I thought about running away, but another, more extraordinary idea thrilled me. I walked into the room, my heart beating rapidly.

'Great,' said Omar. 'Now the kid knows everything.'

'Is this Jon's son?' Sasha asked, her voice tender. 'Don't you look like your father!' She gazed at me with a curious affection, so my that cheeks turned pink and then – as she touched them – a violent red.

'Stefan,' Raf said in a polite voice, 'this is a private meeting. I'm afraid you can't attend.'

I stared around at the group and for the first time in a long time, my loneliness felt like a skin I might shed. Standing here with them made me feel strong. My fear of the State was intensifying into anger. I wanted to strike back at it for what it had done to my mother. I wanted to stick up two fingers at it, publish Banned Books, smash CCTV cameras – anything that would destroy the machine.

'I want to join,' I said, and then repeated, more loudly: 'I want to join the Words.'

There was surprised laughter. Sasha beamed at me and went to touch my arm, but Omar stopped her. He stared at me intently.

'What happened to the boy who believed in the Rewritten version of *1984*?' he asked. 'Who said he hated his dad and thought he was an idiot?'

I stared back at him, feeling the inadequacy of words, wishing I could prove myself in some way. Then I had a flash of inspiration.

'Give me your lighter,' I said. When Omar didn't reply, I picked it up. They all looked slightly nervous. I drew my ID card out of my pocket and held the flame against it. My ID, my last anchor, my last proof of who I was, began to melt and bubble. The photo of my face became a scorched blur.

I looked up at Omar. There was a ghost of a smile on his lips. The rest of the Words began to clap. Omar didn't join in, but his smile became real. He reached out and shook my hand.

'Your dad would be proud of you.'

I felt my heart swell; I felt close to tears.

'Are we going to free him?' I appealed to them all. 'I thought you were planning a raid on the prison ship – when is it going to happen?'

I thought that they had been hiding their plans and would reveal them at once. But they all shifted uncomfortably.

'You should tell me – I deserve to know!'

'It's not that, Stefan,' Sasha said. 'It's just that we're still planning it – it's a difficult operation. We care as passionately as you about releasing your father.'

The silence was broken by one of the other men saying brightly, 'Well, why don't we all take a look at Raf's new book!'

I felt disappointed but I joined in with the applause. Raf flushed as several of them clapped him on the back and Sasha gave him a hug. Omar, however, looked incredulous.

'So you decided to—' he began.

The man heaved a box up onto the coffee table. They all helped to tear off the strips of thick, brown tape. Then Raf reached in and pulled out a book. It had a red cover and I saw Raf's name flash across the spine.

'Fifty copies!' he beamed. 'My very own book!'

Omar took a copy from the box and began to flick through it, his face hardening.

'You know, we'll easily sell these fifty in a day on the underground,' Sasha said in a low voice. 'Waterstone's in Liverpool have said they'll sell a few under the counter for us.'

Omar snapped the book shut and turned to the synopsis on the back cover, reading aloud:

'*Raf Gokkaya's first novel is an outrageous and controversial black comedy that explores the life of a Muslim man who is struggling with his faith. When he is arrested for terrorism on false charges, deported and tortured for thirty consecutive days, he begins to wonder if atheism is an easier path. This is a rare book that dares to poke fun at Islam while also raising serious spiritual questions . . .*'

'I agree that some people might be offended by my ideas,' Raf said loudly. 'But my argument is that we are all in the Words, so we believe in freedom of speech no matter what, don't we, Omar?'

Omar smiled and then nodded sharply, downing the rest of his drink.

'After all,' said Raf, though there was anxiety in his voice, as though he was trying to convince Omar that all was well, 'ideas are just ideas. The views of my hero are not necessarily my own. I've always felt that books are the most peaceful way of fighting for a cause. A form of passive resistance.'

Omar smiled at him, but shook his head and said, 'You know, when I was first arrested over my book, I felt indignant. I thought, I'm just a philosopher, a man exploring ideas – why the hell should I have to carry the blame for people who twist my words and act on them? But, you know, recently I've began to change my mind about that. I feel proud that my book made an impact. Because there's no such thing as people who just *believe* in ideas. Once people get ideas, they want to *act* on them. They want to share them with other people. People become *idealists*. And idealists are always dangerous. People who can see grey areas, who live beige lives, will always be the safe members of society. But they will never change anything.'

'Nobody is going to act on this book, Omar,' Raf said hastily, 'it's just a comedy.'

'But it offends the Prophet,' Omar said in a stony voice.

I stared at Omar, feeling upset. I didn't like to hear the Words arguing; I liked the idea of a group who worked against the State as one powerful entity. Raf gazed over at me and gently suggested that I go upstairs to bed. He said they had one or two issues to talk about alone.

'I promise they don't concern your father,' he added, seeing me hesitate. 'Omar and I just need to sort a few things out.'

I nodded, forcing a smile, even though I felt rather left out. Upstairs, I went into the bathroom and stared at my reflection in the bathroom mirror. My dad had always told me that I had my mother's face – except my eyes. My eyes were the same shade of green as his, he said. I gazed out of the bathroom window at the bright lights of Liverpool. I felt frustrated at the thought – for I had to face the possibility – that if the Words didn't hurry, or if their escape plan went wrong, I'd never get to see him again. I wanted to talk to him, to just sit and talk and find out more about this fascinating man. We had to find him.

Down below, I heard the bang of the back door as the meeting ended. They seemed to go one at a time, with short intervals between departures. Then I heard the sound of rock music. I was surprised that Omar was taking the risk; curfew was close and the music was loud enough to be heard out on the street. Frowning, I went out onto the landing. I could hear raised voices from downstairs.

Once more I crept down the staircase, hanging back nervously in the hallway. Raf's voice was high and angry; Omar's replies came in low, intense whispers.

Then I heard a crash and a terrible scream. I stood in the hallway, staring at a picture of a pretty field on the wall opposite, my heart trembling. They had stopped speaking but I could still hear strange, horrible noises: cries and a low, rasping, gasping noise. I turned to run upstairs, hide under the covers, pretend I hadn't seen anything. Then I caught a scent from the clothes I was wearing; the smell of another boy's skin. I remembered that Raf had a son, to whom these clothes belonged. I pictured how he might feel to come home and find his father in a pool of blood. I hurried to the living-room door and looked in.

I stood very still.

Omar looked up at me. He started and in his moment of distraction, he lost his grip on the tie that he'd wrapped around Raf's neck.

'Go away!' he yelled.

Raf flailed about, his eyes bulging, his hands clawing the air. Omar quickly tightened his grip on the tie and yanked it even tighter. Raf's face turned a violent beetroot colour and his eyes disappeared into their whites. Was Raf a traitor? One of the men Omar was searching for?

'Stop!' I pleaded. 'If you don't stop, I'll call the police!'

'Oh, sure you will,' Omar gasped, for he seemed breathless and exhausted with the pain of what he was doing. 'Raf's book – it offends the Prophet – he must die!'

A furious disbelief surged through me. My dad had always said that the Words stood for two things: freedom and peace. They were different from all other groups because they refused to advocate violence. And now Omar was trying to kill Raf, all over a few words! His hypocrisy was insane. I wanted to ask Omar how he'd felt when he'd stood in Trafalgar Square and nearly been stoned to death. If he felt someone else should suffer that same pain. But there was no time to reason with him; I had to shock him into letting Raf go. I ran to the phone and dialled 999, crying, 'Police!' when they asked which department.

'You have to come, someone's about to die,' I gabbled out the address in one gush and then hung up.

Omar came into the hallway, his expression thunderous. 'What the hell did you do that for?'

I ran back into the living room. Raf was lying on the floor, gasping. When he saw me, he reached out, whimpering. I tried to take his trembling hand but he batted my fingers away, gesturing. I realised he was trying to grab at *Paradise Lost* – trying to get me to take it.

I grabbed the copy of the book, hugging it to my chest. I turned to see Omar waiting in the doorway, his eyes glittering.

'You're not going anywhere with that book,' he shouted.
I turned and ran to the window, fumbling with the latch.
I heard Omar behind me, but I didn't waste any time looking back; I jumped out onto the damp lawn, then shoved
the broken front gate to one side and started to run.

Twenty-four

I pounded down the road, Omar following at my heels. I could see the streetlamps flicking off intermittently. Which meant that in fifteen minutes' time, curfew would begin. The streets would be swarming with police and anti-terrorism units.

We reached the end of the road, clutching our stomachs, heaving rasping breaths. Across the road, an anxious woman was calling her sons for curfew; her voice quivering with poignancy. I turned to look at her beautiful face. And then Omar's cruel one. When he had tried to strangle Raf, his expression had been a mixture of self-disgust and evil delight. Now he was staring at me with cold fury. He reached out and grabbed my arm, trying to yank me down the left road. I struggled away.

'You're not going to kill me,' I cried hoarsely, hysterically. 'You can't, the police will be here soon, they'll stop you, they'll get you if you try to kill me!'

'I have no desire to kill you,' Omar said, laughing a little hysterically too. 'You're really not that important. Despite what you just did I still have to follow your father's wishes and look after you. So will you bloody well follow me!'

'No!' I cried, as he grabbed my arm again. 'You disgust me! You don't deserve to be in the Words! You're a murderer! You crazy, you're— Don't touch me, just leave me alone.'

I yanked away my arm and started to run again. As I fled, one by one the streetlamps began to go out, as though I was being chased by darkness.

Once again, I heard Omar's footsteps pounding behind me. I tried to push myself faster, but my body was breaking up in exhausted protest.

I felt him grab me from behind and we fell in a clumsy heap to the ground. The gravel scraped my temple and cheek and I let out a cry. I felt him clamp his hand over my mouth.

'Look,' he whispered furiously, 'curfew is starting. You're sixteen years old. Do you really believe you can survive out here on your own?'

His words resonated inside me. I was hungry, exhausted, sick.

As he stared into my eyes, the streetlamp above us reflected orange demons in his pupils. Then it went out, plunging us into darkness.

A new, white light appeared, circling over the garden wall behind us. It lingered on our bodies and we both froze.

Omar swore violently and jumped up to his feet, grabbing me up by the scruff of the neck.

'Run!' he yelled, shoving me forwards. When I hesitated, he hissed, 'I'll tell them you're with me! I'll say you're one of the Words and you'll end up back in the Institution!'

We ran. Houses, gardens, walls flew past. Our panicked reaction was the worst possible one: the police car smelt prey. It speeded up, lights blinding, a computerised megaphone warning us: 'STOP, OR WE WILL BE FORCED TO USE PHYSICAL ACTION IN THE NAME OF THE TERRORISM SECURITY ACT.'

Which translated that it was legal for them to shoot us.

I was in so much pain I almost didn't care. My lungs felt punctured, stomach torn open by a stitch, my wounded cheek throbbing, sweat stinging my eyes.

Then Omar grabbed me and tugged me down a side alley. We pounded through, hearing shots behind us. We trespassed across a front garden, burst through a back gate, tore across a back garden. There was a large blue trampoline and a swing which I knocked and sent flying up-down-up in the air.

We reached the bottom fence. I kept looking back nervously – I couldn't see any police, but were they hiding? Ahead of us was a stretch of long grass, full of dark shapes. It looked as though the neighbourhood was using it as a dumping ground for their rubbish.

'Come on,' Omar said.

We climbed over the fence and ran on. Grass scratched my legs and I felt the greasy skin of fried-food packets rub my ankles.

Halfway up the garden Omar stopped, panting. He pulled *Paradise Lost* out of my hands, ignoring my protest. Then he lifted up the seat cushion of a blue sofa dumped right in the middle of the lawn and shoved it underneath. I realised he was taking no chances in case we got caught.

The grass led up to a house. There were no lights and the windows looked cracked and burnt out. We slammed through the back door into darkness. I wrinkled my nose at the acrid smell.

Omar pulled a lighter out of his pocket and the flame shook violently.

We edged through a kitchen and into a hallway. A doorway beckoned us; we tiptoed over and looked in. The room was a curious mixture of luxury and stark dirt. Food wrappers littered a fancy carpet and a few crumpled beer cans nestled next to a stylish cabinet. It seemed deserted . . . until we heard a groan from the corner.

A tramp. Buried under a patchwork of cardboard and rubbish. His face was filthy, his beard matted.

'You're very welcome to share with me,' he said in a slurry voice, 'so long as you leave me in peace.'

'You're the only one here?' Omar asked.

'Just me . . . just me . . .' the tramp pulled his corrugated cover up over his head. 'Just me and my little rats.'

Omar flicked his lighter on again and I followed the yellow orb upstairs. By now, I felt quite exhausted and close to collapsing on the floor in defeat. Omar flicked his lighter across doorways, then led me to a small bathroom. Like downstairs, it was quite fancy despite the dust and the dirt. Omar tested the water from the tap and told me it tasted clean. We took it in turns to duck our heads down and suck sluices of water into our parched throats.

Then Omar said something that surprised me.

'We need to wash that wound on your face – I wouldn't want it to get infected.'

He tore away the hem of his shirt, rinsed it under the tap and then held the rag to my cheek, holding up his lighter with the other hand. I was surprised to see a tenderness in his eyes. For a moment, it felt as though I was looking into the eyes of my father. I lowered my gaze, overwhelmed with sorrow.

As Omar gently scrubbed away, he talked rapidly in a low voice, as though reassuring himself.

'We're in trouble now though . . . neither of us was wearing a cap, you didn't have your hood up . . . the CCTV will have caught our faces, no doubt . . . I don't know if we should stay here or just keep moving . . . now they know we're in Liverpool . . . bloody CCTV . . . in Victorian times, they moralised, now they have this synthetic moralising, these cameras that watch us and remind us to be good . . . I don't know if I should have left *Paradise Lost* out there . . . maybe I should go back and get it . . .' He went on like this for a while, ranting and philosophising.

I stopped listening, for my body was behaving strangely. I tried to hold it still, but it kept erupting into spasms and twitches, as though it couldn't hold my panic in.

'Why did you do it?' I suddenly burst out. 'You're a member of the Words. You stand for liberty and freedom. How – how could you?'

'I love Allah,' Omar said sharply, 'and I must obey him and defend him against blasphemers. I agree with complete freedom and no censorship, but there is a difference between writers who express themselves and those who insult my God! Raf's book was the act of a *kafir* who deserves to burn in hell. He makes fun of the Qur'an on nearly every other page.'

'That doesn't make any sense.'

Omar stopped dabbing my cheek and his lighter flicked off, plunging us both into darkness. He turned away and washed his hands in the sink. I stared at his silhouette in painful bewilderment. Then I remembered something my father had once told me: *People don't make any sense.* It didn't make me want to spend any more time with Omar, but for a moment I understood him.

'Come on,' Omar said, 'I need to pray and you need to sleep. Maybe we can see if the tramp downstairs can spare us a few of his scraps – we both should eat. We might need the energy to run again.'

I felt miserable. I wanted to be back in the warmth of Raf's house. I had found a brief sense of security in the

Words and now we were out in the cold once more. I felt nervous about approaching the tramp, but I followed Omar down the stairs all the same.

We were halfway down when a white circle of light spilled through the warped glass of the front door, hovering a few inches above my head. I froze and Omar hissed, 'They're here!'

I turned, ready to run upstairs, but Omar cried: 'No – down here.'

I hesitated, then followed him back down. Omar went up to the front door and knelt down by the letter-box. He slipped his fingers in and tweaked it slightly. Light fell in. Very gently, he let it fall flat and stepped backwards. Ignoring me, he went into the living room. I followed him nervously. The tramp was singing softly.

'Any chance of us hiding under your duvet?' Omar asked. 'We're having a spot of bother with, er, a few people.'

'By all means,' the tramp said in a cracked, drunken voice. 'The more the merrier.'

As we approached him, the stench rolling off him made me recoil. Omar clambered over him, lying down next to the wall and patting the space in between. Great, I thought, I get to lie down between a murderer and a tramp. I climbed clumsily over the tramp, apologising as I trod on his beard and he let out a hiss. Then he pulled the cover up over our heads. We lay in a muffled, smelly cocoon of darkness.

Waiting.

Waiting.

Out bodies seized up with collective tension as we heard the front door burst open.

Then the slam of footsteps.

I heard Omar's breath quicken. The footsteps got louder. And then more distant as they rang up the stairs and across the bedrooms above.

The wait seemed to go on for ever. I became so tense I couldn't sustain it. My body went limp. And just as I had relaxed, the footsteps magnified once more.

There were voices by the front door. Omar whispered to me – I think he was so engulfed with panic that he had to speak – 'I think we've got away with it.'

And then the cold air was clawing our faces. Omar and I hissed at the tramp to get down but suddenly he wasn't a tramp any more. He was standing above us. He was tall. He was sober and had stature.

'I've got them,' he called out in a cool voice. As he turned to face the hallway, I saw the a blue flash of uniform under his dirty mac. 'They're here.'

'Oh great,' Omar cried. 'Oh, just great.'

As the policemen pulled me to my feet, fear punched my stomach so hard that I vomited. One of them shook his head. I looked at Omar, searching for reassurance in his face, a way of getting out of this. But he was just gazing out through the window at the garden and I could tell he didn't care about me; all he was thinking about was that copy of *Paradise Lost*, left behind, wedged in the sofa.

Twenty-five

The Catcher in the Rye.

199

Twenty-six

I woke up. Something hard was jabbing into my cheek. I pushed it away fiercely, then heard the *thwack* as it hit the floor.

I blinked. I was back in the squat, lying in a bedroom. I looked at my watch in confusion. My ordinary watch – which had a thin brown strap and an old-fashioned face, for it had belonged to my father's father – had been replaced by a chunky black digital.

My new watch told me that it was nearly midday. It also confirmed that the police catching us hadn't been a dream. A shard of memory tore through the blankness: an officer leaning over me, fat fingers unbuckling the strap. Yet here I was, lying in bed. Safe and sound. Back at the very house where we had been arrested. In my ordinary day clothes. I pulled up my T-shirt, checking for bruises, but there were none.

I pulled open the curtains. Outside the sky was a deep blue and clouds floated about, dreamlike.

'Omar.' My throat was very dry and my voice crackled. 'Omar?'

I called quietly, still feeling on edge. What if the police were still in the house?

I tried to remember the police interrogating me. But other than the watch, I couldn't think of anything. I couldn't even recall them bringing me home. There was just a blank, slightly floaty feeling in my head. A little how I used to feel when I'd taken the Good Behaviour Pills.

I swung my feet onto the floor. Then I saw the book. Instinctively, my hand flew to my face. This was what had been on my pillow; I could feel the indent the pages had left on my cheek. I turned it over and excitement coursed through me:

The Catcher in the Rye by J. D. Salinger

> *The Catcher in the Rye.*
> Top of the list of Banned Books.
> The book even Mr Kelp hadn't allowed me to read.
> 'Omar,' I called out faintly.
> No reply.

I stared back down at the book. I knew I ought to look for Omar, but I felt like a starving man who had suddenly come face to face with a three-course meal. I drank the words in like a magical potion; they bubbled and fizzed in my brain. The voice that kept nagging me to find Omar grew quieter, then disappeared. A curious sensation came over me. It was as though the book was so powerful, my ego had been obliterated. The past and future failed to exist. There was just the present, and me holding the book, and the words filling me up, and the silence around us.

I heard footsteps creaking on the stairs. A voice in my head told me that I ought to respond and hide. But then the voice sailed away like a cloud. I kept on drinking in the words.

'Stefan?'

I carried on reading. *In a minute*, I thought, *in a minute*.

'STEFAN!'

I looked up with a sigh.

Omar was standing in the doorway. Like me, he was wearing ordinary clothes, though his hair was slightly mussed.

'You . . .' he trailed off. 'I . . .'

I felt as though I ought to talk to him, but the book had gripped me utterly. I carried on reading.

'I . . . you . . .'

I was beginning to feel slightly impatient. Couldn't Omar see that I needed to reach the end of the book?

'Well, we're okay, we're back,' Omar said finally. 'They obviously thought we were just . . . that we were willing to comply, that we weren't in the Words . . . that we had no new information to give them . . . I think . . .' He frowned uneasily, as though he couldn't quite believe that it had all been so easy.

'Yeah,' I said, turning to page 162.

'What the hell are you reading?' Omar cried.

I suddenly felt very protective, as though the book was a cub and I was a lion, ready to roar and claw if he came close.

'*The Catcher in the Rye*,' Omar read from the cover. 'What! What the hell are you doing with that?'

I snapped it shut and hugged it hard to my chest.

'I found it,' I cried. 'It was under the bed. I found it and it's *mine*! Finders keepers!' I didn't care that I sounded like a six-year-old.

'It was left under the bed?' Omar asked. 'Hey, maybe the Words left it for us. Maybe it has a coded message. Let me see it.'

'No.'

'Give it to me.'

I passed it over, barely controlling my fury. As he turned the book over, bending the cover roughly in his examination, I felt as though he was handling my private diary. He flicked through the pages for an agonising length of time, then passed it back.

'We'll examine that properly later.'

I gulped and shoved it under my pillow. *Don't worry*, I found myself reassuring it, *I'll read you in a minute. Just let me deal with Omar first.*

Omar and I stared at each other with hollow, dazed eyes.

'We should eat,' Omar said, but in rather a vague voice, as though he was motivated not by hunger but by finding something practical to do.

'Yeah, I guess.' I couldn't envisage any food that would satisfy me as well as *Catcher*. It was like drinking in chocolate and chips and pizza and all the best food in the world melded into the most beautiful combination.

As I got up from the bed, my weak knees gave way. I clutched the bedstead and Omar caught me from the other side. Dark beetles clicked before my eyes; words and voices and memories whirled.

'Are you okay?' Omar asked.

The dizziness passed and I nodded.

'Yes,' I said. 'I think so.'

♔

Downstairs in the kitchen, I felt a change coming over me. As though I'd been in a deep sleep and I was slowly coming out of the mental fog. As I searched for plates in the cupboard and rinsed the dust off them, a clarity began to flow through my mind like a cool liquid. Omar seemed to have woken up too: he was running his hands under tables and chairs, searching for bugs.

'I can't find anything,' he said, frowning.

We were surprised to find fresh food in the kitchen.

'When we came into this house, it seemed like a squat,' Omar said slowly, fingering a jar of pesto as though it might be poisoned.

'But it looked nice too,' I argued. 'Maybe they've just gone away on holiday and left this food behind. Maybe that tramp got the food in before he rumbled us.'

'I hate that bloody tramp,' said Omar.

We were too hungry to keep analysing the situation any longer. We cooked up some pasta and a tomato sauce with basil, then sat down to eat.

We ate in silence. The food tasted dull; the clink of my knife and fork irritated me as though they were nails on a blackboard. I was getting that itch again, to get back upstairs and back to the book.

'We need to go out tonight,' Omar suddenly said. 'Sasha Brooks is giving a talk at Waterstone's, in the city centre, at around six.'

I frowned.

'But we're meant to be getting my dad back,' I said slowly. 'We are, aren't we? And – and – if we go into Liverpool, we'll have to walk past several hundred CCTV cameras, *and* then we'll sit in Waterstone's, where any member of the public can recognise us, and then the police might be about . . . I mean, I know they let us go, but we must surely still be in their bad books.'

And if we get stopped tonight, I realised, *I won't get to see my father and say sorry for betraying him.*

'We should go to the talk,' Omar insisted. 'Sasha needs our help, and she can help us to get to another location. The police will be back after us soon.'

'She's in the Words, though,' I said. 'How can she give a talk and not get arrested?'

'She's producing two editions of her book,' said Omar,

smiling. 'One for the public, and the underground copy. The one that sells in the shops brings in money – and she donates that back to the Words.'

I wanted to raise more objections, but my mind was being seduced by the thought of yellow: the beautiful yellow cover of *The Catcher in the Rye*. I pushed aside my plate and got up, ignoring Omar's request that I help with the washing-up.

Up in the bedroom, I picked up the book and discovered something terrible. There was only one more page to go.

I read it slowly, savouring every sentence. I could hardly bear to finish. But there it was. THE END.

I closed the book, turned it over, smoothed the front cover.

I stared at the title and the letters seemed to get bigger and bigger and bigger:

THE CATCHER IN THE RYE

Twenty-seven

I closed the book and felt a smile spread across my face.

That was a good book.

I suddenly felt so happy.

I was aware that I had been worrying about something, but I couldn't recall what it was.

There was no reason to be sad, for there was a gun under my bed. I reached down and found it there. There was also a red box of bullets.

My hands worked as though they were puppets being controlled by a greater force. I stared down at them with a feeling of faint surprise as they opened the box and slotted a bullet into the gun.

And then another and another and another until every slot was full.

As though loading a gun was something I did every day, automatic as cleaning my teeth.

I spun the chamber, then locked it shut.

The click triggered a feeling of comfort, of rightness, like the feeling you get when you dot the last full stop on a school essay that you know will earn you a good mark.

The Catcher in the Rye.

Twenty-eight

Omar and I left the house and began to head for the city centre. Overhead, gulls were circling, making harsh noises. On the horizon, the sun was losing its warmth. It was two hours before curfew would fall.

'We have to be careful,' Omar had warned me once again before we'd left. 'We can use a safe path until we get to the city centre. But once we hit the city, we'll be in a no man's land. The Words have no control. When we hit the high street, you must keep your head down. You have to picture all the CCTV cameras lining the way as lions in the undergrowth, waiting and ready to pounce.'

Now Omar kept chewing his lip and pulling his hands in and out of his pockets. I kept thinking that I ought to be nervous. But my heartbeat was as slow and steady as a metronome. There was just the faintest ripple of irritation: a feeling of something I had forgotten, something I had to do to make everything perfect. I was conscious of something bulky in my pocket, rubbing against my thigh – *The Catcher in the Rye.*

'Just be natural,' Omar murmured. 'Just be very relaxed.'

For we were close to the city now. We turned over the peak of the hill and there it was, spread out before us: a network of lights and noise.

'There's something you should know,' Omar said in a low voice, 'about Sasha Brooks and your father . . .'

I wanted to listen to Omar. But my mind seemed to slip away from his words and when I looked up at him all I could see was his mouth moving. I was conscious of the weight in my pocket, its bang increasingly hypnotic, like a prelude to a march.

Then I felt Omar nudge me and heard him say, 'Are you all right? It's difficult to take on, I know. Your father didn't want me to tell you, but I felt you deserved to know.'

The Catcher in the Rye.

'Yeah,' I said.

The shops were open until 7 p.m. and we found that the streets were busy. Mannequins stared out of windows with glazed eyes and shoppers stared back with glazed eyes. I found myself becoming fascinated by faces. A grim pair of lips. A pug nose. A heavy pair of eyebrows. It began to feel as though the beat against my thigh was a drumstick and it wanted a face to bang against. A longing rose up inside me to find the right face, the right face that would say *The Catcher in the Rye.*

'God,' Omar shuddered. 'Will you look at that?'

'What?'

He pointed to a shop where two girls were fighting over one of the best bargains – a pair of designer jeans. The stronger girl was tearing at the hair of the other one and a pair of security guards had to separate them.

'Shopping is the opium of the people,' Omar winced. 'Doesn't it make you feel sick to watch them?'

I watched them. I felt nothing.

And then Omar told me that we had reached Waterstone's.

When I saw the black exterior and the pale gold lettering,

I suffered a strong sense of déjà vu. *The Catcher in the Rye The Catcher in the Rye The Catcher in the Rye.* I felt happy and relieved. I felt that we had come to the right place.

Inside there were lots of people with dull faces sipping water from paper cups. There was a black stage. There was a table, a chair and a microphone. There was a stack of books waiting to be signed.

Omar whispered that we should move over to the side, keep a low profile. But I could not stop staring at the stage. I felt as though time had rewound and I had stood here many times before.

The Catcher in the Rye.

Then a voice behind us cried, 'How lovely of you to come!'

We turned to see a beautiful woman with a heart-shaped face.

'Sasha!' Omar leaned in and kissed her cheek. She blushed and lowered her eyes.

'Is it safe for you to be here . . . ?' she whispered, her eyes darting around the bookshop.

'Who's going to notice us?' Omar whispered back. 'The wanted lists are endless. We couldn't miss your book reading.'

Sasha turned to me, touching my cheek.

'I still can't get over how much you look like your dad!'

I jumped, frowning.

I felt as though I'd been underwater, everything muted and colourless, and had suddenly burst up, up into reality. I blinked at her and glanced around the bookshop. Suddenly I felt confused – what the hell were we doing here?

Sasha reacted as though I'd burnt her. She quickly drew back and wrapped her shawl tight around her shoulders. Then someone called for her to go up on stage.

'Sure,' she called to him. Then she turned back to us and whispered, 'Have you heard about Raf? Yesterday the police went into his offices – at the law firm – in broad daylight – and arrested him. They know he's in the Words. Someone's talked!'

Omar blinked, shocked. I tried to feel shocked too, but instead all I felt was *The Catcher in the Rye*.

'You were right,' Sasha dipped her voice. 'We should have found out the list of traitors. We should have broken the *Paradise Lost* code and taken control. Who knows if they'll come after me next, or any one of us—' She broke off as someone called her again. 'We'll speak later.'

Sasha climbed onto the stage.

The Catcher in the Rye. Why did I keep thinking that?

'Let's sit down,' Omar said.

'We should sit at the front,' I heard myself saying, even though a quieter voice underneath it warned: *At the front? But that's a stupid place for us to sit.*

'Are you kidding?' Omar hissed. 'And draw attention to ourselves?'

'We should,' I repeated, hearing a firmness in my voice.

I led the way to the front. As we sat down, the bulky thing in my pocket shifted. I slipped my hand in and felt cold metal. *The Catcher in the Rye*. I closed my eyes. *The Catcher in the Rye*. I opened my eyes.

'I'm so glad that you've all come here tonight,' Sasha said. Her voice was slightly shaky and she paused, swallowing. Her eyes flitted over me and then to the rest of the audience. 'It means so much to me, in this day and age, when everyone is discussing the death of the novel, to have such a warm and enthusiastic turnout . . .'

When she started to speak, it seemed as though a spotlight shone on her, casting the rest of the room into darkness. I became fascinated by the quirks and textures of her face: the dimples when she smiled; the way she raised her left eyebrow, lifting a small mole on her forehead; the way she used blinks like exclamation marks. The metal thing in my pocket seemed to warm against my palm, as though waking up. She opened her book and began to read from chapter one.

You mustn't do this. You're going to do something terrible.

But it was as though the voice of reason was pushed back by the commands, into a little cupboard in the back of my mind.

Please don't, please don't, why are you doing this, why?

'"Sheila stood in her daughter's bedroom. Her daughter was sleeping . . ."'

The Catcher in the Rye.

Please . . .

'"Sheila looked down at her affectionately."'

The Catcher in the Rye.

The metal in my pocket; her voice; the silent room; sweat on my brow.

The Catcher in the Rye. Yes. *The Catcher in the Rye.* Yes. Wait for it, wait for it . . .

'"Above her daughter's head was a beautiful dream-catcher—"'

I stood up, pulled the metal object from my pocket and pulled the trigger.

BHAM!

Silence.

Sasha slumped. Cries and screams lacerated the air.

The Catcher in the Rye . . .

I looked down at the gun I was holding and felt as though I'd woken up from a terrible nightmare.

Twenty-nine

I'm not sure how I ended up in the hut.

I found myself running towards the docks, taking the path that Omar had showed me, safe from CCTV. *The Catcher in the Rye.* I stood on the rim of the docks, searching, searching for the prison ship. Without the binoculars, it was just the tiniest black dot on the horizon. *Dad*, I said silently, *I'm a murderer. Your son is a murderer. What do you think of that, Dad, what do you think of that?* I heard myself let out an inhuman laugh. Then I saw the boatman who had chatted to Omar and me a few days ago give me a cheery wave. I panicked and hurried down towards the shanty-town. To the makeshift huts where the refugees who had lost their houses to the sea had been forced to live, before the water began to seep into them too. They were boarded up and I yanked away a piece of rotting wood, splinters biting my hands. *The Catcher in the Rye.*

Inside the hut, there were several inches of muddy water on the sandy floor, polluted with seaweed and rubbish. It was hardly bigger than a small kitchen. The only furniture was a rotting chair with three legs, propped up against a wall, and a board, nailed high above the ground, which served as a bed. I lay down on it, the cold seeping into my hot pumping body. The dark ceiling grimaced over me. Over and over again I saw Sasha fall; I saw myself shoot her a thousand times. Why didn't the police catch me? I almost wished they had. I yearned to be back in the Institution, to feel the spotlight shining onto my face, piercing my irises, forcing my brain to find an explanation, to remember, to rationalise. *The Catcher in the Rye* – stop, stop, I screamed, get out of my head, get out of my head. I looked down and realised I was clutching the gun to my chest. The barrel stared up at me. I thought of my father and how I might never reach him now. I thought of Sasha, of her dying thoughts, of the people who loved her. My fingers curled around the trigger . . .

I tossed it to one side with a clatter and curled up into a ball. My heart felt cold and still with the shock of this new me, this new future chained around my neck. I felt tired and sleep became a temptation. But I didn't want curfew to fall and trap me in the hut for the night. I needed to get back to Omar. Omar had nearly murdered Raf. He would understand me; he would take pity on me.

I left the hut and hurried back towards town. I tried to memorise the path Omar had showed me, to avoid the CCTV, but in my blundering confusion I took a wrong turn and ended up back on the high street. CCTV seemed to be everywhere. My heart began to tremble. I kept my hood up tight and my eyes on the pavement, on the cracks and dirt, the high heels and brogues, the lost euros. As I passed a hardware shop, however, something made me look up.

A bank of TV screens. I saw, in a montage of shades and sizes, the same image: a bullet firing across a bookshop. *That's a very violent movie to be showing in public*, I thought. And then I turned back.

I realised the bullet had come from my gun. When I stared at the boy on the screen, it felt as though I *was* watching a film, that he was an actor I had never met in my life before. The headline scrolling underneath warned: YOUNG TERRORIST IN BOOKSHOP ATTACK.

I began to walk away very quickly.

I still couldn't believe it. *I'm sixteen years old*, I thought, *and I'm officially a terrorist*.

Back at the squat, I found Omar. He was sitting at the kitchen table, staring into space. I stood in the doorway, trembling, waiting for him to notice me. When he finally did, he let out a furious bellow. Terrified, I backed out into the garden. As he came charging at me, I saw the passion and the pain screaming in his eyes and realised just how much he'd loved Sasha. What a stupid, stupid mistake I'd made to come back. I turned to run, but Omar flung himself on top of me, slamming me onto the wet ground. Winded, I gasped for breath, grass meshing into my mouth. He rolled me over violently, then curled his hands around my neck.

Was this how it had felt for Sasha when she had seen the bullet coming towards her? Had she suffered the same quiet voice – as though her mind had separated from her body, becoming narrator to its destiny – observing, *So this is what it feels like to die*? Omar's palms tightened. It felt as though he was trying to squeeze my neck into a tiny tube. I heard the hissing of my dying breath and closed my eyes, feeling myself thrash about in the darkness. My dead heart told me I deserved to die, but the life force shocked me with its angry defiance. My hands flew up, clawing his shoulder blades; my legs kicked against him. I stared up into his raging eyes, pleading mercy.

And then, suddenly, he let go and the cool air was rushing into my throat. I found myself coughing, retching spools of shocked saliva into the grass.

Omar burst into tears. He sat hunched over his knees, rocking himself, his ribs shuddering with sobs. Every so often a small moan came from his lips.

'She's not dead,' he said shakily. 'Sasha's in hospital. I saw her before I came back here. She might still live.'

'She might?' I cried hoarsely. So I wasn't a murderer. The joy of relief must have shone on my face, for Omar reached out again. My hands flew to my neck, but he surprised me with a stinging blow to my cheek. I fell back on the grass, tears stinging my eyes again. The sing of the blow tunnelled through my skin and muscle until it struck the bone. I held my cheek and cried, 'I didn't mean to do it . . .' I broke off, rubbing my throat, for it still hurt to talk. 'It was just that *word* – it was like I was hypnotised or something. When she said the word *catcher* it was as though something just took over me and made me shoot. I don't get it – I just—'

'What?' Omar rubbed his eyes and scowled at me. 'What are you saying?' Suddenly he was alert. Then he stood up. 'Let's get back inside.'

Inside the kitchen, I collapsed on a chair. Omar began to pace about as though we were in a courtroom and I was under his interrogation.

'What are you saying, then? Explain clearly. You're saying that a *word* triggered your shot?'

'It's just that – I remember – I remember reading *The Catcher in the Rye* and the last line made me take this gun – it was there under my bed. I know this sounds insane, I know you think I'm just making up some story – but I just reached under the bed and the gun was there. And then I felt as though I was in a bubble until Sasha said *catcher*, and then – it made me fire the gun.'

'*The Catcher in the Rye*? The one you were reading the morning after we were dropped off by the police . . . ?' Omar shook his head. 'I don't believe this.' He sat down on a chair and burst into ironic laughter. Then he began to trace the grains and whorls in the table, muttering to himself. 'Maybe they got to me too . . . I can't believe it . . . I was so stupid, not to realise . . . but I suppose that was part of it too.'

'What?' I raised my voice, desperate to understand.

'That's why the police picked *The Catcher in the Rye*, don't you see?' He laughed again. 'Someone there has a sense of humour, I suppose. The famous book favoured by assassins. God. What a way of sticking up two fingers at the Words. I expect they're laughing now, laughing at us—'

'I don't understand what you're saying. What are you saying?'

'I'm saying you were brainwashed. That's what happened when the police picked us up. That's why we were so disorientated when we woke up back at the house, why nothing made sense, why they let us off so easily. Keeping us for questioning, locking us up – what would that change? They'd get some information from us, but not much. But using us both as pawns to shoot our own – it's a sick joke. No doubt it was all unofficial . . .'

'I was brainwashed . . . ?' I repeated, stunned. I'd always associated brainwashing with stupid stage shows and mercenary magicians. 'But they can't – that doesn't really work . . . I mean, you can brainwash someone to just, I don't know, make chicken noises – but you can't brainwash them to *kill* . . .'

'They wouldn't have just swung a clock in front of your face and spoken in a deep voice, Stefan,' Omar cried savagely. 'They've been developing various drugs for some time to produce the so-called criminals of society. You've probably had a cocktail of Valium and various other sedatives and serums in your bloodstream.'

'I . . .' It was true: even now, with shock pumping adrenaline through my system, my mind felt woozy, as though stuffed with cotton wool. 'I . . . I just can't believe they'd do that to me . . .'

'You were brainwashed to kill Sasha; I was brainwashed to take you to the meeting,' he said in a monotone. Then passion split open his voice: 'I mean, it's just *sick*, picking on a sixteen-year-old and getting him to kill!'

We sat there for a while in silence; no doubt both of us were replaying the day over and over.

'Of course,' Omar broke the silence, his eyes darkening, 'they say you can't really be brainwashed into doing anything you don't want to do.'

'I'm not a murderer!' I cried, jumping to my feet. 'I'm just – I'm innocent – I mean, why would I want to kill her – I don't even know the bloody woman.'

'But I told you on the way to the bookshop that she was your father's lover!'

'*What?*'

'After your mother died, your father joined the Words and met Sasha. They had a love affair that went on and off for years – he kept it quiet from you, fearing you'd feel jealous or betrayed.'

I shook my head, unable to digest this news. It was all too much to take in.

'I need your help,' I begged Omar. My voice was hoarse with exhaustion and I had to force my words out with great

217

effort. 'Please. You have to tell the Words I'm innocent, they have to hide me from the police.'

'The Words? You want the Words to *hide* you? The Words will instruct me to kill you – I have no doubt about that. You're a traitor.'

'But . . . but . . .' I took a step backward, horrified. 'That's not fair – I want to be *part* of the Words – I want to join!'

'Look,' Omar said, 'I'm not going to kill you. I might hate you right now . . . but I owe your father this. But if they find you, they will. So I think you should go – go now.'

I couldn't believe it. When we had been running, the thought of the Words had become a safety net. A shield between me and the State. Now I was stripped naked.

'But my dad was with them – and I'm his son – and we were going to get my dad out of the prison ship.'

'It may still go ahead, but you can't be involved,' Omar said.

'But – *please* – my dad said you should take care of me.'

'You said a few days ago that you wanted to get away from me.'

But that was before I had truly tasted how big and bad the world out there was.

'I'm sorry, Stefan, but you're on your own.' He slumped over the table, running his fingers through his dark curls. Then he added in a gruff voice, 'You take any leftover food from the fridge, if that helps.'

I grabbed an old carrier bag from the surface with a loud, deliberate rustle. I paused, my eyes burning, staring hard at Omar. But he didn't look at me. I swallowed and went to the fridge and took out the bread. I opened up a cupboard and took out a tin of baked beans. I grabbed an apple, then his lighter, which was sitting on the sideboard.

He didn't object. I knotted the handles of the carrier bag and stood in the doorway.

Omar stared at the table.

'Okay then,' I said, swallowing. 'I'll go.'

Omar continued to stare at the table.

Outside, I stopped in the garden, standing in the flattened grass where we had fought. I stared at the houses, full of people eating and sleeping and doing the housework and watching TV, all decent, ordinary men and women who would turn me in if they caught one glimpse of my face. I stared up at the sky, brooding with the incoming twilight. I felt as tiny and helpless as an ant. I had no idea where to run, where to go, how to begin a new life. And so I just stood there, half-hoping Omar would come out after me and say he'd changed his mind.

Omar didn't come out. I wanted my life to resemble a book; I wanted a solution to appear from nowhere, a magician to materialise and tell me he could take away my problems with a wave of his wand; a policeman to pat me on the head and say it was a mistake; a preternatural sign in the bushes and trees to guide me to somewhere I might hide. But the universe just carried on with its indifferent story, the wind blowing softly through the grass, the gulls cawing overhead, the sky becoming a little bit darker.

I told myself to start walking. Finally, my shaking legs began to move. Halfway up the lawn, I felt so sick and weak with the shock that I had to lean on the dirty old sofa that sat, abandoned, in the middle. It was then I saw it: the fray of pages poking out from under the bottom cushion. I remembered the night – only a few nights ago, though now it felt like years – when Omar and I had run from the police and he'd stopped to hide *Paradise Lost*. It was still here; he must have figured it was the safest place to stow it. I glanced back at the house. I reached out and grabbed it, flung it into my bag.

Then I began to run.

Part Three

Thirty

There were a number of places I could have gone. I thought about breaking into a church and sleeping under a pew on a cold stone grave, my forehead kissed by rats' whiskers. I thought about tucking myself under the corner of a railway bridge, deep in the coarse bushes, lulled to sleep by the rumble of trains overhead. But every choice involved the same problem: too many cameras.

There was only one place I could think of that wasn't watched 24/7: the deserted shanty-town. Nobody wanted to hang about in a place where the floors were carpeted in salt water. I followed the same path I'd taken with Omar the day we'd visited the docks, through the back streets where the cameras were few and far between. By now it was late afternoon and the pavement by the docks was busy with tourists queuing up for the boats. I ducked my head down, terrified of being recognised. Then a woman with two toddlers spoke to me and I nearly jumped with the fright. I guess she saw a lost look in my eyes, for she gave me a gentle, pitying smile and asked if I wanted her to pay for me to join her boat. I grinned and shook my head, but I found tears flickering in my eyes and said a grateful 'Thanks'. I had a feeling that I wouldn't get to talk to another human being for quite a while.

I quickly slipped down over the dunes of debris and discarded planks to the shanty-town, where I hid in the shadowy gap between two huts. When the tide came in, the water eddied around my trainers, but I didn't dare move. The woman had unnerved me; I decided to wait for the docks to clear, for I didn't want to be seen going into my hideaway. My fear of being recognised sewed up my pain, but the stitches kept bursting open, memories spurting up. I pushed aside a piece of driftwood with my foot and saw Sasha's blood spraying over the sand; the seagull overhead haunted me, its caws carrying an echo of her screams.

Finally, just before curfew fell, the docks emptied. I crept over to my hut, melting into the darkness, and clambered inside.

I took out *Paradise Lost* and laid it down on the wooden bed for my pillow. I flared my lighter once, took a slice of bread from my carrier bag and chewed it down. There were holes in the roof of the hut and in the dying gloom I could see my remaining provisions: one last piece of bread, an apple, and a tin of baked bins with no ring pull and no tin opener.

Then what? a voice asked. *Then what will you do?*

I don't know, I don't know.

The solitude of the hut was horrific. I'd been able to hold back my shock in the business of running away; now it sprang at me, ripping and tearing me apart. *I shot someone. I nearly killed her. She might still die. She might still die.*

It was strange – when I looked back, I could see that ever since the police had returned me to the squat, I'd existed in a peculiar bubble. My head and my heart and conscience had been wiped clean, filled with white smoke. Now the bubble had burst, I could remember the police station far more clearly. The questions, the spotlight. They'd told me that I'd go back to the Institution unless I helped them. *Just a little experiment*, they'd said. I'd thought they'd just make me read a Banned Book. But I'd ended up in a dark room, strapped to a chair. A doctor sliding a needle into my arm, soothing me as I'd tried to jerk away from him. Neon images flashing before me, until they were branded on my retinas. Liverpool Waterstone's. Sasha Brooks. A gun. And that refrain, over and over. *The Catcher in the Rye*.

Just repeating the trigger made me shudder. I still couldn't believe they had played such a cheap trick on me. Once again, I had been used as a guinea pig.

That filled me with as much sadness as the thought that Sasha was lying in hospital because of me. I could hardly believe that I once loved the State as though the State was my heavenly father. That I had believed that the government existed to help me grow and the police were there to protect me. The rage of cynicism burnt inside me. I wanted to do all I could to help the Words fight back, but now all the Words wanted to do was kill me. How could they desert me when I was a victim of the State?

Sasha Brooks and your father were lovers, Omar had said.

Was that even true? Or just a lie, concocted by Omar to wind me up? I thought I ought to be angry at my father, but instead I found myself thinking, *He's only human*. My memories of my mother were too vague to be sure if she and my dad had ever been in love. Maybe he had found something true with Sasha. Maybe my dad loved Sasha as I had loved Sally.

Oh, Dad, I wept. And my betrayal, which had been stabbing at away at me, now plunged even deeper. *I still can't believe that I have passed you to over to the very people who tortured Mum. I'm sorry, I'm so sorry.*

There was one argument that I thought might persuade the Words of my innocence. I had analysed the shooting so many times over that a revelation had come to me. I had been programmed, precisely, to kill Sasha Brooks with a single, lethal shot. Instead, my aim had been off-target. Feeling desperate with hope, I stood up on my bed, the top of the hut grazing my head, and whispered out loud, as though I was addressing Omar:

'I *do* have a conscience, you see. My conscience fought the commands, it blurred my judgement. *That's* why I didn't shoot to kill, I only injured her . . . oh God, I shot her. I shot someone. I'm going to have to live with that for the rest of my life . . . but I think she's going to live, oh God, please let her live . . .'

Through the small holes in the hut's roof, I saw the stars looking down on me, cold and indifferent.

I collapsed back down in despair. I had a feeling that even if I went back to Omar, he wouldn't listen. Maybe he was in trouble too. I remembered the guilt on his face when he had told me I had to run. After all, he had failed both of us too. He had been the one to take me to my target . . .

Dawn came and my last piece of bread was eaten and I still had no idea what to do next. I took the can of baked beans and dashed it against the sharp edge of the bed. Several of my nails broke and I cursed out loud, then licked the sickly orange sweetness from the label.

I ought to save the beans. I thought the shock was making me hungry; I was desperate to blot out the yawning pain in my stomach with food. But, as the hours went by, a stronger sense of where I might go began to take hold of me.

226

Oh, Dad, I whispered, *all I can think of is coming to find you. If I can get to you, then you're the last person who can believe in me and look after me. Even if the guards catch me and shoot me, it won't matter. I've got nowhere else I can go.*

You're my last hope.

I wept then until I had no energy left for tears. The sound of the sea seemed familiar. As though my father could sense my closeness, as though his reassurances were folding into the waves, shushing me gently, telling me it would be okay.

Thirty-one

My teeth were chattering so hard I thought my jaw might break. The night had been mild, but the daytime tide was bringing in a new, icy wind. I tried curling up in a foetal ball, rubbing my arms and legs, slapping my skin until it stung red. Soon I became exhausted with the effort, and the moment I relaxed the cold began to creep back up over me again. At this rate I would get pneumonia. I needed to light a fire – but what with? I crept out of my hut. It was still early and the boat-rides hadn't started up yet. I gazed out over the brief shoreline of mud and rubbish, towards the waves, searching for the black dot of the prison ship, but the horizon was covered in cloud.

The tide was out and my hut floor was only mildly damp. I carried in some rocks and created a little circle for a base, then draped some seaweed over it and a piece of corrugated cardboard. I knew it was crazy, lighting a fire in a wooden hut, but I was so cold, I didn't care; I figured if I burnt the bloody thing down, I'd just make a run for it. I flared my lighter. The cardboard was too damp and the flames died quickly. The seaweed crackled and popped, emitting an acrid smell, then melted into black lava.

In my desperation, I grabbed the copy of *Paradise Lost* and tore off the front cover. I threw it onto the fire and the small flames flickered up. I leaned over them in relief, savouring the warmth as it licked my chin, leaning so close the flames were practically singeing my skin.

For the first time in hours, my taut body relaxed, the warmth kissing my muscles.

Then, within fifteen minutes, the fire was dying into embers.

I turned to grab the remainder of the book – a thick sheaf of white pages – and then suddenly stopped.

If I wanted to find my father, then could *Paradise Lost* help me? I thought about the meeting of the Words where Omar had looked for the code. He'd mentioned that it contained the list of traitors. But then it might also contain a list of higher members of the Words. Omar had claimed they would kill me, but maybe he was just being cruel, taking out his rage on me. Surely if I went to them, if I explained what had happened, they might believe me and help? If the Words were planning a raid on the ship, I could go with them. I could help free my father.

Maybe it was a foolish thing to do – given that Omar himself had spent hours trying and failing to unlock the code – but I was suddenly gripped by the absolute determination to crack it. I was also desperate to find something to focus on, to shut out my demons of doubt and terror. Something that might help me forget the cold for at least a few minutes.

And so I read and read and read. I found a pencil in my pocket and scribbled on the title page, trying to work out every possibility.

I took the first letter of every sentence on the top of each page. I came up with OOFANFHBO before I gave up.

I tried to read it backwards. I tried to see if there were any pages turned over at the corner. There was one. Page

49. It described Eve's temptation. It had to be this page, it had to be. I decided to keep reading over and over until I knew it by heart. Until the words were all so familiar they would bind into a key and unlock the code. My eyes were burning and my stomach was screaming for food. But I heard a voice inside that sounded like Dad's, telling me to keep going. I felt my head lolling forward and I quickly snapped myself awake.

'Concentrate!' I yelled out loud.

I held my head in my hands, rubbing my eyes. They were so hot they left a burning tingle on the skin of my palms. I curled up into a ball and heard myself let out a faint moan. *Concentrate. Work out the code. Find Dad.*

I forced myself to sit up and picked up my pencil again.

What about converting the letters into numbers?

A = 1

B = 2

C = 3

And so on.

I spent another hour coming up with a string of meaningless numbers. The distant babble of tourists by the docks rose and fell. Darkness was smudging into the hut. I reached for my lighter, rubbed it against the ball of my thumb. Nothing. I yanked my thumb against it over and over until the skin broke and bled.

My lighter fuel had run out.

Which meant I couldn't light a fire tonight. Which meant I'd freeze.

I could risk creeping up onto the mainland, but there was the immediate danger of a camera spotting me. I tried to think of another way I could get fire but my thoughts kept swirling into a tired grey murk. I rolled up on my side, pulling my trackie hood over my head, curled up tight. I knew it was dangerous to fall asleep if the temperature fell too low. But I couldn't resist it; it filled my mind with the relief of deep, forgetful black . . .

The whole world is contained in a grain of sand . . .

The whole world is contained in a grain of sand . . .

The whole world is contained in a grain of sand . . .

Euphoria woke me up. It sparkled through me, taking the edge off my chattering teeth and shivering body.

The whole world is contained in a grain of sand.

I knew it. My subconscious had computed the answer in my sleep and it was so simple, so simple.

I'd got it.

In the pitch black, I felt around for *Paradise Lost*.

My fingers encountered wood and I panicked irrationally that someone had stolen it. Then I felt the book knock against my knuckles. I fumbled for my lighter again, trying to flick up the flame.

Nothing.

It was so dark I couldn't even see the time on my watch.

I slipped outside the hut. It was just as dark outside. There was no moonlight, nothing but pitch black; I could only tell I was in the shanty-town by the feel of damp rubbish under my trainers and the smell of salt in the air.

I leant by my hut, shivering, rubbing my hands and arms and legs. There was no point in even considering sleep – I was way too excited now. I couldn't check to see if my theory was right until the light dawned. All I could do was sit and wait, and wait and wait.

Gradually the darkness lost its thickness. Colour trickled into the sky. I opened up the book. My heart was beating like mad. I was scared I might be wrong, that I'd just come up with some stupid theory. But I kept remembering the conversation Omar had had with my father back home, echoed in his chat with Raf: *The world is contained in a grain of sand . . .* Omar hadn't understood what the clue meant. But I did.

There. The final full-stop of *Paradise Lost*. I'd noticed it before. It was much larger than all the others. As big as a beauty spot. I ran my finger over it – it felt thicker, as though something had been glued onto the page.

A microdot. I'd learnt about them in Surveillance classes at school, when we were learning about terrorist communications. It was a tiny photograph of a document which could then be read in full size if you found the right equipment.

I'd worked it out.

The Words' secret messages were contained in that one dot. Now I would be able to reach them, to help save my dad.

Excitement whooshed through me. I stared out at the sea and it seemed as though the waves were laughing. As though from his prison ship my father was laughing through them and saying, 'Well done.' I ran down to the waves and shouted back, 'I've done it, Dad, I've got it!'

And then, as I began to calm down, reality hit me.

For now I needed to work out how the hell to find a machine to read a microdot.

Thirty-two

It was a scrap of newspaper blowing across the mounds of debris that solved the problem.

I'd sunk into a state of despair again, trying to work out if I'd have to leave Dad behind and go back to London. There had to be some special place there that would have machines to read microdots.

The sun was coming out and the warmth was a relief. I could feel my nose running and I was worried I was getting a cold. I had to slip into my hut again when someone brought their dog out for a walk. Their dog veered away from the pavement and danced down inquisitively towards the shanty-town; his owner called him back. The dog dropped a half-eaten dog biscuit by my door. I wiped the drool off and ate it. It tasted bitter but the meaty substance was good.

Then I saw the newspaper. I took it back to the hut, thinking it would be good for future fires, when I saw the headline: *ENTS: Museum and galleries for suggested day-trips out with your family: The Merseyside Maritime Museum; The Lady Lever Art Gallery; The Liverpool World History Museum – just opened.*

The Liverpool World History Museum.

Omar had asked for directions to that museum, hadn't he? Maybe he'd had a tip-off about it. Maybe it was related

233

to *Paradise Lost*. Maybe that was part of the reason we'd come to Liverpool . . .

I turned back to the newspaper, examining the article once more.

Liverpool World History Museum – just opened. A wide range of exhibitions, including 'The Egyptians', 'Ancient Texts' and 'A History of Spy Technology'.

My heart leapt. That was it. It had to be. No exhibition on spy technology would be complete without a microdot machine – would it?

♛

I was going to have to risk it.

I spent a nervous hour building up my courage. I opened up my hut door and stared out to the sea, assessing its mood. Earlier it had seemed angry but now it was calm, as though Dad was whispering through the waves, *You can do this, you can do this* . . .

My apple and the last of the cold baked beans had been digested hours ago. I was so hungry I felt dizzy. I even tried picking up some seaweed and nibbling it. It tasted rank. I kept wondering if the museum had a café in it. I ended up obsessing more over the thought of sandwiches and cakes and Cokes and crisps than the machine itself.

I took the copy of *Paradise Lost*, hugged it to my chest and then pulled up my trackie zip over it. I yanked the hood over my face as far as it would go.

It was late afternoon when I walked up past the dock towards the lights. I'd been so used to the solitude of the hut that it was a shock to see the rush and buzz of human life. The tourists queuing up had never seemed so loud, nor dressed so brightly. I stood on the rim of the road, scared and excited by its scrape against my raw senses. Cars, people, shops, music. Everyone aware that curfew would fall in a few hours – everyone wanting to make the most of the day.

I'd thought about waiting until curfew and slipping through the shadows – but a solitary figure would show up on the CCTV. In a daytime crowd, with my head down, I was harder to spot. Even if there was a recognition flash from a camera, I figured they'd have to rewind the tapes a few times and search for me in the throng.

When I walked into the crowds it was like diving off a high cliff into the sea. My heart was beating like mad. I made eye contact with a few people. Then panicked and reminded myself that I had to keep my head down.

I remembered the man at the docks had advised Omar that all we had to do was follow the signs down the high street. Even so, I was afraid I might get lost, and I was relieved when a cluster of signposts pointed me in a clear direction.

As I strolled down the high street, I began to relax. Nobody was looking at me. Everyone was engrossed in buying as many goods as possible for as little money as possible. I wondered why I'd endured my hut for so long, trapped by my own mental boundaries.

And then I saw it. The black windows, the gold lettering. I tried to hurry past the store, but I couldn't help but stop and stare. There was now red tape across the door and a sign saying, *Police crime scene. Do not enter. Waterstone's is closed until further notice.* And then, suddenly, I felt the sensation of something red flashing across my face.

I glanced up in panic.

A CCTV camera stared down at me. There was another red flash. *The recognition program!* My head spun. All the CCTV cameras down the street, perched at the top of shops and lamp-posts, were swivelling their black heads to stare at me.

Then a metallic voice cut across the street, 'Suspected terrorist located on Liverpool High Street. Please vacate the area immediately. Vacate the area now, for your own safety.'

I quickly merged with a crowd so that the cameras couldn't single me out, mimicking the shocked expressions of the people around me, glancing at everyone else in paranoia. An elderly man who was carrying a walking-stick fell under the glare of the cameras; a woman cried out, 'It's him, it's *him*!' The elderly man dribbled in shock and then turned on her teenage son, prodding him with his walking-stick and yelling, 'It's you – isn't it? Don't try to blame me when the cameras are pointing at *your* son.' The boy protested as an adult yanked back his trackie hood to examine his face and his mother protested, '*How dare you do that to my son!*' Meanwhile, the rest of the crowds were streaming north, and I quickly joined their flow. In the distance I could hear the aggressive bark of security dogs as anti-terrorism guards spilled out of the malls and shops and the scream of a siren arced across the city centre.

And suddenly, it was there. A shiny, metallic skyscraper. The Liverpool World History Museum.

I had to fight against the crush of the crowd to reach the entrance. I noticed several people shooting me puzzled glances and I turned away, rummaging through my pockets as though I was searching for a mobile to call my mum.

I felt too scared to risk walking right through the entrance; I followed the wall round to a side street. There wasn't another official entrance, but some men were yanking up a dirty grille that led towards some sort of basement. A lorry was backing out. A mechanical voice warned, 'This vehicle is reversing . . . This vehicle is reversing . . .'

The lorry stopped. A man came out and opened up its

doors, then pulled down the tailgate. Then a van pulled up and they transferred a box from the lorry into it. I thought about jumping into the back of the lorry, then lost my nerve at the last minute. My nose was running again and I wiped it on my sleeve, sniffing hard. I reached the end of the street, then circled back towards the loading bay. I was scared the men might notice me but they were distracted by the sound of sirens; I saw them wander to the end of the street to check out the commotion. I realised I had a few seconds to make a decision. I took the plunge. I hoisted myself up into the lorry, clambering through boxes and antiques. There was a large bronze bust; I recognised its face from music history lessons. I ducked down behind Mozart's head just as the men returned. I heard the doors slam and then I was lost in darkness.

As the truck revved up, a terrible thought struck me: I was expecting it to pull back into the basement, but what if it was *leaving* the museum? What if I was about to be carried on a long journey halfway across the country?

I felt the truck backing up, then going forward – into the museum, or the street? I tried to calm down by reassuring myself that either was safer than being outside.

Then there was a banging noise and the truck juddered to a halt.

Silence. Stillness. I heard the bang of the doors at the front; I heard voices, tired but cheerful. Then suddenly the infinite darkness revealed its boundaries and light filtered in. *They were opening the doors of the truck*. I quickly crouched down. I watched my warm, shallow breaths making circles of moisture on the back of Mozart's bronze neck. I could hear the pants and groans of the men as they heaved out the treasures concealing me. Every so often, they broke off to say 'Where does this go?' or 'Steady with that one.' There was also a prim, female voice, a little further away, which sometimes interjected: 'Careful, that's *fragile*.' The voices were torturous, for in my weak state I desperately wanted to call out to them for food. I had to bite my lip and slap myself back to sanity, fiercely telling myself that if they found me I would only end up starving in a cell.

My eyes squinted as more and more light flowed into the truck. There were now only three objects concealing me from view: Mozart's bust, a sarcophagus and a large ancient globe. I heard a sliding noise and a felt a waft of cold, dusty air hit my face. My eyes watered and my throat tickled, but I forced the cough back down into the middle of my throat, squeezing my knuckles tight as I resisted the urge to free it. Then I realised in horror that the sliding noise was the sarcophagus being pulled out of the truck. Now my trainers and the bottom half of my legs were only being veiled by the gloom. I froze, waiting for voices of shock and accusation. But there were none.

Then I heard one of the men say, 'Right – you take Mozart's bust,' and I knew my moment was up.

Run, was all I could think of. After all this, I couldn't give up without a fight. I tensed my body, ready to spring out and surprise them, hopefully buying myself time to flee.

And then I heard a voice say, 'Isn't it time for our tea-break?'

'Oh, must you? We've so much to prepare for the exhibition,' the prim female voice objected.

'We've been working four hours straight – according to the law we should have got a fifteen-minute break half an hour ago. Sorry, but that's the way it is.'

I heard their footsteps echo and fade; heard the slam of

a door. I stood up, and Mozart nearly overbalanced. I hugged him, just catching him in time before he became a bronze bombshell. I crept to the edge of the truck, checked it was safe, then climbed down.

I stood there for a few minutes, drinking it all in in wonder. So many, many treasures. There was a huge statue of an Egyptian cat, sleek and mysterious; there were large coffins decorated with elaborate patterns; there were sculptures, large white balls that looked like giant marbles, spooling and scattering eerie patterns of light across the walls. In between them all were shards of cardboard and folds of bubble wrap. It was a crazy risk, but I couldn't resist it. I took a bubble between my fingers. The *pop!* echoed loudly in the silence. I let out a quiet laugh.

And then I noticed the coffee cup.

A Starbucks beaker was sitting by the big coffins. I reached down and curled my fingers around it. Still warm.

I tore off the lid and downed half of it. Hot caffeine jack-knifed my stomach and made my head spin. A huge, giddy smile spread across my lips. A few sugar granules lingered on my tongue. I felt them dissolve into one of the most blissful tastes I'd ever experienced. Then I downed the rest of it and put it back down on the floor.

The shock of calories hit my system. My whole body felt as though it had lit up neon. I walked slowly up the door that led into the museum. When I first tried it, it wouldn't open and I panicked that I was shut in. Then I saw a red button next to the door and above it a sign reading *Press to Enter*. With a beating heart, I pushed it open and stepped into the museum.

Thirty-three

I crept down a corridor with lime-green lino on the floor and beige walls. Colourful signs directed me towards the *New Egyptian Exhibition* or *Ancient Texts*. I didn't want to look at the CCTV cameras, but, like something out of a horror movie that magnetises your gaze, they drew my eyes irresistibly upwards. *Idiot*, I berated myself, waiting for a red warning flash.

No flash. And the cameras didn't rotate like the ones on the street. I realised they were the old-fashioned, inert ones that just sat and filmed.

This might buy me time, at least. The security guard must have so many rooms to monitor, and he'd be looking out for people damaging the cases – after all, what kind of terrorist breaks into a World History Museum for a browse? Then again, my face had been on the news. I pulled my hood up. Then, fearing it looked suspicious, I pulled it back down.

I came to a main hallway with a high, domed glass roof. It was milling with people, mostly schoolkids being shepherded about by teachers. The panic that flared up outside on the street seemed to have calmed; I couldn't even hear sirens. I kept expecting everyone to stare at me and point. But I looked like just another kid. Trying to appear casual, I went up to the large, colour-coded sign.

There it was:

A History of Spy Technology: Level 3

I saw a lift across from me, and dashed towards it just as the doors were closing. A smiling mother held them open for me. I muttered a breathless thanks, then stood very still, facing the metallic greyness, convinced a dozen suspicious eyes were boring into the back of my neck.

The doors slid open and we spilled into the 'Spy' section just as a voice on the tannoy announced:

'The museum will be closing in half an hour . . .'

Feeling frantic, I examined a few exhibits about the origins of spying, looking for any mention of a microdot. *Spying*, I read, *goes as far back as the ancient writings of Chinese and Indian military strategists such as Sun Tzu and Chanakya. In today's society, spying is still a useful deterrent against terrorism. Try some spying yourself when you next go out onto the street. You are permitted, by law, to record someone's behaviour if you feel they are behaving suspiciously. Many teenagers have helped to prevent acts of terrorism with just a few minutes of footage on their mobile phone.*

Then I noticed that a museum attendant was giving some kind of talk; he was holding up a lemon and a sheet of paper. An arc of schoolkids surrounded him, silent in their awe. I watched as he passed a lemon half to one of the kids. Immediately I jostled my way through the group, ignoring their protests, until I was right at the front. I stood and watched in amazement as the attendant dipped a pen in the lemon the kid was holding, then wrote something on the paper. The writing remained invisible. Then he handed the boy a lighter to wave gently beneath the paper. Within seconds, ghostly brown lettering began to appear:

THIS IS A TRICK
TO SHOW YOU
HOW INVISIBLE INK
WORKS

'Lemon can work very well as invisible ink,' the attendant explained. 'And it can be revealed by applying heat. You can press the paper against a radiator, or iron it – or wave a flame under it – as long as you don't set the paper alight! The reason it works is because the invisible ink chars at a lower temperature than the paper.'

'Wow,' I said out loud, realisations singing through my mind.

'Here, you can have a go,' the man said, excited by my enthusiasm.

I wanted to object, for I needed to get to the microdot machine fast, but he pressed the lighter into my hand. As he turned away to get a new sheet of paper, I quickly took flight, tunnelling back through the crowd.

'Here, where'd he go?' I heard his voice behind me. Then, to my relief: 'Oh well. You look like a nice young chap. What's your name? Keith? Well, Keith, you have a go. Here's another piece of lemon.'

I slipped the lighter into my pocket. *Paradise Lost* was becoming heavy beneath my top; I was tired of its bang against my ribcage. I had to find this machine, and I had to do it fast.

Stenography . . . Cryptography . . . Undercover Surveillance . . . Bugs . . . I found every type of spy technology you could think of, except microdots. Then there was 'The Brainwasher', a small, dark booth with a curtain pulled across it like a Truth Box. The schoolkids seemed particularly enthralled by that one. I overheard one of them whispering: 'Once you go into the booth, you never come out the same!' and his friend jostled him, laughing nervously. A plaque next to it said: *Brainwashing is now a popular technique that is being used to fight terrorist organisations.* I turned back to the booth, feeling sick. At the bottom of the curtain, I could see a pair of small shoes dangling. The boy was being drilled by a mechanical voice: *'You will be a good boy and help us to root out terrorism. You will be a good boy and help us to . . .'*

It was clearly meant to be comic but I wasn't amused. My dad had once said that sometimes the most powerful weapon the government could use was laughter; by turning brainwashing into a fun game, these schoolkids would grow up feeling there was nothing really wrong with it. I wanted to smash the machine to bits but I forced back my anger, focusing my energies. The microdot machine. I had circled the whole room and I hadn't found it. I'd assumed it had to be part of the exhibit – but what if, in fact, there wasn't one here at all?

'The museum will be closing in fifteen minutes' time . . .'

I performed another frantic lap of the room, checking to see if I'd missed anything. I saw that the museum attendant who had performed the lemon trick was now alone; the schoolkid group had moved on to the queue to look at the large microscope. I hurried up to him and said:

'Is there a machine here that can read microdots?'

'Well now,' he laughed, looking enchanted, 'microdots are so very fascinating, aren't they? Do you know they were first used as far back as the Franco-Prussian War? When Paris was under siege, a photographer there called Dagron developed a photographic shrinking technique and the compressed messages were sent by pigeons. But, my dear boy, you don't need a machine to read a microdot. A simple but powerful microscope will suffice.'

'Really?' I stammered. 'A microscope? That's all?'

'Yes but –' he checked his watch, '– I'm afraid I don't know if you'll have time now to see it before we close . . .'

'Thanks,' I muttered, joining the queue of schoolkids.

A microscope. *A microscope.* I could have just broken into a school science lab for a microscope. I felt confusion riot through my mind. I'd assumed from Omar's references to the museum, from the advert, that this was the place to come – but what if I'd just been putting two and two together and made five?

'The museum will be closing in ten minutes' time . . .'

'Come on, come on,' I muttered. Five more schoolkids to go; five more stupid, snotty schoolkids who didn't even really care about the machine at all.

'Come on,' their teacher clapped, 'do hurry, we don't have long.'

She had obviously assumed that because I was on my own, I was older than sixteen, for she gave me an apologetic grin, then ordered the two boys in front of me to share their turn. I grinned back, though I was feeling increasingly sweaty and dizzy with anticipation. The two boys examined the writing, taking turns to shove each other out of the way.

Finally, it was my turn.

I unzipped my tracksuit and heaved out *Paradise Lost.* I'd burnt the hardback cover back in the hut, and now pages were coming loose from their elderly binding. Several clumps fell to the floor and I picked them up with damp palms. There was already a sheet under the microscope. I gave the attendant a sidelong glance and saw that he was engrossed in packing up his display. There was no way my baggy, fraying manuscript was going to fit under the lens, so I carefully tore the last page out of the book, pulling the full-stop into focus.

Fear held me back. What if it was nothing more than a dot on a page?

If there's no microdot, I told myself, *you'll have to give up. Surrender yourself to the State and let them punish you. This is it.*

'The museum is now closing,' came the voice over the tannoy. 'Please proceed towards your nearest exit immediately . . .'

'Hang on,' I breathed out. 'Just hang on.'

When I looked back through the microscope, I nearly whooped out loud. Tears of euphoria pricked my eyes. That little full-stop exploded under the lens, a bud flowering into beautiful knowledge.

CLASSIFIED INFORMATION
FOR THE EYES OF THE WORDS,
FACTION ONE ONLY
THIS YEAR'S TEXT FOR WEEKLY UPDATES
IS *BEOWULF*, LOCATED IN THE LIVERPOOL
WORLD HISTORY MUSEUM, LEVEL 5
INSTRUCTIONS ARE IN
LEMON-JUICE INK ON PAGE 53.

What floor was this? Level 3. Just two floors up and I could do it. I had the lighter in my pocket – what a complete stroke of luck! I was completely prepared—

'Excuse me, young man.'

I felt a hand clamp my shoulder and I whirled round with a gasp.

It was the museum attendant who had organised the lemon-juice trick.

'I'm afraid you'll have to go now. The museum is closed. You're the only one left.' He flashed me a gentle smile. 'It's great to see how much you're enjoying yourself.'

'But – but – can't I just – I really just want to see Level 5 – it will take *five minutes*. Seriously, if I can just—'

'I'm so sorry – but we do close promptly at seven,' he said, with a note of regret. 'We already cut it fine with curfew. Once upon a time, when new exhibits were delivered to us, we'd work round the clock, sometimes all night, to get them ready. But that isn't possible any more – we have just a brief window of time between closing and curfew to get the entire place cleaned and prepare our exhibits. But look, I can organise a free pass for you – how's that? You can come back tomorrow. I can even give you a little tour myself, since you're so keen.'

Tomorrow? The moment I walked out of this museum, every CCTV in the high street would flash hysteria. By tomorrow I'd be in a cell.

'Hey, thanks,' I said, managing a trembling smile. 'That would be great.'

'I'll just get one for you.'

The moment he left the room, I whipped my page from the microscope, gathered up the rest of *Paradise Lost* and shoved it into my trackie, then pulled the zip up tight, papers bustling against my chest. Out in the corridor, my heart leapt as I spotted a lift. I jabbed the call button several times, watching the green pointer light flash across floors.

Ping!

The lift had just opened when the attendant reappeared, slightly out of breath, carrying my pass.

'There we are. Great.' He gently cupped his palm around my elbow, guiding me into the lift, then pressed ONE. I felt the whooshing sensation of the lift plummet through my stomach. I'd missed my chance, and I'd been so close.

We walked back through the central hallway. The lights had already been dimmed and our footsteps echoed magnificently across the deserted floor. He tried the front doors and then frowned, realising they were locked.

'We'll have to take the side exit, where the trucks deliver.'

We headed back down the corridor where I had first entered the museum. He punched in the door combination and winked at me, promising, 'I think you're going to like this.'

As we entered the room strewn with exhibits, I didn't have to feign my awe, even though I was seeing it for a second time.

'Andrew?' a woman's voice called down the corridor. 'Andrew, are you there? I need you urgently in the Egyptian section – we can't get the marble to sit steady!'

'All right, just a sec,' he called back. He grinned at me and said, 'I'm going to be back in five minutes – you can take a quick look round, but I'm afraid you really will have to go home then, okay?'

I nodded eagerly, thanking him several times over, and his face lit up. I wondered if he had a son like me. I listened to his departing footsteps, then got into the nearest hiding-place I could think of: a large sarcophagus. It was filled with bubble wrap and cardboard and I chucked them out and climbed inside. I took a moment to savour my last moment of light and fresh air before I pulled the lid back over. It was extremely heavy and I wanted to pull it as tight as I could, so I pinched my fingers painfully as I drew it to the very edge. Then I lay still, worrying if I'd left enough space to be able to breathe. I was about to reach up, when I heard footsteps again and Andrew's voice calling, 'Hello? *Hello?* Where've you gone now . . . you . . . I said I'd be back in five minutes . . . I . . . oh . . . oh well . . . you've gone then . . . have you?'

Silence.

The disappointment in his voice tugged at me, but there was nothing I could do.

Tonight he'd go home and go to bed, wondering what had happened to the mysterious boy he'd befriended in the museum. And then, no doubt, the next morning he'd wake up and put on the news and spit out his cereal in horror when he realised who I was. He'd redraw my character; any good qualities he'd seen in me would become the surface lies of an evil charmer. I shook my head sadly against the coffin, silently telling him, *But I'm not like that, really, if only you could really see who I am . . .*

Andrew stopped calling and I figured he'd left. I lay there for a while, wishing it wasn't so dark, for I couldn't even see my watch. I'd have to judge how long it was until curfew, and then add on an hour at least before I dared creep out.

I became aware of how exhausted I was. Though the coffee had given me a boost, I hadn't eaten properly for around forty-eight hours. My body relished the dark comfort of the coffin. It fell slack. I told myself fiercely that I must, I must stay awake, but my body was too tired to care . . .

I suddenly came to. *Someone was lifting the sarcophagus up.* My heart began to race and my breath grew hot. Through the small crack between the lid and the coffin, I could see the red-striped shirt of one of the men. I was being carried. Then we stopped. I felt myself being set down. I sensed a change in the air, tasted the metallic coolness of a service lift. There was a *ping!* and I felt the sensation of moving upwards. Then that swaying movement again, as though I was on a ferry. A pause; the sound of a lock. Voices saying, 'Put it there, there – for goodness' sake, *hurry*, we've got five minutes . . .' The bang of the sarcophagus, juddering through me, as it hit the floor. The sound of footsteps, the lock grating once more. Voices fading. Silence.

I let out a long, trembling breath of relief.

What I should have done is to get out right away and search for *Beowulf*.

But my body, having had a taste of sleep, moaned in protest at the thought of getting up. Realising how exhausted I was, aware that I needed to preserve my strength, I told myself I'd lie here – just for ten minutes.

The next thing I knew, I was sinking, sinking deliciously, ignoring the panicked voice that hissed, *No – you need to stay – awake . . .*

I woke up, drenched in darkness. My body was aching all over, as though I'd been in a fight. I lifted my head and – *bang!* – it hit something hard and I yelled out in pain. As I reached up to rub my aching forehead, my elbow knocked against an equally hard surface, pain now competing in my arm. It was then that I remembered where I was. How could I have been so stupid as to fall asleep? Then again, surely I'd just been out for a few hours?

I strained my ears, but I couldn't hear any voices. I pulled my arms up to my chest, then lifted my flattened palms up, up until they hit the lid of the sarcophagus. I paused, sweat beading on my forehead, terrified they might have nailed me in during the night.

I pressed up. Nothing moved. *I'm locked in, I'm locked in*, panic began to whimper and I told it fiercely to shut up. I pushed again. I heard a grating noise. Relief poured over me. The sarcophagus was just very thick and heavy, that was all. I splayed my palms against the stone, mustered up one last burst of energy and, emitting an animal groan, I shoved the lid to one side. Light fell over me; noises, dangerous noises, warned me that I was not alone. I looked down vaguely, saw *Paradise Lost* in the tomb, and then gazed around.

I gawped at them.

They gawped at me.

About thirty or so schoolboys. Different from yesterday's lot – and yet so similar. All the same types, just dressed in a different shade of uniform. Some of them pointed and stared; a few laughed; one came right up to the glass and breathed against it with a loud hiss.

Glass.

Between me and them.

I looked around wildly. There was the sarcophagus; a Pharaoh; a statue of a cat; the large white marble. They all had small white plaques in front of them. *I was standing right in the middle of an exhibit.*

'Oh God,' I said out loud, cursing in shock.

I ran to the window, searching wildly for a door, a lock, some way out of my glass cage. The schoolboys' cries grew more exuberant. Then I turned and saw their teacher. She was wearing a nice suit and, behind her tortoiseshell spectacles, her eyes widened. I stopped panicking and gave her a slight wave, as though I was a helper, just trying to sort out the exhibit, everything fine and dandy. I saw a confused smile flicker across her face in return.

Then one of the kids cried:

'He's a terrorist! He was on TV last night!'

'Yeah!' another cried, recognition igniting on his face. 'He is too! He's the terrorist who shot that writer!'

The teacher went pale. She pushed through the sea of boys and came right up to the glass, peering at me. There was fear in her eyes, and also curiosity. As though she was wondering how on earth a sixteen-year-old boy like me could be infected with such evil. I stared back at her, my eyes pleading for understanding and help. She frowned uneasily and for one brief moment, something passed between us, and hope flickered inside me. Then she turned away, clapping her hands together and crying, 'I want you all to follow me in silence. We're leaving the exhibit at once.'

'But he's a terror—'

'I said, *quiet*! We will depart from this room in a calm and orderly manner.'

The boys lined up in obedient silence, but their eyes kept swivelling towards me.

I let out a groan and buried my head in my hands. I was just a few levels away from *Beowulf*, from the coded message, and now I would never know what it was. Within minutes she would have called the security guards, and I would be heading for the Institution.

The Institution. I could already hear that voice, that insidious yet impersonal voice that flowed from the cell camera. I let out a cry and tore off my tracksuit top, wrapping it around my hand. Then I smashed my fist against the glass.

I fell back, pain singing in my knuckles. I hadn't even cracked it.

The last schoolboys were hurrying out of the room; I saw them looking back at me in horror. I turned wildly, searching for ammunition. The sarcophagus was too heavy; the Pharaoh was too big. The white marble . . . I ran up to it, kicking away the small prongs that held it in place, trampling on its explanatory plaque.

I got behind the marble, gathered up every last drop of energy into my arms and then, with a gigantic effort, I pushed it forward.

It rolled and rolled . . .

. . . and hit the glass.

And stopped.

But the glass didn't hold up. The impact had been strong enough to zigzag large cracks across the pane. I ran up to it and shoved the marble once more. The glass burst open and I stepped backwards, shielding my face. The marble rolled right through, spun across the floorboards and then hit the wall with a loud *thwack!* A trail of glass followed it; the air was incandescent with tinkling pieces. I stepped through the jagged hole with care, feeling one of its edges snag my top. I yanked myself free. I could hear heavy footsteps thundering from the direction of the south door. I turned, saw an exit to the north, and ran for it.

Thirty-four

I pushed the call button for the lift, waiting impatiently as the pointer trawled through the floors. Too slow. I took the stairs, pounding up them two at a time. Level 4 – *Space Exploration* – flashed past. Another twenty steps circled above me; I pushed my aching legs on and on. Here it was: Level 5. I noted signs for male and female toilets, then the *Ancient Texts Exhibition*.

It was virtually empty, except for an elderly couple dressed in expensive clothes. There were cases displaying old books and wrinkled, cracked manuscripts the colour of weak tea. *Oh God*, I thought, *what if it's locked up inside a case?* I saw that the elderly couple were standing in front of a large book laid out on a lectern. Surely they wouldn't leave it out on public display? Words from the past floated inside my head; my father telling Omar why he kept the precious copy of *Paradise Lost* out on the bookshelf: '*It's always safer to have something right under their noses than hidden away suspiciously.*'

'Extraordinary,' I heard the elderly man saying in a grave voice. 'Just extraordinary. I mean—'

'Is that *Beowulf*?' I burst out.

The elderly woman turned and looked down her powdered nose at me. I ignored her attempt at a withering silence and stared past her to the plaque: *Beowulf is an Old English epic hero poem about a warrior who battles the dragon Grendel* . . .

'Yes!' I cried. The manuscript was in a glass case and I couldn't see a way to open it up. I grabbed a fire extinguisher and yelled at the couple to step back.

'What on earth do you think you're doing?' the woman called out, but she stood back all the same.

I heard her cry out as I crashed it against the glass. I reached out, removed a shard of glass from the cover and grabbed it, pieces tinkling to the floor.

'You can't do that!' she cried. 'That's an eighth-century treasure! You – you can't – put it back right this instant!'

I could hear distant footsteps and commotion. If I headed for the stairs, I'd only run into them. Maybe there was a fire exit, a passage up to the roof. I ran down a corridor, panicking, unable to see any signs. Then I spotted a sign saying *Toilets*. I ran towards the blue door with a stick man pencilled on it. Then I chose the pink one instead. They'd never think of looking for me in here. I dashed in; the mirrors halted me. I realised how long it had been since I'd looked at my reflection. A triptych of dirty, bruised faces stared back at me. It was the face of a stranger; he looked years older than me. I turned away from him uncomfortably, checking the cubicles. One was engaged; the other two were empty. I dived into one and locked the door. Slamming down the toilet lid, I sat down and flicked through the pages. My hands were shaking so violently I kept tearing the ancient text, silently swearing and apologising. Page 53. Here it was.

I reached into my pocket for the lighter, but it wasn't there. I glanced around in horror, then saw it had fallen out and rolled to a halt next to the door.

I smoothed open *Beowulf*. Page 53. *Go slowly*, I told myself. *Don't set the damn book alight.*

The page shook in my left hand. I flared the lighter flame underneath, trying to hold it as close to the paper as I could without burning it.

'Come on,' I murmured out loud, 'come on.'

And then, as though by magic, the words started to appear.

Grendel gongan godes yree baer

RECENT COMMUNICATION OF THE WORDS FOR FACTION ONE MEMBERS

Mynte se manscaoa manna cynnes

In my excitement, I forget everything: the guards, the police, the cameras. *Who accessed this book?* I wondered in awe. Presumably the Words had someone working at the museum as a mole. The guard there must have regularly replaced the book with a replica while he was organising updates or allowing the Words to look at it. How angry would the Words be, now that I had shot Sasha Brooks and stolen a book that only their highest members were supposed to know about? If I could just get hold of the names of the top members, I could go to them and explain that I was on their side. They'd understand that, in the end; they'd forgive me, surely?

My nose kept running; I sniffed and tore off a bit of toilet roll, giving it an impatient wipe. Another flare of my lighter revealed a little more:

summe besyrwan in sele pam hean

PRISON SHIP 'LUCY', LIVERPOOL DOCKS:
18.00 HRS, 12 SEPTEMBER
PRISONERS TO BE RELEASED:
TOM HARGREAVES
LUCINDA EVANS
ETHAN JONES

September the 12th was tomorrow. I felt myself exhale a deep breath of relief.

'Oh thank God,' I whispered.

They would free my father.

There was no way Omar and I would have ever really got to the prison ship and saved him. Not with all those guards wielding guns; we'd have ended up in a cell ourselves. But I had faith in the Words. They were organised; experienced; they would know how to get him back. And then I'd find out where his safe house was and I'd go to him. He'd forgive me for Sasha. I know he would.

Except . . . my father's name wasn't actually on the list.

My head flew up as I heard the bang of the toilet door. I crouched down, peering through the slit, and saw shoes that looked dangerously masculine. I held the lighter under the final paragraphs. As I heard the men checking the other cubicles, I prayed for the message to hurry up, hurry up and appear:

wod under wolcnum to paes þe he winreced

ELIZABETH WARREN
JON BURNS AND SAM MILLS ARE PRISONERS
TO BE CAPTURED BY US AND KILLED. THEY
ARE ENEMIES OF THE WORDS AND HIGHLY
DANGEROUS . . .

My lighter flame died.

My heart stopped.

I read it over, several times.

I waved the lighter frantically under the rest of the page, looking for more words. Contact names. I could go to them, I could beg them to spare Dad, explain just how dedicated he was to them –

There was no more invisible ink.

THEY ARE ENEMIES OF THE WORDS AND HIGHLY DANGEROUS.

'Open up!' someone banged against my cubicle. 'Who's in there? Open up!'

I stared at the door in dazed shock.

Then a voice above me said, 'Here he is.'

I looked up and saw a policeman in the next cubicle, peering down at me. I stared up at him numbly and then let out a large, explosive sneeze. He yelled at me to open up. I backed up into the corner, holding the lighter under the page one last time, praying, begging for one last clue, not caring that he could see what I was holding. Nothing. He lunged over the cubicle wall, his boot catching me in the stomach as he landed. I let out a bellow. The lighter and the book fell from my hands. As he grabbed me, I heard a crackle, tasted the first tendrils of smoke. He tussled me out of the cubicle, and I looked back to see the fire eating through the pages, turning words to ashes, censoring secrets.

Thirty-five

I sat hunched up in the cell, on a bed with a hard, thin mattress. There were no windows and the grey light was dim and sickly, as though all the suffering of past prisoners had created a palpable atmosphere. On a small table sat a bottle of Good Behaviour Pills. And then there was the camera, perched in the corner, staring at me. It had been just the same when they had first put me in the Institution. For the first two, three days, there had been nothingness, no communications, just the sensation of being watched, until the camera seemed to mesmerise me, to grow and grow until it filled the room, so that when the voice behind the camera finally spoke the interrogation came as a relief.

I wasn't as scared as I'd thought I'd be. When the police had caught me back in the tramp's house, I had thrown up at the thought of having to go back to the Institution. But the fear of the place, magnified by my imagination, was worse than reality. I felt relatively calm. Or maybe I was just so exhausted I didn't have the energy left for fear.

And this time, when the interrogation began, I'd know how to play the game. Protest a little, squirm a little, then give in. Let them think they had me.

The thought gave me a glow of secret power.

I lay down on the mattress, shivering slightly. I kept

automatically reaching out for *Paradise Lost* and pawing thin air. The thought of those flames eating through its pages made me sick. If only the police had seen the secret message, they could have prevented the Words' mission to kill my dad. And I might have destroyed years of messages. Now the Words would hate me even more.

But – the thought had churned through me a thousand times over – *why the hell did the Words want to kill my dad in the first place?*

Had his name been put on the list because I had shot Sasha Brooks? That didn't entirely make sense, for the Words surely couldn't think that he was guiding me or involved in any way. I'd always thought that, with the exception of Omar, the Words were a peaceful organisation; I'd thought that their way of protest was through pen and ink and the printed page. After all the years of dedication and loyalty my father had given them, how could they treat him like this? At the end of the day, were the Words really any better than the State?

Through the gloom, the bottle of Behaviour Pills glinted temptingly. A simple, easy way to drown out my misery.

I reached for them.

And then I pictured the guard behind the CCTV and his smile of satisfaction as he watched me take them. I debated whether to shower the pills over the floor and stamp them into a pink crush. Then another thought crossed my mind and I slipped the pills into my pocket, lying back down on the bed.

Another hour passed. I began to think that there was no worse cage than the prison of our minds, no worse torture than our own thoughts. Over and over, the events of the day – the chase – high street – museum – case – *Beowulf* – thumped through my mind in a relentless hammer of memory. Worries and fears multiplied. The police might stop the Words' rescue mission, but what if the Words had undercover guards on the ship helping them? I pictured them entering my father's cell, holding a gun to his head, delivering a single shot . . .

I sat up and crawled over to the camera.

'I'm ready,' I said. 'I'm ready to confess.'

Silence.

'The Words are planning to blow up the Liverpool prison ship. I'll tell you all the details. You need to vacate the ship at once though,' I improvised.

Silence.

Frustration burnt through me. They'd taken my shoes and watch, so I had no hard objects to use as weapons. Then I remembered the bottle of pills in my pocket. I drew them out and smashed them against the camera. Victory beat in my heart as its lens shattered into pieces. How I'd ached to do that the last time I'd suffered the Institution – how wonderful it felt now!

Immediately a siren shrilled through my cell. I shoved the pills in my pocket and clambered back onto the bed. Footsteps pounded down the corridor and there was a grating noise as my cell was unlocked.

Two guards were standing at the door. One of them strolled in and silently examined the shattered camera. Then he stared at me sullenly.

'Whoops,' I said lightly.

Rage flashed in his eyes.

'You're coming with me. We can show you a cell that you might find a little more comfortable.'

He yanked me off the bed and together they dragged me down the corridor of cells.

'You have to – you have to stop the Words from blowing

up the prison ship,' I jabbered wildly. This wasn't meant to happen; they were meant to take me to an interrogation room and make me tell them everything about the ship. 'Where are you taking me? . . . I didn't mean to . . . I just have to tell you about the prison ship . . .' I broke off, hating the shrill desperation in my voice, feeling the brevity of my triumphant rebellion.

The guard grimaced at me and said, 'The prison ship? After the stunt you've just pulled, you're *going* to the prison ship.'

Thirty-six

Darkness. My new cell was so tiny that I could only lie in a foetal ball. Pain hardened into curves throughout my body; I was scared that, if I got out of here, I'd never stand up straight again and my spine would be forever bent like some doddery old man's. The flexicuffs on my wrists were so tight I could feel bracelets of raw red forming on my skin. I squeezed my eyes shut, bombs of terror exploding across my mind. Why the hell had I provoked them, why hadn't I thought my plan through? *What if they come and pull me out and torture me?* I whimpered inside. *Not the mild pain they inflicted on me in the Institution, but the real thing – waterboarding and beatings and stringing me up and pulling out my nails?* They won't, they won't, I tried to reassure myself; the State would never allow such a thing to happen to a sixteen-year-old. *But it's naïve to believe the State has a conscience*, my fear argued back. *They can show a blind eye, pretend they didn't authorise it or know anything.*

I needed to be ready for the moment that cell door opened. I could tell them once again that the Words were planning to kill my dad – but they probably wouldn't even care. No; they'd want names.

Names. The darkness of panic emptied my mind. I knew no names, no names—

Sasha Brooks.

But I couldn't do that to her. She might be lying in hospital, but they'd happily go to her bedside, ready to interrogate her the moment she woke up. I begged and prayed for the strength to bury her name so deep inside me they couldn't pull it out. I tried to concoct some fake plan the Words were going to enact, but the more I attempted to make it sound convincing, the more I thought they'd never buy it. Finally, exhaustion overwhelmed me, flowing through me like black ink and I found myself passing out . . .

♛

Light. Piercing my eyes; a baptism on my face. The guards pulled me out of my cell.

'I don't have any names,' I cried, collapsing onto the gravel. I curled up, cringing, waiting for any angry blow. But one of them helped me to my feet.

'Rub your limbs – it'll help,' one of them said.

I rubbed my legs painfully, feeling the shock of blood and energy flow through them. I was standing in a gravel courtyard; in the distance, a small queue of prisoners were filing out. I trembled with relief that I had survived the night. After the cell, the fresh air tasted like nectar. The dawn was dreaming orange across the sky and in the distance I could see the glinting silhouette of the World History Museum.

'I don't have any names,' I muttered to the guards, 'I don't have any—'

'What's the kid jabbering on about? Get a move on.'

I realised I was supposed to be joining the queue. They were all in orange jumpsuits and everyone was about twice my age. They ushered us towards the docks. There was no chance of even thinking of escape. On either side we were escorted by columns of officers accompanied by savage Alsatians. The breaths from the prisoners puffed out in white clouds.

At the docks, we stood in a long shivering line. In the distance I could hear the boatmen calling, 'Just ten euros to see the ruins', still wooing tourists to visit the drowned houses.

When I first saw the motor-boat, I was surprised. I'd been expecting a boat thick with steel doors and multiple locks and chains. I'd expected us to be held in individual cells. Instead, we shuffled into the motor-boat and sat down on benches, our cuffed hands on our laps. One of the guards shook his head and made a mutter about 'bloody government cut-backs'.

The prisoners started flashing looks of hope at each other, savouring the possibility of escape. But the guards instantly quelled us; they stood in lines along all sides of the boat, their guns and batons ready in their hands. We waited for five minutes and another line of prisoners filed down the docks to join us. This lot were wearing blue jumpsuits, which meant they were considered less danger-ous than us in our orange ones. The oranges began to jeer, until the guards screamed and swore they'd shut us up.

Then another group filed onto the benches opposite us. And that was when my heart stopped.

Across from me, wearing an orange jumpsuit, was Omar Shakir.

The police must have arrested him soon after they'd got me. I gave him a wobbly smile. His eyes were two flints. My smile faded. I swallowed and stared at the sunlight glinting on my cuffs.

The boat set off. The wind clawed our face and the sun beat down heavy on our heads. I didn't dare raise my eyes.

I could sense Omar staring at me, feel the waves of his anger emanating across the aisle.

I had a nagging feeling that the man sitting next to Omar looked familiar. I quickly flashed my eyes over him. I *had* seen him before. At the meeting of the Words, back in Raf's house. They had been debating whether the Words were a peaceful organisation and this man had clapped Omar on the back and agreed, 'The Words must always use force where necessary.' I glanced at him again and felt alarmed when he glared back.

Now I had two prisoners staring at me. What if they were on this ship to enact the escape mission and kill the traitors? What if the police hadn't stopped them at all?

Suddenly Omar whispered, 'I know about your dad, Stefan. Last night, before the police got us, the Words got in touch with me directly with the list of traitors' names. Your—'

'Hey, you! Quiet there!' one of the guards called over.

Omar pressed his lips together and I lowered my eyes, my heart frantic. A few minutes passed and Omar whispered again, 'Your father was on it. You want to know why? He gave up Raf's name – *he* got Raf arrested. Raf might be a blasphemer but we in the Words don't betray each other. We—'

'I said, shut up!' the guard snarled.

'He wouldn't do that,' I hissed. I opened my mouth to say more, but the guard raised his baton and I quickly swallowed the words back.

All I could do was shake my head passionately and stare at Omar, pleading at him with my eyes. My dad would *never* betray anyone. He loved the Words like a family. He had risked his life to hide Omar in our house; he was in a prison *because* of him. How could Omar believe it?

But Omar just stared at me blankly and I knew that, even if I was allowed to speak, nothing that I could say would convince him. I was so mad at him for being so stupid that I felt like standing up, twinning my cuffed hands into a fist and punching him. I heard my dad's voice in my head telling me, *Calm down*. I took control of my anger and tried to see the situation from Omar's viewpoint. He had lost Sasha; lost Raf; the Words were being torn apart and now he was on a prison ship. I could sense how he felt because I'd been through it myself; his world was falling to pieces and he wanted to lash out and gather them back together. He wanted someone to blame, and it was easier to get revenge on someone helpless like my dad than on the massive machine of the State.

I looked into Omar's eyes once more. His rage was cold now. A door had closed inside him. He'd decided my dad would die and that was that.

Fury spurted up inside me again. When the guard turned away, I leaned down and spat on Omar's shoes. It was petty – but worth it for the look on Omar's face. He yelled out and the guard raised his baton. Omar cowered and then glared at me with such intensity I thought his eyes might turn red.

I turned away from him and stared at the sea, watching the waves part frothily as the boat drove through them. The prison ship was coming closer and closer. *Dad*, I said silently, *I'm coming for you. I'm not going to let them kill you, I swear I won't let them.*

✦

We were taken from the boat to the prison ship one by one. When it was my turn to go, Omar took his revenge. He surreptitiously stretched out his boot and I half-tripped, causing the other prisoners to jeer and shout. His friend flashed me a malicious half-smile. The guards yelled at me to quit playing games and get a move on.

A guard tapped me on the elbow with his baton, guiding me up the ramp towards the ship. I was slightly seasick and I stumbled a few times, my footsteps echoing loudly on the grille. I was taken to a small office to be assessed by the warden. He looked as though he had spent all his life on the ship and never come off it; his skin was bleached nearly as white as his hair and, behind his round spectacles, his eyes were the flat grey of the sea on a windless day. He took my name and examined my file with an indifferent face. Then he tapped several details into the computer, signed and stamped a form, and rattled out my new ID number and the location of my cell. Before they took me away, the guards removed my cuffs and frisked me, patting me down roughly and taking off my boots. When one guard heard the rattle in my pocket, his eyes lit up – until he saw what they were.

'Good Behaviour Pills.'

'I thought they might help me,' I said.

The warden examined them silently, then screwed the lid back on.

'Fine,' he said. 'Let him have them.'

The bottle was pushed back into my pocket and the guard jabbed his baton into my ribcage, winding me.

'Get a move on, then.'

They led me through one set of heavy gates, then another, then another. I felt as though I was slowly walking into deeper and deeper circles of hell. The cell doors were dirty, yellowed and thick, without any windows. At the end of the row my cell lurked like a monster waiting to take me in and devour me with its teeth of boredom, exhaustion and pain. For all my bravado, a great dread came over me and I wondered if I would be able to bear my future.

They unlocked the cell door and I saw the shadow of another man. *The Words have organised this*, I thought in shock, *and I'm in a cell with Omar.* Then I saw his face. Not Omar. I could hardly believe it.

The cell door clanged shut behind me and we stared at each other.

'Dad!' I cried.

Thirty-seven

I opened my arms to hug him tight, but he didn't stir. He just sat on the bed and stared at me. He looked so different from the Dad I had known, the one who had pottered about the shop and nagged me about binding old books. He looked as though he had lost about ten kilos in weight; his cheeks were gaunt and his wrists, which had always been so delicate, were now skeletal, his fingers fragile twigs. He had grown a thick beard that brushed down over his neck, while much of the hair on the top of his head had fallen out. His skin was a horrible, pasty yellow and one of his ears had a horrific, jagged edge, as though the lobe had been torn off. His eyes, however, told a different story. They shone out of his face like beacons for the last pieces of his soul that hadn't been trodden down. They blazed with anger and passion and sorrow.

'Stefan,' he said at last. Even his voice was different – a rasping, ill sound punctuated his words. 'What are you doing here?'

'I . . . I came to save you.' Even as I spoke the words, I realised how stupid they sounded.

My father blinked in astonishment. Then, slowly, a smile crept across his face. I smiled too, feeling my eyes burn. His smile turned into ragged laughter. He cried out my name, then stood up and enveloped me in a hug. As I held him, I smelt the acrid, sour stench coming off his skin, felt the painful thinness of his ribs. But nothing had felt so good in months as the bang of my dad's heartbeat against mine.

He stepped back and stared at me, looking anxious.

'You look thin . . .' he touched my cheek. 'And what's this bruise?'

'Dad,' I laughed, 'I'm okay! . . . I mean, compared to you . . .'

My father glanced down at himself in surprise. Then his eyes crinkled up.

'I'm not so bad, Stefan.' He frowned, staring at my mouth. 'You've lost a tooth.'

'I was in a fight and Omar made me take it out because it was a fake and he thought it was bugged.'

'Omar?' Fear coloured his face. 'What were you doing with Omar?'

'I think he wants to kill you, Dad,' I blurted out.

'Of course he wants to kill me, I don't need you to tell me that,' he snapped, to my amazement. 'But how—' he broke off as coughing interrupted his words. 'But—' he tried again but the coughing overwhelmed him and he sank down onto the bed, clutching his stomach.

'Dad? Are you okay?' I asked, feeling scared.

'Stefan, I'm fine,' he said, patting the bed. 'Sit down. I want you to tell me everything, from beginning to end.'

I sat down next to him, chewing my lip. I ached to tell him the whole story, but the beginning was the hardest place to start. It meant that I would have to begin with my betrayal . . .

'I . . . when Omar was hiding with us . . . I got scared . . . and at school they said we should tell teachers about terrorists . . .' I trailed off, aware of my father's eyes on me. 'I

270

didn't know, Dad,' I blurted out, 'I just didn't realise what I was doing when I told Mrs Kay. I'm sorry.'

'It's all right, Stefan,' he said, his eyes liquid with compassion. 'It's my fault. You were confused, you didn't understand what was going on. I should have explained more to you – there's so much I kept from you . . .'

'I know about Mum,' I said awkwardly. 'I know how she died.'

He fell silent for a while. I feared that I should never have mentioned her. I heard a noise spill from his lips, saw the shake of his shoulders. When I realised that he was crying, I began to cry too. Once the release came, we couldn't stop. We both wept for her loss, for the years he had been forced to lie to me, carrying his tragedy alone in his heart, for our misunderstanding, for my betrayal. I felt him clench his hand around mine, so tightly that my knuckles hurt. I looked up at him and managed to smile. When he smiled back, it was more of a grimace, his teeth bared in pain.

'It's all right,' he said at last. 'We're going to be all right.'

I suddenly felt strong. Together it seemed as though nothing could defeat us. And then I remembered my journey to the ship and shook my head.

'Omar's here, Dad, he came onto the boat too . . . he wants to kill you. They've got it all so wrong, there's been this big mistake – there's a list of traitors in the Words and your name is on it. And he believes it – he's so stupid.'

I waited for Dad to look angry or surprised. To jump to his feet and pronounce his innocence. Instead, he just looked rather sad.

'That's because I am a traitor,' he said at last. His shoulders slumped. 'I'm the one who put Raf in jail. I gave up his name.'

'What! So Omar was right? It was you?'

'Yes, it was me.'

I remembered Raf's kindness when Omar and I had broken into his house. His gentle eyes and warm chuckle. I remembered the horror in Sasha's voice when she had told us Raf had been taken in.

It took me a long time to ask the next question, for I was scared of the answer.

'So, are you – are you working for the State? Is this some kind of trick that you're on the prison ship or something?'

'No, never.' Dad's voice was taut with disgust. 'I'd never work for the State after what happened to your mother. You have to know that, Stefan.'

'Sorry, sorry,' I said, with a rush of guilt. 'But . . . you gave them Raf's name . . .' I trailed off, feeling sick. 'Oh God, Dad. They tortured you.'

Rage burnt through me.

'You could have died,' I said. 'Like Mum.' I felt tears swim in my eyes; I found myself lashing out, punching the bed. Dad nodded.

'Which is why I gave them a name,' he said. 'I saved my own life – and gave up Raf. It wasn't an easy decision. But Omar always predicted I'd cave in – he had his doubts about me.'

'Why should Omar say that?' I cried fiercely. 'You're strong, you had to do it – you would have died.'

'Omar sees me as being weak. Well, perhaps I am. When I took him into our house, I was glad to take the risk. But we'd regularly sit down to discuss politics, the Words, our way forward – and every discussion turned into an argument. At the time, I tried to persuade myself that we could still believe in the same principle, from different angles. But I've had a lot of time to think in jail, Stefan, and it's clear to me that I was fooling myself – Omar and I are very different people with very different ideas.'

'Why? What did you disagree on?'

'Well, when the Words first started, it was a very simple organisation, with pure, innocent aims. But nothing was as easy as we thought it might be. Omar was the most idealistic of us all – he thought that when we first printed Banned Books and sold them underground that we would change the world. He thought that people would read them and see everything differently. That they would turn against the State and demand a return to the freedom we once enjoyed here in England. But I've come to realise that the State isn't necessarily an oppressive, detached regime that is here to beat us down. The State, unfortunately, reflects the collective consciousness. The reason we voted in such a government was because of fear. And fear leads to more fear. As a nation, we became trapped by it. So, you see, a few forbidden books weren't going to change everything . . .

'But Omar was impatient. We had always felt from the start that we ought to be a peaceful organisation – that printing books was a form of passive resistance. Omar came to believe that peace wasn't the answer. He told me that he had deliberately written his book in the hope that it would provoke a terrorist attack; he had given copies to a cell. In my naivety, I kept believing that I could win him round; I didn't take him seriously. I didn't realise that he was starting to contact other members of the Words who were also restless, who also felt that the only way to make people listen was to resort to violence . . .'

'He – he got me to run away with him,' I cried. 'After you were arrested, they put me in the Institution and he got me to run away with him – d'you think that was because he wanted to kill me too?'

My dad paused.

'I think that he was honestly torn between wanting to protect you, for my sake, and wanting to destroy you. Omar has
many good qualities. Beneath his anger, he does have a sense
of responsibility. But the problems of the Words have begun
to eat away at him too. Just before my arrest, I was shocked
to hear rumours that the more violent factions of the Words
planned to kill the peaceful members.'

'But why?'

'Because once the Words started to commit acts of terrorism, the peaceful ones wouldn't want to be involved any
more. We'd leave, start talking to the police, giving up
names. The potential schism was a dreadful thing . . .
There was Omar on one side, me on the other . . . and
those in between.'

'So do you think Omar added your name to the list of traitors?' I asked. Then I frowned. 'But he couldn't have done –
he didn't crack the *Paradise Lost* code. I found a microdot
on the final page, Dad – and then I found *Beowulf*!'

'*Beowulf*?'

'The higher factions of the Words keep their top-secret
messages written in a copy of *Beowulf* – the one that sits in
the World History Museum.'

My dad laughed.

'That's brilliant. Right out on public display, of course.
And you cracked the code. Well, of course you did,' my dad's
face shone. 'You're a genius. You take after me,' he grinned.

'But . . . your name was in that book,' I said, more quietly, circling back to the terrible truth.

'News must have got back to them about Raf . . . they
wouldn't forgive that.'

'It's just not fair – you were being tortured. You're only
human, Dad.'

'Various other members of the Words have been tortured – including Omar. They've stood up to it.'

'You're only human,' I repeated stubbornly.

'I'm a father,' he said. 'That's why I did it.' He lowered his eyes, as though he felt too embarrassed to look at me. 'If it had happened just after your mother died, when I was torn apart with rage, I would have held out, I would have let them kill me and I would hardly have cared. I would have been happy to be dead, to be reunited with her.'

The savagery in his voice shocked me; I saw a terrible flash of an alternative fate, whereby I would have been brought up with a family like the Kelps from an early age.

'But . . . you see, Stefan, there was one person who made me realise that life *was* worth living after your mother died – and that was you. Not at first – when she was first taken from me, I couldn't care about anybody. It was looking after you, having to put you to bed and tie your laces and read you a bedtime story – that slowly enabled the life to leak back into me.' He lowered his eyes, his voice thick with emotion. 'When they were torturing me, I kept blacking out and coming round, and each time I blacked out, the darkness became an invitation – I realised that death was hovering nearby and I could let it take me over, release me from the pain. I could have died for a cause – but my heart wouldn't allow it. Because I thought of you, how much I loved you – and I knew that you were far more important than anything the Words stood for. So I gave up Raf's name and it satisfied them. I remember that my interrogator kicked me off my chair and as I lay on the floor, he gave me a look of such victory, as though he had succeeded in breaking me down, making me betray my principles. He didn't realise that although every cell in my body was singing with pain, I felt euphoric because I knew I had made the right decision – I was alive, which meant that somehow, someday I'd see you again.'

I remained very still. I wanted to hug him again but my emotion felt too strong; I feared I'd hold his fragile body so tightly that I'd crush him.

We were silent for a while, and then my father sighed, 'I wish Sasha was here. She was always the most level-headed member of the Words. If Omar had just spoken to her, she would have made him see sense.'

The name Sasha made me tense up. My father picked up on it immediately.

'Did you meet Sasha?'

I tried to look him in the eye but found I couldn't raise my head. I nodded slowly. I wanted to say it; I wanted to explain, but I just couldn't bear to. It was bad enough that I had betrayed my father, but how would he feel if – after everything he had done for me – he knew that I had shot his lover?

I reached out for him and gave him a tight hug, burying my face in his chest, hiding my horror and my shame.

Once more my father said, 'We're going to be all right.'

The ship rolled heavily and my stomach churned. My father said the sensation of being at sea made him feel constantly dizzy. I felt as though the sea was warning us that there was trouble ahead.

I lay on the mattress, staring up at the ceiling. There was only one bed in the cell and no other furniture except a bucket to piss in. My father had insisted I take the bed and now he was lying on the floor. I was so overwhelmed to be back with him, I couldn't bear to sleep. Every time I was about to drop off, I kept wanting to get up and look at his face. Occasionally nightmares twitched across it. He looked so vulnerable, as though the sleep had taken away the veil of adulthood and revealed the boy he had once been. I felt bad about having the luxury of the bed, so I took the single blanket off me and gently draped it over him.

Of course Omar wants to kill me, Dad had said. He had sounded so matter-of-fact. But was his bravery just an act? I began to ache with worry that I should have told him everything about Sasha; then my father would see just how much danger we were in.

The ship rolled again, as though the sea was becoming violent in her temper. I sat up, gazing round. In the distance I could hear shouting and noises. My father stirred, waking up. For a moment we listened, exchanging nervous glances. Heavy footsteps thundered down the corridor, followed by loud bangs. Under the door began to creep grey tendrils.

My father stood up in alarm.

'Can you smell it?' he cried.

'D'you think it's the Words?'

'I don't kn—' he was cut off as the fire alarms started to shrill.

The smoke began to thicken, tendrils becoming plumes that swirled about our legs. My father went to the door and hammered his fists against it. 'Come on!' he said to me and I shook myself out of my dazed shock and joined him. We knocked on the door until our knuckles cracked, called for help until our voices bled.

And all the while, the smoke grew thicker and thicker.

'Here.' My father tore off a strip from his uniform and tied around the bottom half of my face. 'Try not to breathe it in.'

My father banged and banged until his fist weakened and he slumped against the door.

'Oh God,' he said, his eyes wet. 'Oh God, please help us, please.'

'Don't give up, Dad, don't give up!' I cried.

He remained slumped against the door. I smashed my fists against it in fury. I'd only just got my dad back and I wasn't going to let anyone take him away from me; we couldn't die now, it wasn't fair, it wasn't fair –

Suddenly I heard a key turning in the lock. My father stumbled backwards, clutching my arm. The door opened and a guard screamed at us to vacate the cell and follow him to the lifeboats.

All the cell doors in the corridor had been flung wide open. The shrill of alarms sounded muffled, as though choked by the thick black smoke. We followed the guard, running up onto the top deck.

Up here, it was chaos. Shouting; sirens; dogs barking; guards panicking; prisoners jumping overboard. We could see the fire; the left half of the boat was pure yellow, flames billowing brilliantly against the night sky. We could also feel it; it warmed our bodies with a threatening heat; I felt my eyes burn and water.

'Should we jump over?' I asked my father.

'Let's not panic, let's be calm. They'll get us onto a lifeboat.' But I saw him look back at the fire, saw the flames reflected in his fearful eyes.

The guards ushered us into a line. We'd just missed the first lifeboat, which had set off with twenty prisoners on board. The next boat came and as I stepped onto it, I thanked God in relief. My father sat down next to me and squeezed his arm around me, saying, 'See? We're all right, we're all right.'

And then, through the haze of crackling flames and sirens and voices, we heard the shots. I looked up and saw them. Omar and his friend. Omar was pointing a gun at the guard, yelling instructions that this was their boat. Some of the prisoners yelled protest and Omar fired bullets into the air; they fell back in horror. A guard in the distance fired a shot and Omar fired back, killing him.

Then he and his friend jumped down onto our boat, starting the motor.

'These men belong to us,' Omar called up. 'The rest of you can wait for the next boat.'

Thirty-eight

I twisted my head back, staring at the prison ship. The motorised lifeboat was cutting sharply through the waves; within a few minutes the ship would be no more than a yellow dot. I wanted to scream at the prison guards, *Why aren't you chasing us? Why the hell are you letting four prisoners escape?* But the fire was so intense that a thick mushroom cloud of smoke had enveloped the moon and stars. All anyone on that ship cared about was staying alive.

'Hey!' I felt a butt jam into my chin. Omar frowned at me. 'Keep your head facing me, okay?'

I stared at him sullenly. Dad and I were sitting side by side in the motor-boat. Omar's friend was standing at the front, steering; we'd heard Omar address him as Roger. Omar stood above us, his eyes on my father.

'Is this really necessary?' my father asked politely.

'Is this really necessary?' Omar mimicked him, laughing. 'Look at you. Look at the state of you. They've reduced you to this, to skin and bones and bruises, and you still think that the problems we're facing can be solved by a few books. In fact, in a few minutes' time, you're probably going to try to persuade me not to kill you by throwing a few quotes at me. Something from the Bible, something from Gandhi, something from *Crime and Punishment*. I can tell you now, they won't help.'

My father pinched his lips together. I wanted him to quote his favourite books, to fling them in Omar's face and make a proud and idealistic speech. Instead, he said wearily, 'I don't mind what you do with me, I just don't want you to harm my son.'

'Your son,' Omar laughed. 'Your son, your innocent sixteen-year-old kid is a big part of the problem. He stole *Beowulf* and deliberately set light to it. What's more, the police put it out in time and were still able to decode the secret messages – as a result, several of our highest members have been arrested. McGills is in a cell.' Omar waited for my father to react; my father just shrugged.

'So find a new text,' he said, his voice glinting with sarcasm. 'Try *Le Morte d'Arthur*.'

'You and your son seem to be doing very well at getting the Words arrested,' Omar lost his temper, his voice rising to a shout. 'Stefan is just a stupid kid – I see that. But you – *you* gave up Raf. You gave him up and now they have him. You coward.'

Silence.

'And Sasha.'

Finally my father reacted. I felt my cheeks burn. *No*, I pleaded silently with Omar. *Please don't say it, please don't tell him—*

'Sasha's still in hospital. They think she's going to make it – but who knows?'

'What?' My father cried, his voice ringing with astonishment.

Omar saw the gap in my father's knowledge and a savage glee gripped his face.

'Remember Sasha?' Omar asked softly. 'Remember the

woman who wanted to marry you and become your next wife – except you always held back, pushed her away, absorbed yourself in your books—'

'Nobody could replace Caroline,' my father defended himself fiercely.

'Well, your son went into a bookshop reading that she was giving. And then he shot her.'

'Stefan?' My father cried. 'No. Stefan would never do that . . .'

'It wasn't like that!' I cried. 'Dad, you have to listen to me – the police – they did it really, they made me do it, they kidnapped me and brainwashed me. I know it sounds crazy but it's what happened.'

'You shot her?' my father asked me, his voice barbed.

'But it wasn't like that, Dad, it wasn't really me – they *got* me.'

My father turned back to Omar.

'And she's still alive?'

'Only just,' said Omar. 'She has woken up from her coma – she may just survive. So before you come at me again with your arguments about peace – then take a look at your son. The police did brainwash him – they got me too. They took a sixteen-year-old boy and turned him into a killer. D'you think peaceful tactics can compete with that? We *have* to fight them, we have to take an eye for an eye.'

'You mean you think the Words should become a terrorist organisation?'

'We're not terrorists, we're freedom fighters! You can see everything's changing – you can see it every day. There are new laws, each one getting more and more paranoid. Parents can't adopt a kid if they're obese. Teenagers are being given permission to film other people on their mobiles if they think they look suspicious. Nobody's allowed to protest, nobody can send an email without it being read, nobody can make a call without it being overheard. The government have the power to enter and search our houses any time they like. All Rewritten books are about to be called in and Rewritten again – yes, I thought that one might get to you. We're not winning the fight for freedom at all – we're losing, every minute. We can't let it happen! We have a responsibility to fight and to fight with shock and awe and make the bastards sit up and listen to us.' Omar broke off, shaking. He sat down, nursing the gun in his lap. Despite the cool of the night, his face was bright and shiny with sweat. 'We're out here, on the ocean. This doesn't have to end in a bullet . . . if you want to save yourself, then join us. Come back to the Words.'

'And plant bombs and shoot innocent people?'

'If that's what needs to be done, then yes, that's what needs to be done.'

'There's no reason to kill us,' my father tried to keep his voice even but it shook a little. 'You can let us go. We can just go and get on with our lives, and you can get on with yours.'

Omar slowly spun the gun around the circle of his kneecap.

'Let you go? When you've already told the police about Raf?'

'I was selfish, yes,' my dad declared. 'But they nearly killed me in there, Omar. And I did want to stay alive, yes I did – to stay alive for my son!'

'A feeble excuse. And yet . . .' Omar looked at my father and a brief fondness flashed across his eyes. 'You didn't tell the police everything. You gave them just one name, no more. If I let you go – what incentive do you have to hold anything back at all? We need you with us. We need you back on our side, fighting fire with fire. Now you've seen what they've done to your son, how dirty they play it – you must want to join me.'

'Give me time,' said my father quickly. 'Just let me think it all over – let me think about what I'd like to do.'

Silence. Omar stared at my father. It was a look of raw tenderness and rage. Then he got up without speaking and went to the front of the boat, talking quietly to Roger. My father stared down at me and I saw the pain in his eyes.

'I'm sorry about Sasha,' I whispered. 'I'm sorry, Dad.'

I wanted him to tell me it would all be all right, but he just lowered his eyes sadly.

From the front of the boat, Omar kept his gun trained on us.

'Don't try anything,' he warned us. 'Don't speak. And don't go thinking that if you jump out, you can swim to safety – we're miles away from the coast, you'll never make it. The only weapon on this boat is the gun I'm holding now.'

We sat in silence, watching them confer. Words were bursting up inside my chest. I wanted to tell him that I thought Sasha was a beautiful angel. That I'd never meant to harm her. That we might die tonight and I couldn't bear it if he didn't forgive me.

Roger walked down the boat, training the gun on us.

'Omar's resting now,' he said.

He had cut out the engine and now we were drifting on waves of inky blackness. I could see the glimmer of lights on the horizon. They made me feel both hopeful and despairing; they were close enough to supply comfort, but it could only be false; there was no way we'd be able to swim to shore.

Roger balanced his gun on one knee, watching us with narrowed eyes, and undid a flask. The rich smell of coffee spiced the cold air. He winced as he burnt his lip.

'We're thirsty too,' my father said.

Roger told us to shut up and put the cup down next to him.

The boat drifted a little further. I could see black humps in the distance which looked like a sea monster. For a while I wondered if I was hallucinating with shock and exhaustion. Then I realised they were the buildings that had drowned in the floods. I could see the distant outline of a sign, faint lettering advising tourists that they were not allowed to take photos and could only buy authorised ones at the docks.

At dawn, the boatmen would bring tourists out here. They would coo over the drowned houses. And perhaps someone would spot a ripple of red in the ocean waves. A kid would point and nudge his mum. They would peer over the edge and screams of horror would fill the air as they saw us: a man, floating in the waves, and his son, drifting further and further away from him . . .

The thought made my chest burn with pain. I began to pray desperately, but the more I prayed the more distant God seemed. I gently nudged my dad. I just wanted him to look at me and say I was forgiven. But he just gave me a stern look. I wanted to weep, then I told myself to get a grip. We had to do something. I thought about reaching out and trying to grab the gun off Roger's lap. I hardly cared if he killed me, as long as I saved Dad. Then I slipped my hands in my pockets and the idea struck me.

The bottle of Good Behaviour Pills was still there. Unscrewing them with one hand wasn't easy. The lid had been put on tight and I didn't want my fumbling to attract any attention. Minutes passed; the clouds crossed the moon; the boat rocked gently; the moon shone full again; next to me, my father let out a long sigh. Millimetre by millimetre, I managed to unscrew the lid. Roger sniffed and took a sip of coffee. I eased the lid off and took out two pills. They felt cool and plasticky between my fingers. I stared at Roger, willing him to turn away for just a moment. He frowned and I coughed and stared down at my lap. My father, as though sensing I was up to something, shifted uneasily. Another cloud passed over the moon. Roger stretched and glanced out over the waves. My hand shot out, released two pills into his cup and quickly slid back into my pocket.

Roger's head spun back to us. I stared into the waves, feigning blankness. I could feel my father's silent bemusement. But there was a warmth in his curiosity, as though he sensed I had a plan and had faith that I might be able to pull it off.

Roger reached for his coffee and took a few sips, then put the cup back down.

Another five minutes passed. There was a brief noise in the distance, a quickening ripple in the waves that distracted all of us. It looked like another boat on the horizon. 'Help,' my father whispered, but he didn't dare jump up and shout the word out. Roger turned to stare at the silhouette, his face tense. I reached out and dropped a few more pills into his cup. I curled my hand around the bottle, wondering if I dared put the whole lot in. I yanked it out, sprayed about fifteen into the cup before I lost my nerve and shoved it back into my pocket. The pills dissolved instantly in the hot liquid. Beside me, I felt my father's elbow gently nudge mine. *Well done*, his nudge said, *that was brave*. And despite the fact that we were floating in the middle of the ocean and about to be killed, I felt as though my heart might burst with happiness. I was dying to turn to him, but I knew that just one look would send us both into fits of terrified laughter.

We both hoped we wouldn't have to wait for the pills to take effect. We prayed that the boat would slow and head towards us.

But the silhouette glided on and my father's shoulders slumped.

Roger let out a sleepy yawn and picked up his coffee. Then he yawned again.

And a third time.

I pressed my lips together tight to prevent a howl of nervous triumph from escaping. We sat tight. We waited . . .

And waited . . .

'Omar,' Roger called out. 'I think I need to sleep.'

I wailed inside. If Omar woke up, then our chance was over.

'Omar . . .' he called weakly. He stood up, swayed. The gun fell off his lap and banged to the floor. My father and I froze. Then all three of us reached for it at once. Roger tried to strike my dad, but his aim was too dulled and soft. He tried once more to punch him, lost his balance and keeled over into the sea with a loud splash.

My father stood up in alarm, gazing down at him. Roger's shirt had got caught on the half-submerged roof of a block of flats; he lay slung across the tiles, water lapping around him.

I reached down and grabbed the gun.

'Hey!'

Omar had woken up. He came storming down the motor-boat, yelling, 'Where is he?'

I pointed the gun at him and cried in a shaky voice, 'Put your hands up!'

Omar's fists remained by his sides.

'So you're going to shoot me?' he sneered.

I couldn't reply. Even though I was the one holding the gun, in that moment I felt weaker than Omar, as though I was the victim. He knew I couldn't do it. I knew I couldn't do it. Not after Sasha. When I had shot her, I had suffered a sense of innocence – not just from the brainwashing. I had only ever seen someone fire a gun in a film, and only once. I could never have imagined what it was like to break open someone's body and let the blood flow out, to shut down their mind, to slash their soul, to hurt their loved ones. I knew the reality of how it felt to hear someone's screams in your ears, to suffer that terrible feeling of having crossed a line you can never turn back from. I heard my father gently telling me to give him the gun. But I couldn't let go of it. I couldn't let my father become a murderer either.

'You can't shoot me,' Omar said, taking a step closer, swaying as the boat bumped against a house. 'You stand for peace. You've said you don't believe in violence.'

'Just leave us alone,' my dad cried, 'Just leave us alone. We can swim to shore from here. Just let us go.'

'You see,' Omar went on, 'peace can't win. I'm going to grab that gun off you and I'm going to shoot you. That's power.'

He reached out and grabbed for the gun. A shot went off and horror screamed through me. I heard a splash and then everything went black. Then I heard voices, my father yelling and Omar yelling. The gun had fallen into the sea. Omar dived in after it and my father followed.

'DAD!' I yelled. 'DAD!'

I saw two figures fighting, the waves frothing around them. They climbed onto the roof, still wrestling, slipping and skidding on the tiles as they threw punches. Omar was the stronger of the two. I saw him plunge fist after fist into my father's face. I felt as though I was suffering the blows myself.

'DAD!' I screamed. I saw my father look over at me, his face bloodied and bruised. I saw him close his eyes as though he was going to give up.

'DAD!'

And then he found it. A last muster of strength. He reached up and shoved Omar away. Omar's head hit the edge of the roof and I saw the impact of the blow ricochet through his face. My father jumped up and dived into the water. Omar stood up, blood trickling down his temple, and dived in after him.

'Oh God, oh Dad,' I whispered. I stood on the edge of the boat, waiting, waiting for one of them to come up. *Come on . . .*

The sea remained still and silent.

'DAD!'

Still and silent.

I jumped to the edge of the boat, took a deep breath and dived into the water.

I swam down into the wonderland of drowned buildings. I couldn't see them anywhere. I grabbed the tiled rim of a roof, pushing myself down, down, down. I could see the edge of a bedroom window and I grabbed it, staring through the pane. An eerie bedroom; a wardrobe; clothes tied to the hangers, billowing gently in the water. My throat was beginning to hurt; a bubble of pain was pressurising my chest. Then two figures smashed into the bedroom. I could see Omar trying to strangle my father, the blur of angry faces. The bubble of my chest expanded until I thought it would burst. I kicked back up, up, up, and gasped a huge gulp of air.

'DAD!'

I saw a figure break the waves, gasp air, so quickly I couldn't see who it was. And then, as though someone was pulling him under, he disappeared back below the waves.

Once more I pushed myself down. Past the tiles, past the bedroom, clinging to a plastic tube of piping. Fish tagged past me in a yellow line. I could see a figure in the distance. A dark, sinking shape. I couldn't see who it was. I couldn't see who had won the fight.

Thirty-nine

I burst up, up into the bright harsh air, gasping it in. Salt scratched my eyes and I rubbed them, glancing round, left, right. The water rippled softly before me. Dawn was breaking, glinting off the sides of the boat. A seagull arced overhead. Everything silent; peaceful with the promise of a new day.

'Dad?' I cried. '*Dad?*'

A burst of wind took my voice and carried it away.

'DAD! DAD!'

I took a huge breath and ducked back down into the water.

And then I saw a figure. Swimming towards me.

I burst up again.

'DAD!'

He gave me such a deep hug that we both forgot to tread water. The waves submerged us and we came up again, spluttering and laughing. Then we stared at each other. At the boat, the sea and the big sky above. The drowned buildings; a clock-tower, shiny with water; the shanty-town on the horizon; the docks; the world beyond that.

'Come on, we'll get back onto the boat,' Dad said. 'Are you all right?'

I nodded.

'Is Omar . . . ?'

'He's out, but he's alive. I left him with Roger, on top of the roof. They'll wake up soon enough.'

I laughed and thought then that I had the best dad in the world.

We plunged into the waves. The morning mist glinted gold with sunshine. We climbed into the boat and shivered.

'Where now?' I asked.

Dad gazed out across the sea, and then he looked rather helpless.

'Well, I don't think we can go back to Liverpool.' He started up the engine and we cut into the waves. I felt relieved as the shore shrank away from us until it was only a thin line on the horizon. I thought, *Dad will have a good plan. He'll have contacts, he'll know where to go.*

My father cut the engine off and we began to drift. I saw him looking around at the sea as though wishing it might guide us. Unease filled my stomach. And then I stared up at the birds flying overhead, shooting through the clouds. I thought of the world we had left behind, with its strait-jackets of CCTV and censorship and laws on every little thing we did. And I smiled, happy to just be sitting in a boat with my father, feeling free as a bird, letting the current take us . . .

Epilogue

So – you, brave reader, have decided to take the risk.

You've sat in a school lesson or behind a desk at work and heard the whispers. *Blackout*. It's been published as a novel but everyone knows it's a true story. It claims that all the books we know and love, the books in our libraries, our bookshops, our schoolrooms, aren't better because they've been Rewritten. It suggests they were better in their original forms. Temptation has brushed its fingers over the back of your neck, tingling possibilities. You've looked up at your teacher or your boss and you've realised the grey feeling in your stomach is boredom. You've found yourself saving up your lunch money, every bit of your savings, in return for a forbidden gift. A book, wrapped in brown paper. The book, of course, doesn't have *Blackout* on the cover. It's got *Jane Eyre* or *Oliver Twist* or even – I've heard the rumours – a Mills & Boon cover with a couple kissing on the front.

But you know better than to judge a book by its cover.

Maybe there are some things in this book that you believe, maybe there are some things you don't. *The truth will set you free.* But the truth is also a bomb that explodes in your brain and rearranges circuits; it takes a while for the dust to settle. Maybe you'll never be able to believe that

1984 – that set text we've all read – doesn't end with Winston getting happily married and enjoying life in harmony with the State. Maybe you'll always be convinced I just made that up. It's up to you to believe what you want.

All I can say is: be careful. You're holding a Banned Book in your very hands. In fact, I'm proud to announce that *Blackout* is now renowned for being in the Top 10 most dangerous Banned Books of all time.

It means, of course, that the sentence for being caught with a copy in your hands is doubly tough. I've heard that someone was stupid enough to read a copy with a fake cover on the bus. Someone glanced over their shoulder, reported them to the Security Guard and that person has spent the last few years in a cell.

Despite this, people keep buying *Blackout*. Tens of thousands of people. My father and I are in hiding now, so when we're not eating and writing, we feel cheered up by the news from the outside that the book keeps on being reprinted and reprinted. We're not with the Words any more; we've formed our own small group who are genuinely committed to nothing but the printed truth. Sasha – who is alive and well – joined us a while back. I can see from the way my dad looks at her that she is his Muse and I've got used to calling her Mum.

I just hope you've been more careful. If you're stupid enough to be reading this book on the tube or the bus, I suggest you close it quickly and hide it now. If you're at school, stash it in your desk. If you're lying in bed, then look out of the window at the CCTV camera smiling outside your window. Is it trained on you? If so, it may be time to go and light a fire in your back garden and add this book to the flames.

Don't worry – I won't be offended if you burn it. I like

the idea of my words becoming ashes that float up on the breezes, carried through the air, tangling with people's skin and minds, carried near and far . . .

Acknowledgements

Thanks to my wonderful editor Julia Wells for her thoughtful editing and patience during the slow gestation of this book, and to all at Faber, especially Emily Hardy, Helena Zedig, Rebecca Pearson and Trevor Horwood. Thank you to my super-agent Simon Trewin, Ariella Feiner and all at United Agents. To Zoe Pagnamenta in NY and Tessa Girvan at Intercontinental Literary Agency.

Thanks to all my family, especially my mother for reading a first draft despite a serious bout of flu. Thanks to Alexander Hewitt for listening to me as I bounced around ideas and, for all their support and friendship: David H, Tomazi, Victoria, David W, DBC Pierre, Kate, Tristan and Tansy.

Thanks to all the cast and crew on the April 2009 film shoot of *The Boys Who Saved the World*, who all, in their own unique way, influenced my final draft: Ufuk Gokkaya, Sarah Boezalt, Ali Genc, Doug Garside, Kemal Aslan, Matt Dodimead, Yildiz Adiguzel, Diyar Akar, Haco Cheko, Oljan Genc, Chris Waller, Felix Still, Dan Sales, Beka Ghosh, Luke Baldwin-Smith, James Webb, Ozkan Lysander Koyuncu, Tom Johnson, Chloe Blackwell. (Thanks in particular to Doug for discussing coastlines, Kemal for discussing Game Boys, Tom for a wonderful soundtrack that I listened to while I was writing and, of course, Ufuk for translating my book into a great film!)

A special thanks to Philip Ardagh for thinking up my title.